Motorcycles, Madness & Miracles

A Badass Journey
to Empowerment

Rowan Glaser

Logo design: Shanna Hoffman
Custom Chopper Photography: Randy Brown
Website design: Scott Bohler
www.McMMbook.com
A special thank you to
Karen Davis
Dan Mansur, airbrush artist
Composer & artist Michelle Kaye
Adam Hagen, The coolest contributor!

Copyright © 2013

Library of Congress Cataloging-in-Publication Data
Glaser, Rowan
  Motorcycles, Madness & Miracles / by Rowan Glaser – 2nd ed.
  Includes Toolbox
    1. Personal Growth   2. Visionary Fiction   3. Spiritual   4. Reference guide
ISBN 978-0-9971446-8-0
Second Edition, Second Revision

Let us believe in the good things coming.

→ ● ←

CONTENTS

→ ● ←

→ ● ←

→ ● ←

"The Unbroken"

by Rashani Réa[1]

There is a brokenness
out of which comes the unbroken,
a shatteredness
out of which blooms the unshatterable.
There is a sorrow
beyond all grief which leads to joy
and a fragility
out of whose depths emerges strength.

There is a hollow space
too vast for words
through which we pass with each loss,
out of whose darkness
we are sanctioned into being.

There is a cry deeper than all sound
whose serrated edges cut the heart
as we break open to the place inside
which is unbreakable and whole,
while learning to sing.

→ ● ←

8

Preface:
The Broken Ones

An infant lies in its own excrement in a crib. It ceased to cry. It ceased to care. A bottle placed in its hands like clockwork serves as its only nourishment. The child's misshapen head struggles to comprehend that it has been born into a world that appears to be barren except for food. No love, no nurturing; only actions that allow survival, so it may fulfill its role of being a living body to collect a welfare check.

Time passes. The toddler is alone on the city streets. The fast pace and loud noises are exciting! This new world is tall, so the child uses its small size to remain unseen. Food can be found strewn about. Water is a bit more challenging, but the dark places keep it from evaporating. The shadows become a dear friend in the quest for life. But shadows can't hide the boy forever. Authorities discover him and deposit him in an orphanage.

Another front door opens, revealing a foster family within, the fifth one this month. The child walks in with a smile on his face, a mask of confidence. Meeting different children, he feels jealous that they belong. Some are so happy he wants to hurt them, but

9

he tries his best to hide the anger … to play the game. Clutching a plastic toy gives him something to hold on to, and that's better than nothing. But, when they try to snatch your something, fighting skills are learned and manipulation is developed. Whispers become important; they teach the landscape of each new location …"not quite right" … "worthless" … "a lost cause." Always feeling rejected, the mirror reflects anger, and another foster home is found.

The flick of a nipple creates arousal ... a curious new feeling that is pleasurable. Slowly, the child is initiated into the rituals of sex. The pain and surprise of penetration gives way to confusion. The perpetrator's eyes, lost in a trance, are no longer the seemingly safe haven they once were. An object is given to placate, to reward, and to thank for the silence that is demanded. A discovery of seeming purpose, which yields a room of his own. A clue to how this world operates. Secrets must be kept, but with them come a sense of belonging. The power to say 'no' is stripped away, but there will be others who can replenish that which was stolen.

Shame! Guilt! An adult who is not a member of the game discovers the secret and he is ripped away from those who have been satisfying the need for connection. The mind begins to spin

- thoughts, images, rejections, abuse, faster, and faster and heat begins to radiate outward in waves. The mental turbulence becomes too much, the unreleased anguish has reached its peak; the child's mind is broken into fragments….

→ ● ←

→ ● ←

Chapter 1: **Custom Chopper Show**

The piece-of-shit van rolls slowly through the parking lot, crunching gravel under its bald tires. Rust has eaten most of the paint away, along with some of the metal in the rear wheel wells. The lower panel flaps slightly as the tire rolls into a small dip. The rear bumper, which is also spotted with rust, sports a bright yellow sticker reminding people to 'Start SEEING Motorcycles.'

This is my van, and I know it is a total eyesore, but I really don't care. I think of it as being a sleeper - not that I have an impressive engine under the hood but, because of what I have strapped down in the back - my first custom built motorcycle! She's riding like a queen in the cargo area. Or perhaps, I should call her a bondage queen? Ha! Today is a day I've been working towards for nearly two years, and my excitement is at an all time high. It was a long road getting here, and I don't know what the competition will look like, but in the present moment I have so much joy flowing through my body that I feel like I could fly! I'm bringing her to the world famous Rat's Hole Custom Chopper Show during bike week in Sturgis, South Dakota. It's time to see how she'll do in competition with the big kids. But, first things first, I need to park this van so I can bring my lady out to play.

I scan the parking lot hoping for a hill to make the unloading process go smoother, but it's totally flat and filling up quickly with registrants like me. I notice an available parking spot. As I pull in, I read 'Edinburgh Racing' printed on the side of the white trailer next to me. A quick glance tells me the owners have already locked up and moved on.

To my other side is a new black Ford F250 with an enclosed tandem axle cargo trailer hooked up to it. The trailer looks sharp with its gloss black paint and diamond-plated panels. The rear ramp door is open, revealing a huge motorcycle with a foot wide rear tire in the process of being unloaded. I figure they must have a Boss Hoss[2] with either a 280 or 300 series tire. I rotate the van's ignition key to the off position, as I throw open the driver's door and hop down to determine if they are running the 4 liter Chevy V6 in that frame or the V8 big block.

"Hey guys, nice bike!" I call out to the three bikers that are starting to roll the Boss down the ramp. I try to get a closer look while also being mindful to stay out of their way. Oh - this is a small block; they are running a Chevy ZZ4 350 cubic inch motor ... a high performance engine similar to what's in a Corvette. Then, I start to wonder why they didn't just start the bike and back it out, since these bikes come factory-equipped with an automatic transmission with reverse, but hey - not my call.

"Thanks…" they respond. They look up once the bike is stopped on level ground. The largest biker is a mountain of a man. His face lights up when he sees me. I feel recognition of kindred souls, although I'm sure we've never met before. To his left is the scrawny, wispy haired, sidekick. A snicker is heard from the third man, drawing my attention to a handsome biker with a beard. From the sneer on his mouth, it seems he's judging the condition of my van, and then he turns to look at me. I'm an attractive female with shoulder length curly hair, slender build, and a happy, yet reserved demeanor. I'm wearing flare-legged jeans and a company t-shirt to justify writing off travel expenses. The once black shirt is faded from years of washing, but nicely softened so that it feels good against my skin. I rarely wear makeup and today is no exception. Basically, I'm a tomboy that's grown into a woman. But, not wanting to flaunt my sexuality, I continue to dress the part of the tomboy.

I give a half-smile in response to his snicker while thinking to myself, yeah, my van is a piece of crap, but I purchased it just to make this one trip and it's doing what it's supposed to - so that's good enough for me. You don't know my story, so don't judge.

Turning back to the gentle giant whose frame casts a shadow over the smaller man, I ask, "Is this your bike?" I'm guessing that it is, because he's just so big that he would look right at home riding it. He must be over 6'4" and around 250 pounds, and by the look of his chest and arms, enjoys working out. His face is gentle and his eyes are equally bright,[3] a beautiful blue with a twinkle that lets me know he's kind, yeah … this is someone I feel comfortable talking to.

"You got that right!" He replies with a booming voice. "And my wife says I must have a screw loose to spend so much money on a bike like this. And I do! Come here and look!" He points to the back of his bald head and turns a little, so I can see what he's referring to. It's a tattoo of a screw coming out of his head!

"Nicely done!" I laugh.

He returns the laugh, "Ya see? I've got a screw loose! Bwahahahaha!" And he throws his head back and laughs so hard that his entire body jiggles! What a character! I really like this guy!

The laughter subsides and I direct the conversation back to the Boss, "I've heard these bikes are really excellent to drive because of the lack of vibration. Is that true?"

"Oh yeah, it's a super-smooth ride." He responds in his deep voice. "Between the weight of the bike and the exceptional

16

engineering, this bike is pure power once you grab a fist full of throttle. I won't let you ride mine, but they've got demos set up just outside Sturgis."

"Maybe I will, but with my weight and that much horsepower, I'll probably be horizontal and hanging onto the grips with my legs flailing out behind me in the wind!" We laugh at the visual. "Well, I won't keep you. I'll take a closer look at your bike once it's set up in the staging area. I'd better get unloaded myself …," I say with a wave of my hand. "Nice meeting you all!"

I turn and make my way to the back of the van and become focused on the task at hand. Opening the double doors, I proceed to slide out a 2'x10' wood plank with aluminum transition plates that I had screwed onto the ends of the board earlier that week. I position the plank against the lip of the floor and shift it back and forth a little to ensure that it's secure. Then I walk around to the side doors and open them up to gain access to the front of the bike. While fabricating the ramp, I also installed a front wheel chock[4] and some tie down rings[5] into the floor of the van - luckily the floor still had solid metal! There's nothing better than peace of mind that the bike is staying exactly where it's supposed to, while traveling long distances. The ratchet tie downs[6] are connected to some soft loops,[7] which are then secured around the lowest portion of the handlebars. I had compressed

17

the forks[8] a little to minimize the suspension from moving, but not so much that it was going to damage the fork seals. Taking a close look, I don't see any leakage so everything appears to have made the road trip without mishap.

"Hey, are you planning on unloading this bike by yourself, little lady?"

My reverie is interrupted as I realize that someone is talking, trying to gain my attention. I look up to see the three bikers from next door peering in the back doors.

The giant offers, "We can give you a hand, if you'd like."

I look at them in surprise, almost as if weighing the decision. Why was I hesitating?! Of course I'll take their help! I break into a wide grin that hopefully offsets my surprise, and lets them know how appreciative I really am.

"Sure!" I respond, and then take charge of my new assistants. "I'll hop on the bike, and if you ..." I motion with a nod of my head to the silent guy, "could hop in here and gently release this tie-down and you ..." I nod to the bearded guy "could release the right tie-down here at the same time." Then I motion to the giant, "and if you could make sure the ramp doesn't move and that I don't descend too quickly, then we should be able to roll this out no problem." They all take their positions as indicated, and as a team, the four of us ease the motorcycle out of the van, down the narrow ramp, and onto the gravel lot. I put the

18

kickstand down and dismount while explaining, "I knew this might be a challenge unloading the bike being solo and all. But, when I drove in here and looked around for an incline to lessen the angle of descent, I couldn't find one. So, I really appreciate this. I swear you're all heaven sent!"

"It was our pleasure. This is a beautiful bike you've got here … and you are?" The giant holds out his hand for an introduction.

I take his burly hand in a firm grip and reply with a smile, "My name is Katarina Zora. And you?"

"I'm called Groovy J, and this here is Hollywood," he says, using his free hand to slap the chest of the pretty boy biker. And this is Mike." He motions with a nod to the silent guy.

"Pleased to meet all of you." I release Groovy J's grip and shake hands with the silent guy, who now has the name of Mike. I'm not expecting to remember his name, I have a hard time with that - it's never anything personal. But nicknames, those are easier to remember. I turn to Hollywood, yeah, his name suits him. I hold my hand out to shake his, and he takes my right hand into *both* of his and then rubs his middle finger on the inside of my palm. What the hell?! I remember learning that signal back in school as a way to tell someone you're interested in hooking up. I'm shocked and slightly amused to come across this little flirtation from the past. Then he holds my hand a little while longer and gives it an extra squeeze just before releasing.

"If there's anything else I can do for you...." He lets his voice trail off suggestively.

I ignore the innuendo and jerkily turn my back on him, addressing the other two guys, "I really appreciate your help. And good luck to all of us in the show today!"

"Well, hold on there, little lady ...," Groovy J begins.

"Katarina." I correct him.

"Okay, Katarina ... sorry." He says with a slight incline of his bald head as if tipping his hat. "How about telling us a little about your bike here? This is mighty beautiful. I take it that you are the proud owner, is that correct?"

A smile returns to my mouth from his politeness and kind words, "Yes, I finished her up this spring and thought she was really beautiful. But, I wasn't sure just how nice until I took her to the Motorcycle Madness show this summer and she took 1st place, Best Paint, AND Best in Show! So I thought I would try my luck at The Rat's Hole and here I am!"

Groovy J laughs at my excitement, "Well, I'm glad you made it! This paint *is* outstanding. What color it is?"

"It's a girl's color." Ah, so the silent guy does know how to speak.

20

I smile kindly at Mike's words, "Yes, I have heard that before, and I guess you could call it a girl's color, which is appropriate since it *is* a girl's bike." I tease Mike lightly, because I imagine him to be a little addled in the brain. Then, I turn back to Groovy J, "The color is called gold to magenta pastel, because it's one of the color shifting paints from PPG's Harlequin line.[9] House of Kolor used the name Kameleon[10] to designate their color shifting paint, so most people call these paints Kameleon. But, that's not correct. Do you see how it looks like magenta …"

"It looks pink." Mike says matter-of-factly.

"To an untrained eye perhaps, but I can assure you the color's name is gold to magenta pastel." I inform Mike with an

21

air of gentle authority. "But, do you see how it picks up the gold tones at the edges, almost as if it's glowing?" The three bikers move their heads around, and then start bending their bodies in awkward positions to see the shift.

"Yeah, that's really beautiful …" Hollywood stretches the word 'beautiful' out, while turning to gaze at me. I look away, starting to feel a little irritated. What's this guy's deal? There are thousands of women here. Why can't he flirt with someone who wants it?

Groovy J points to the rear fender, "It also looks like you've got a lot of clear on this."

"How about 30 coats," I reply. A whistle of amazement is heard from more than one pair of lips. "I know it's a lot of clear, but this was the old DAU82 that PPG[11] used to make. And, I brought it on slowly with proper dry times between each session. Plus, if you look here, you'll see why I did that." I direct the other two men to come around to the rear of the bike where the giant is standing. Then I point out the brake light and turn signals, which are flush-mounted in the sheet metal. Each of the three sections is shaped like a diamond. The turn signals are smaller, and sit on each side of a larger, reverse diamond which is the rear brake light. "I had wanted the surface to be as flush as possible, so I used the clear to fill in the difference. The lens is from an old 1984 Mustang tail light. I brought the rear fender to a

22

salvage yard and looked through a ton of different tail light assemblies until I found the perfect curvature. Then I cut up the lens and notched the edges in a step-down fashion so they would fit into the openings that were laser cut in the fender, and then glued everything in place. Then to fill in the level difference, I started applying the clear - until I hit around 30 coats and my intuition told me it wasn't a good idea to go any further! As it is, with this much clear on the parts, I have to make sure the bike doesn't experience any sudden temperature changes because metal will contract and expand with hot and cold, but the paint will do so much more slowly. To prevent any sort of cracking, I can't splash the bike with cold water on a hot day or anything, but I think it's totally worth it. I really like how this all looks."

The men nod in agreement, and Mike reaches out his hand to feel where the lens meets the sheet metal. "Niiiice…"

"Whoa! You don't touch someone else's bike!" I scold Mike. "I don't want the paint to get scratched if there's any dirt on the surface or on your hands!" Mike recoils his hand quickly and steps backward, almost losing

his balance. Oops, didn't mean to scare the poor guy!

Then, Groovy J notices the airbrushed mouse underneath the taillight assembly, on the bottom portion of the rear fender. "And THAT is groovy like an old time movie! Bwahahahaha! Why do you have a gerbil on your bike?"

I can't resist laughing. "That's not a gerbil, it's a mouse!" I answer good-naturedly. "The mouse represents the southern direction in Native American spirituality, although, in some tribes, it's the coyote. But, in the *Medicine Woman*[12] books I read, it's the mouse, which stands for trust and innocence, so that's why I went with it. Here, look …" I direct him back to the gas tank sides. "If you look at the airbrushing here, you'll see several golden eagles flying toward sacred land. Below the eagles are bear footprints painted to look like turquoise stones. I saw a similar line drawing in a book once, although I can't remember

24

the name. Anyway, this represents east and west. The west is the bear, which teaches us intuition and introspection. The eagle is for the east, illumination. This translates to introspection on oneself results in illumination of the Self. Then, on the front fender," I explain as I walk to the head of the bike, "you'll see an airbrushing of the white buffalo. That's for the north, and for wisdom. This signifies how we start in the south with trust and innocence until we gain wisdom in the north, and then we return to trust and innocence after our heads are full with knowledge so we maintain balance and don't end up as egomaniacs. These are

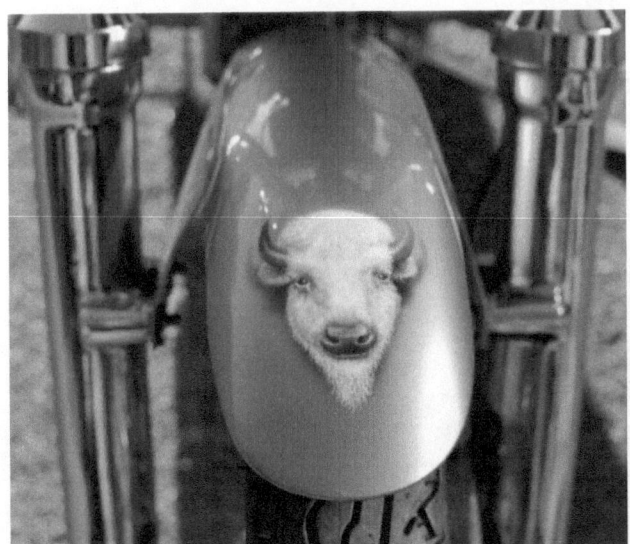

the paths of the medicine wheel, as I understand them. In fact, this entire bike is my tribute to shamanic spirituality."[13]

"So, are you Native American?" Mike questions.

"No, I'm not. At least not in this lifetime, but portions of their spirituality have really worked in my life, such as sage.[14] I used to be really angry, but by incorporating the smudging

25

ceremony[15] I was able to dissipate that anger so I could begin to lead a better life. Sage removes negativity from a person or place."[16]

Groovy J pipes in, "Hey, I heard about sage on Jay Leno years ago when he had Robert Downy Jr.[17] as his guest. For some reason, it stuck in my head that Robert used sage and it was instrumental in getting him over his drug addiction and back on top. This was before the Iron Man[18] or Sherlock Holmes'[19] movies."

"Sage, huh?" Mike says contemplatively. "That could be useful …"

Hollywood interrupts and turns to me, "So *you* painted this?"

Instantly, my stomach tightens. I'm not sure if it's the emphasis on 'you', or that it's Hollywood asking, but I'm really starting to dislike this guy. "What? You don't think a woman can paint?" I hear my voice go out of

26

resonance, and it comes across harsher than I want it to. Plus, they did help me get the bike out of the van, so I try to calm my response. But, just because I want to be polite, doesn't mean I have to look at Mr. Pretty Boy, so turning to Groovy J, I answer, "I started my own custom paint shop back in '91, and I went through auto body school and graduated top of the class, so I definitely know how to paint." My eyes, almost involuntarily,

sneak a glance at Hollywood to make sure he had heard, and then I continue addressing the giant. I motion for Groovy J to inspect my bike once again. "If you look at the frame here, you'll see that every weld has been molded with body filler." I point to several different locations to emphasize just how smooth every weld location

transitions. "See, this bike is one fluid motion from front to back. And every part is one-off, well except for the oil tank and rear fender which is from a FL - but I had to use a BFH to get that to fit. Even the chain guard needed to be altered. The actual airbrushing, I designed it and sprayed some. But, I hired a local guy to do whatever was over my skill level. Then, there are all these ghost graphics …" I continue pointing at different locations on the bike, "the beaded chest plate on top of the tank, these arrows, and an arrowhead around the tail lights. All this is done in the same color as the base, but because there's so much clear in between the top coat and the ghost graphics, the paint appears to float over itself." I stop talking and exhale deeply, willing myself to relax. I'm talking way too fast and my hands are clenched. I glance over in the general direction of the registration table and notice a line forming.

"I know a FL is a large framed Harley, but what's a BFH?" Hollywood asks, making me have to look at him once again.

"Big Fucking Hammer." I answer curtly. My comment is met with a snort as he looks away, and I glance at registration again to give a hint that I need to get going.

"Well, this is just beautiful," Groovy J says with admiration. "I know you are going to do wonderfully in the show today. Actually, do you have a card? I've been tossing around the idea of having some aircraft panels with screws instead of rivets, and then I can have some of those screws loose and others ready to fall off!" A light smattering of laughter goes around the group, breaking the tension.

I smile gratefully at Groovy J and reach into my back pocket to pull out a business card, but the pocket is empty. "Oh wait, I have them in the van. Here - let me grab some." I do a quick half jog to the front driver's door and hop back in. Reaching for the cards that are on the console, I notice that my hand is shaking from the confrontation. I take a moment to calm myself. Then grab a small stack of business cards, just in case anyone else asks.

As I turn back to the guys, both Mike and Hollywood have returned to their trailer, but Groovy J is still waiting expectantly. "Hey, sorry about Hollywood back there. He can be a bit annoying at times, but I don't think he meant anything by asking about the paint."

"It wasn't about the paint. It was because he was flirting with me."

"Oh! Well ... that's just how he is! You know - you should think of it as a compliment. Most ladies really like Hollywood."

Looking at Groovy J defiantly, I couldn't believe this leader of men was telling me to accept the role of sexual objectification because his friend was handsome! I explode, "I am NOT most ladies. I'm the business owner of a successful custom paint shop. I literally built it from the ground up with the help of a buddy - framing, electrical, *everything*, AND I'm a

29

Navy veteran who served 7 years. I HATE being dismissed to a pretty face with *a place to stick a dick*! I mean seriously - if people could see the amount of CRAP I've had to go through to get where I am today!" I glare at Groovy J, whose eyes have grown wide, and realize that I'm out of line, and my anger is coming out sideways. Inwardly, I reprimand myself as I feel my face flush. "Aww … man ... I'm sorry. I should get going … get the bike checked in and set up."

He holds up his hands to stop me. "Wait - what just happened here? What crap are you talking about?" Groovy J says with genuine concern.

I hesitate, preferring to bolt than reveal myself, but since we connected so easily at the beginning, I feel I should offer some sort of explanation for my outburst. I let out a heavy sigh before answering, "In a nutshell, when I was 2, our family took in a 4 year old psychotic foster boy. We didn't know that until later of course, but it really created some interesting household dynamics, to say the least. One of the things he would do was erupt in sudden, intense anger and since I was so young, I observed this and it got programmed into my brain as the way to respond when I want people to back off. So I'm still working on it, obviously." I smile awkwardly. "I apologize for bitching at you. But, at least I can see what I'm doing and why – so with awareness, I know I've got the key to change it." I stop, but then decide to add, "But, in my defense, it's all relative, because when my brother would get angry, he'd grab the largest butcher knife in the block and chase us through the house trying to stab us!"

"Serious?" J asks incredulously.

"Yeah. We'd run to the bedroom at the end of the hall because there was a wall you could brace your feet against and hold the door firmly closed. It was the safe room for my siblings and I. Our foster brother would stab the door. Then throw his entire body against it, trying to get in. There was a pushed-in section where the wood had given way that was located at knee height. Eventually he'd calm down and go away. No one ever bothered to fix the door."

"Damn!" Groovy J responds. "That sounds like something out of 'The Shining'![20] Where were your parents?"

"Out. It never happened when they were home, of course. And, if we told them when they returned, we were informed that we needed to learn to fight our own battles."

"Sounds like my folks there. But, this was a four year old kid chasing you?"

I look at J perplexed, and then I catch up with his line of thinking and laugh at the visual. "No. But, hahahaha! I just pictured him as a freaky little doll coming after us with a knife! Hahahaha!" Groovy joins in laughing also.

I continue, "No, he wasn't four - this happened years later, but I can see how it sounded like that! Hahahaha!" As the laughter dies away and my smile fades, I consider telling him more. Something about this guy makes me want to open up, and since that is a rare thing, I decide to go with the flow.

"This was after he got kicked out of juvy[21] and sent home, around twelve or so. It was all rather confusing actually … he'd be sent off to an institution. They'd say they couldn't handle him and recommend committing him to the state hospital. My mom would refuse and bring him back home. There would be tons of visits to therapists, and then he'd steal a tractor and take it on a rampage through a greenhouse. The police would be called, flashing lights would alert the neighbors that he did something once again, and my tight-lipped family would seclude until the embarrassment died down. The court day would come and some judge would send him back to a boy's home after looking at his huge rap sheet.[22] He'd be locked up for a few years until a suicide attempt would scare the facility and they wouldn't want to deal with him anymore, which meant he'd come back to live with us again … a back and forth type of deal. I never knew when he would show up. But, my mom said we had to be nice to him and not piss him off because no one else wanted him … talk about pressure!" I give J a side glance then add, "That wasn't the worst though … what really sucks is that he sexualized me at the age of five.[23] That continued for three years until he was sent off to the psych ward for the first time."

"For molesting you?"

"No ... for other crazy stuff, there was a lot." I wave my hand dismissing the rest. "Anyway, because of the abuse, all my life people would say 'I look easy' or they share inappropriate sexual stories, or the friends I make always end up revealing sexual abuse in their past, as well. It's like some secret society and we're all drawn to each other. Well, coming here today, I was just so excited to enter my bike in the show. And it's not like I'm half-dressed or doing the Glencoe parade![24] But still, here comes Hollywood with his flirting and back talk and I'm like, really?! I have to deal with this shit today??" I pause to let out a heavy sigh, and then yet another, which helps to release the frustration. With a shrug of my shoulders, I confess, "I guess what I'm *really* pissed about is that I can't just say NO. When Hollywood made the first pass, I couldn't simply say something decisive like, 'knock it off' or 'I'm not interested.' I freeze, then avoid. I think of a good comeback later, but never in the moment. So, it's not so much that I'm pissed at him, I'm pissed at myself and my lack of being able to voice that he's crossing my boundaries." I take another deep breath. "Then, since I can't say anything, he keeps trying - and I keep freezing. *It's very frustrating*! And it all seems to happen in fast motion, so I miss

33

opportunities to stop it. But, at least I'm aware of what I'm doing, so I know that is key to changing it. Assertiveness works better than aggressive or passive-aggressiveness. I'm still practicing on having assertive responses and haven't quite gotten it down yet – but I will." I look at J, wondering what sort of reaction he will have to my telling him my back-story so soon after meeting him. Instead, he asks, "What do you mean by awareness is the key to change?"

I raise my eyebrows because I'm impressed. It seems he has a mind open to learning more. I respond, "If you can see something happening, then you have an opportunity to change it. I've got a bunch of effective techniques that I've learned over the years."

J laughs, "I see myself doing things I want to stop all the time! I wouldn't even know where to start."

"Your Higher Self knows. By sincerely putting out the intention to have something change, things will arrange and appear in your life to fulfill that desire."

"How do you know?"

I'm not sure about the best way to answer him. Do I try to sound scholarly and list the books that I've read over the past few decades? Do I pull out my clergy card? Or do I admit that I live as a hermit, allowing a lot of time for introspection? No … I want to be as direct as possible. "I've had a lot of experience in the healing fields with some pretty amazing results." I respond with a deep look of knowing.

Groovy absorbs for a moment, and then looks away. As he turns to face me again, his voice is gentle, "I'm sorry the abuse happened to you. But, you seem to be doing really well, despite it. There's something extraordinarily healthy about you, like an inner light … maybe that's why Hollywood was flirting with you?"

"I just know that I'm here to show a beautiful bike that I'm proud of."

"Well, if you can create something this beautiful …" He says while motioning to my bike, "that means there's something beautiful within *you*."

I study his face. I'm not sure if his remark is flirtatious or not.

Groovy J looks over at his friends. Mike and Hollywood have some liquid spray wax that they're using on the fenders and tank. Then he looks back to me and opens his mouth to speak, but shuts it again. Then he looks away. When he turns back again, his face shows concern. "Things are kind of crazy right now in my world. It's hard to know what to believe. Your bike there - your tribute to Native American spirituality - it resonates with me. I've always thought that if we hadn't killed millions of

35

them and taken their land; they might have shared their wisdom with us. I mean, this land was *pristine* for thousands of years. Everyone could drink the water right from the stream, and their kids grew up knowing they had a future. Us white guys come along and it's gone to shit in couple hundred years. And now, my little peeps … well, I've got money and a nice house, but if there's no water or Earth – what good is it? I keep hearing about air that's getting more toxic,[25] bees that are dying off all over the place,[26] people getting cancer, and everything is so god damn expensive! Hell, I feel like a fucking cash machine!"

I don't really hear a question in his comments, so I remain quiet.

He continues, "And then, I've seen some weird ass shit with no idea how to interpret it. My buddies over there," J motions to his friends, "they don't want to hear it. They just want me to be good ol' Groovy J, the life of the party, the owner of the bad ass toys. But to tell you the truth, I'm bored with all my toys and sick of worrying about the future. How the hell are we going to fix all the shit that's going wrong?"

"I'm not seeing the same world as you, J. By turning my life 180 degrees from where I started, I'm seeing the world healing and becoming more balanced with nature."

"Really?!"

"Each person who does their inner work makes the path easier for those who follow. And what we focus on, gains momentum. I'm excited for the Golden Age that's dawning! That's the whole symbology of my bike here!"

J looks intensely into my eyes and says, "You must be seeing something that I've missed. I'd like to talk with you more. Some *real* talk. It seems I need to get up to speed. This sort of stuff never caught my attention before, but I could use a crash course. Are you willing to hang out?"

"Yeah, sure, but I can only offer my experiences. I don't know if it will apply in your world, but I'm willing to share what I've learned."

Nodding his head yes, Groovy J has a plan that he feels good about. "How about whoever is done setting up their bike first, finds the other?"

"Sounds good. See you then." I say, giving him a nod in closing.

Extending his hand, we shake, and then pull each other into a half hug, patting each other's back firmly twice. I smell expensive cologne. As we let go, J walks away to rejoin his friends and I turn my attention to my Harley hybrid. I turn the key, open the petcock, lift the choke lever, give the throttle two full turns, then hit the start button. The motorcycle roars to life with that wonderful sound of thunder. Then, I load the ramp back into the van, lock the doors, and return to the bike to close the choke. I hop on the bike, and then … hesitate. Visualizing a piece of paper in the glove box, I quickly assess if it's worth the effort to get off the bike and retrieve it. Shaking my head and laughing a little on the inside, I silently reprimand myself. I *know* intuition is what turns life into a treasure hunt, and still, I scoff … oh well. I double check that the kick stand is down, and then lean the bike to the left and get off. I unlock the van, grab the paper and with a quick fold, place it in my back pocket. Hopping back on my bike, I give a quick kick to the stand, and I'm on my way to registration.

Chapter 2: **Motorcycles**

The Rat's Hole,[27] the world's best-known chopper and trike show, attracts world class competitors from Australia, Japan, Germany, and throughout the United States. There are twelve classes, five places, and a massive table full of trophies. First Place is a four-foot-tall double tier trophy with an angel holding her hands upward, standing gracefully on a golden cup, with four eagles standing as sentry guards. The top winners are invited to return the next year to judge; I am hoping to be among them.

While waiting in line to register, I start to regain the excitement of being in Sturgis for bike week. I survey the space where the motorcycles are being displayed. The scenery is beautiful and I feel pride in how the majority of bikers are so different from the rest of the money-driven world. Karl, otherwise known as Big Daddy Rat, chooses to hold the bike

39

show at Hills and Plains Park, at the east end of Sturgis.[28] Mature trees offer sanctuary from the heat, rocky cliffs are a backdrop against the sky, and there are plenty of places where you can kick off your boots and relax after the ride. The food trailers and vendors are 'mom and pop' operations run by people who are bikers themselves, giving the entire atmosphere one of community. This is in complete contrast to the cement tourist traps I see the rest of the sheeple[29] being led to accept. I hope bikers never allow the money game to seduce them to stray from

what's really important - nature and freedom.

The bikes already set up in the staging area are on the grass in rows length wise, with 2 feet between tires to allow spectators room to walk around and really check out what people are doing to personalize their ride. Bikes are grouped according to model and engine size with a separate class for the metrics. Then, there are the specialty classes like Antique, Bagger, and

Rat bike. The Rat bikes are always amusing. In the old days, they were held together with ingenuity and had little care given to appearance. Now, guys have taken it to the next level of rat-ness, gluing all sorts of junk onto their rides. Skulls, buttons, action figures, you name it. Some of these bikes you can stare at for hours and still find new pieces of crap to point out to your friends! Ha!

People watching here is great, too. I can't see a lot of variety in clothes - blue jeans, t-shirts, and vests seem to be the go to - but those who enjoy standing out, really do so in spades. In the registration line with me is a shirtless old timer with bells on his pierced nipples and cheesy x-ray vision glasses on his face. I laughingly smile at him and he smiles back, teeth stained by nicotine. We both turn to watch as a beautiful, long-haired woman walks by wearing a full Indian headdress and a black bikini under black leather chaps. The chaps accent her shapely, perfectly tanned thighs wonderfully - they actually look silky and it's really her skin … smooth. Looking another direction, I spy a greybeard wearing pig's ears, snout, and glasses. He poses for a photo with a couple of nice young ladies who are topless, but not exposed. They have airbrushing over their breasts to comply with the law. The small breasted one has orange slices with juice dripping down her side; the larger breasted woman has watermelons for her tit camouflage. Nicely done people! Hahaha!

41

Over by the vendors' area where there's a hardtop surface, I notice a crowd starting to gather. A scraggly biker wearing jeans and a tank top has positioned himself standing alongside his bike for a burnout, while holding on to the handlebars. He revs the engine and pops the clutch. The back tire starts to spin, and then smoke. A cheer goes up from the bystanders as he walks the billowing bike in a circle, laying a chunky smear of rubber the entire way. The grayish white cloud starts drifting towards us and we get a whiff of the awful smell of burnt rubber that's simply part of the fun. As he's completing the circle of smoke, while grinning at the attention he's receiving, his momentary lapse of focus allows a loss of grip on the front brake. His bike begins to creep a little. With the brake no longer locked, he starts being pulled forward by the machine while his fingers grasp unsuccessfully. It's too late. The strain pulls the bike into a quick headstand, then a 180 with him being swung around and his feet leaving the ground! His bike lunges at an angle and then hits the cement slab with a crunch, pulling him on top of the hot engine. His buddies run over and pull him straight up and off the bike with his arms and legs splayed in all directions, like a horse fallen on ice. Then, some other guys pick up his bike to halt the gas that has started leaking from the fuel tank. The cheering becomes more enthusiastic, appreciative of the unexpected show of a clown that only hurt his pride.

42

→ ● ←

I laugh again and step forward, as it's my turn at the registration table. "I'm entering a Sportster." I tell the hard body with the clipboard.

"Stock or Radical class?" She asks.

"Probably stock, but what's the difference?" I question.

"Are there any alterations to the frame?"

"Yes, it's been stretched two inches and raked to thirty-three degrees."

"Radical then. Here … fill this out, check this box. Pay Nicole at the cash register right there. Then take this card with your number and put it by the front tire. You'll be parking over in that section." She motions with her pen to where the other Sportys are lined up.

"Okay, thanks." I follow her directions and move methodically through the line. After paying the entrance fee, I start my bike up and head over to my spot. Once I tuck the information sheet securely under the tire, I check out the competition. I know there are more bikes to come, but right now my main rival looks like a Sporty with a Paughco[30] rigid frame that is molded. The tins have some nice graphics in primary colors. The billet[31] wheels are a great touch, especially since my front wheel is a standard spoke and my rear a solid Fat Boy[32] rim. However, my wiring is run through the handle bars - I should pick up points for that. Plus, I have switched to a Wide Glide

→ ● ←

front end with only two dummy lights integrated on top of the triple tree - a green neutral light and red oil light. The Paughco still has factory electrics and controls. Both bikes look good, but I really believe that mine is better. Well, all I can do at this stage is hope that the judging is fair and that the best bike wins. I snap some photos of my creation as a keepsake. Then, I wander around looking at all the other cool bikes being readied for competition, taking pictures of any paint work that I haven't seen before or that's done really well. Later, I'll put them into 3-ring binders for my customers to browse through when needing ideas for their own paint scheme.

Spotting Groovy J's sweaty head bobbing around his Boss Hoss, I make my way over. "Hey J, you all set up yet?"

"Yep, sure am Kat."

I grimace.

He notices. Being a gentleman, he asks, "Okay, what nickname do you go by?"

"My friends call me Zora."

"Zora – I like it! Want to go grab a couple beers and chat, Zora!?"

"Beer? Naw, with this heat I'd rather have some water and then go sit in the shade over there and watch the bikes come in." I motion to the edge of the display area where the tree line starts. "Will that work?"

J thinks for a moment, then replies. "Okay, yeah, I get it … that's healthier. And yeah, I suppose I do feel a little dehydrated. The sun can really beat down on you when you don't have any hair for protection." Raising a hand to rub his bald noggin, he looks over to the vendors' area and points out where water is being sold. We walk over, purchase a couple glass bottles of artesian water,[33] and then return to the grassy area. I scan the land with my eyes slightly out of focus, looking for the most inviting place to sit. One section of grass seems more vibrant than the others and I ask J if he can see that also. Noticing what I'm referring to, we head over. As we sit down, I start unlacing my riding boots and pull them off. Then, I remove my socks.

"Getting comfortable, I see." Groovy J gives me a little shit.

"Yes, I am. My feet don't stink, so no smart ass remarks. I have my reasons."

"And, what are these reasons which you speak of so freely?" J says in a strange accent, trying to be cute.

"I need to massage my feet. It's called reflexology[34]. Any sore spots that I find correlate to an area in my body where some toxins have built up. By applying pressure and working out the knot, I heal myself."

"You can massage my feet next!" J jokes.

45

"I'll pass!" Joking back, I wrinkle my nose.

J watches me for a while, and then leans back on his elbows. This makes his chest jut forward; his shirt clings to his muscles, outlining how powerful this man really is. I begin massaging my left foot and turn to watch a bike putt slowly by.

J starts the conversation, "So, how long have you been riding?"

"I started when I was 15 and except for when I was stationed overseas, I've always had a bike. My first was a Kawasaki 100, then a Honda CB400 Super Sport, then a Kawasaki 750 LTD, now this Sporty, and I also have an Electra Glide at home for long trips. What about you?"

"I owned several gixxers[35] in my younger days. Then, I slowly acquired a stable with a Ducati, my father's old Knuckle, a Hayabusa, and now this Boss." He recalls. "Do most people know what they want to have painted, or do you come up with the ideas?"

"It goes both ways. Sometimes a customer will bring in a design they want reproduced on their bike. I'll use aspects of the original, but change it enough to make it my own. But the best is when the customer gives me a theme, chooses the preferred colors from the thousands of paint chips I have in stock, then allows me the freedom to create whatever the bike tells me it wants to look like."

"The bike tells you?"

"Sort of … it's using i-magi-nation, I am the magi – or magician – because I can see what is possible for the bike to become, in all its glory."

"Very groovy! So have you done a lot of paint jobs?"

"Yeah, I have."

"Do you enjoy it?"

"The process of creating beauty is what I love above all else. That's when time disappears. My favorite is symmetrical graphics using the principles of sacred geometry[36] meaning, I get to create motorcycle art using ancient wisdom!"

"Doubly groovy!" J laughs.

"Yes it is! And what's with the 'groovy' word there, *man*?!" I tease.

"Ah …" In absent minded memory of hair long gone, he raises a hand to his bald head again. "I was a hippie in my younger years. I had luscious man hair that the ladies loved to touch!" He swoons with an imaginary hair flip. "But … things change. Words change too. By holding onto the word, I let people know I'm a groovy guy!"

I smile and give him a thumb's up!

→ ● ←

He smiles with pride, then continues questioning, "You mentioned being stationed overseas. That was with the Navy?"

"Yeah, seven years, right out of high school." I reiterate. "My favorite was boot camp. There was a simplicity and peacefulness to the way we would start each day. You wake up and make your bunk, get dressed in your sharply ironed uniform, put on your freshly polished boots, and then stand in line in front of your locker. Once everyone was ready, we would march outside and go into formation. As a division, we would march to the galley, and then stand in line with other divisions. Going into parade rest, we'd wait for our turn to eat. Standing there, with nothing to do and nothing to think about, was the part that I liked best. Smelling the air; clean, crisp, and fragrant. Feeling like I was a part of something greater. I'd observe the transition of the night sky, variations of blue slowly stretching upward to extinguish the stars overhead, and it made me feel peaceful. Content. Even if my stomach was hungry I didn't mind, I knew satisfaction was near. At the time, I credited the military with creating these feelings of belonging. But now I know that it was the silence and the act of being still, of observing without thought. Even now, when I go outside and the temperature and sky is similar, I return to those Florida mornings during boot camp and smile." I feel myself time travel back a little, just from remembering.

48

→ ● ←

Then, returning to the present, I continue. "The discipline demanded was also a plus - knowing exactly what was expected out of me. No confusion, just cut and dry. If I do this, this, and this, I will be in good favor. I excelled in that environment. First, our company commanders made me the recruit section leader, and then the athletic petty officer. They even raised my rank to E-2 upon graduation, so that was a nice bonus!"

"Right on! A few extra dollars in your pocket!"

"But, once I was in 'A' school, the military turned back into a party so I just went along with it and partied too. I remember feeling disappointed that life was returning to the same old – same old. But if you know about ranks, does that mean you served also?" I was hoping so, because it would make J that much more of a brother.

"Yep – Navy too. My duty was on a nuclear submarine."

"Serious? You're such a big guy! Wasn't that difficult being on a little sub?"

"You get used to it. I'm not going to say I didn't bang my head a few times until the learning curve kicked in. Mind if I tell you my theory about learning curve?" J asks.

"Go right ahead."

J explains, "The first time that you try something, it's pretty much half-assed because you're getting a feel for it. So, it's never that great, but as long as you just say 'hey - learning

49

curve' it's not a big deal and you don't have to get down on yourself. I do this with my little peeps all the time. They'll be learning how to do something and if it doesn't quite work out, they look at me as if I'm going to be pissed. But nope, I just say 'learning curve' and then their little shoulders relax and they breathe a sigh of relief, because it takes the pressure off."

"I like it. Mind if I add that to the Toolbox?"

"What Toolbox?"

"Oh, that's just what I call my collection of healing graphs and articles. It's actually a folder on my computer's desktop where I add anything that strikes me as important."

"Go right ahead!"

"Thanks. So, what made you join?" I ask Groovy J.

"My dad. He was Navy the whole time we were growing up. He'd tell us stories and his voice would come alive as he'd share - like those were the best days of his life. I wanted to experience adventures like that, too. One of his favorites was when he was an airplane mechanic and they were working on the flight line. He was changing fluids, but also watching these two other guys working together on a F6F Hellcat. The propeller switch had been flipped on when the head mechanic told his apprentice to grab a tool. The kid walks over to get the tool and walks directly through the path of the spinning propeller – he didn't get sliced or knocked out or anything! It was totally a miracle!"

"Whoa … I love miracles!" I reply in amazement.

"Yeah, me too! But, he'd also tell us some nasty shit – like one guy who accidentally activated the ejection seat while inside the hangar and got splattered all over the ceiling ..."

"Ewww!"

"… or stuff like what they would do to each other in the pollywog-to-shellback tradition for crossing the equator. They'd save up the leftover food for days, and then put it into a large tube for anyone who hadn't crossed the equator to crawl through - no exception - and if someone bitched, he had to go through it twice. And that would really suck, because there was always someone puking in there. Once through the food and vomit tube, they'd come to the Royal Baby who was the fattest guy on ship. They'd grease his belly up and the poor pollywog had to take a cherry out of his belly button - with his mouth - to pass through and become a shellback."

"Gross! I'm not a big fan of traditions – in the military or even with families. I think they hold us back more than anything."

"And I'm not a big fan of authority. My dad told a story about these two airmen that were sunbathing - guess they wanted to look good for the ladies. Anyway, they didn't realize how

51

intense the sun was that close to the equator and got second degree burns. They went to the infirmary and because the sunburn was so bad that they couldn't work. The Navy court-marshaled them for destruction to government property!"

"Dang! Talk about adding insult to injury!" I exclaim.

"And it sucks being owned! Even though I've been out of the service for a while, I still feel like a slave to the government with all the taxes I have to pay!" J gets pissed.

But, knowing the truth of the Federal Reserve,[37] and not wanting to go there this afternoon, I steer our conversation back to naval experiences. "I almost witnessed some major destruction to government property. Want to hear?"

"Hell yeah! What happened?" J asks with renewed spirit.

"This took place while I was stationed in Rota Spain; I was up in the tower working ground control …"

"What was your rating?"

"Air traffic controller."

"Serious? That's impressive. How'd you get that job?"

"The entrance exam had us look at diagrams of boxes on paper and then fold them into cubes in our mind. I guess I do a good job of visualizing things. I'm also analytical. I spent my early years in a playpen trying to make sense of some really bizarre behavior happening around me."

"I hear you … but an air controller? That means you're smart. I've heard a lot of people wash out of that rate. I've also heard that it's really stressful, is it?"

"Only if you have crap equipment, otherwise, it's kind of like a video game. Put the blips in order; bring them to the runway threshold or to another controller's airspace. It's less stressful than being a check out girl with a long line of impatient customers!"

"Okay, I hear ya." J nods in agreement.

I continue, "So I'm in the tower looking out over the flight line. I'm watching this airplane that was being towed to the hangar for maintenance when I notice that the tow cart made a turn, but the plane didn't turn with it. Somehow, it unhooked and was slowly taxiing uncontrolled toward liquid oxygen tanks at the side of the airport. I alert the local controller who then puts all air traffic into an emergency holding pattern while the rest of us go through our emergency procedures. Grabbing binoculars, we watch the flight crew frantically try to stop the runaway C141. One guy threw a huge metal box under the front wheel, but it was completely flattened by the weight of the craft. The plane continued moving along, and it was slow… but on course for the tanks. If it made it there, we knew the explosion would be intense and we'd be incinerated. Looking at each other in partial shock, one guy suggests running down the stairs to dispatch.[38] But, why

53

bother? So, we return to watching and unconsciously hold our breath. The ground crew is still scrambling for a solution as the plane continues to slow down … closer … slower … closer … slower … closer … and … stop. It took a moment to register, but then we all look at each other in joy, and a cheer goes up as we realize we get to live another day! Woohoo! It was really a good feeling, because I felt like they were my family after that; I guess something about near-death will do that to people."

"Yes, yes it will. You never forget your mates that cross to the other side." We pause out of respect for a moment, and then J asks, "How did you like Spain?"

"I loved it! And … it sucked."

"Let's hear the love first."

"I was 18 years old, finally on my own, and living in a foreign country - that totally rocked! It felt like I was stepping back in time. In Rota, the people would go to the mercada, or market, each morning to buy their food for the day. Pure food is of high priority there. And speaking of fresh, my favorite restaurant was one where upon arrival; you go to the chicken pen and *pick out* the bird you want to eat! Then you play cards and drink while they kill, pluck, and cook the chicken. Talk about farm to table!"[39]

"You're making me hungry!"

"The taste was out of this world! Also in Spain, they serve small portions of quality food, called tapas, which is the opposite of America where people are given large quantities of a cheap product. My health improved there." I pause to recall, "Let's see ... what else was unique...? The phone booths cost a nickel. Household heat came from a small butane heater that had to be turned off at night, just in case the pilot flame went out, otherwise people could die from asphyxiation. The water heater was a small unit that hung in the bathroom. It only held enough water for one person, so if you lived with someone else, you had to take turns going first and getting the warm shower. And yes, I did live with someone else; it was my first experience of consensual love, which is what made it suck since our relationship only lasted two years. Being naïve, I thought once I found that special someone - that was it – we'd be together forever, so it was a bit of a shock to learn otherwise. Um ... okay ... that was an understatement there ... our breakup was actually devastating to me, because I was never taught any skills in regard to relationships. Then, growing up in a household where showing weakness resulted in ridicule – I was clueless on how to process tough emotions. So I drank – a lot. Didn't heal the heartache or solve anything, but, that was the past and now that I *have* done my work, I can remember those times without any triggers or negative impact. I actually feel gratitude for the time we *were* together - because we really had a blast exploring the country, skiing the Sierra Nevada Mountains at Christmas, and running with the bulls at Easter!"

"You ran with the bulls?! Bwahahahahaha! You're the first person I've met to have done that! And you're a lady!"

"This wasn't the mainstream event in Pamplona, but rather in Arcos. It's a city built on the side of a cliff where you can look down and watch birds fly. A bunch of us controllers would turn it into a full day drinking event with boda bags full of wine. The spot we'd witness from was neither the safest nor the best, but somehow a tradition was born so that's where we'd stand irregardless. Partying like a bunch of sailors, we were so drunk by the time they released the bulls we wouldn't have a safe place out of the beast's path like the smart Europeans hanging from gypsy bars[40] and behind barriers. One time, my love and I had to flatten ourselves in a doorway and freeze. Holding our breath and praying for invisibility, the bull passed so close we could see his wide and confused eyes. He charged the very next door, breaking it down and entering a family's home who had chosen not to participate – totally tearing it apart! It was intense, but it wasn't our time to go!"

"Right on! But let me ask you this, if it had been your time … well, what I mean is, what do you think about death?"

"I remember portions of my past lives, so whatever happens is fine. It feels like this whole living thing is continuous, just changing bodies – although spiritual masters say death is a mistake.[41] I don't know … I just do my best whenever I come up to bat, then leave the Earth better than I found it, so next time around it will be a nicer place to come home to."

"You're a reincarnation believer then. I'm not sure what I think yet ... but I'm leaning that direction. I just haven't had any solid experiences to convince me."

"There's this story on YouTube that was aired by ABC Primetime about a 3-year-old boy who remembers dying in a plane crash in a past life. He was 21 at the time his plane was shot down over the Pacific during WWII and that's when his last life ended. His parents in this life are highly educated, but reincarnation didn't fit into the religious dogma they identify with. So they were surprised when their son, at 3 years old, identified the drop tank on a toy plane – and *they* didn't know what that was. He'd tell them other things, as well. It took a while for the father to investigate all the different information that the child was providing, but once he did, the facts checked out. The name of the aircraft carrier, its location, the name of a friend from Iwo Jima who was still alive ... all of it happened the way the toddler recalled from his past life."[42]

"Interesting … I'll check out the video." J says.

57

Sensing that he wants to ask something else, I remain quiet.

With a slow exhale he asks, "And suicide - do you ever think about that?"

Such serious questions from someone who enjoys kidding around, I think to myself. But if he's willing to ask the tough question, the least I can do is answer truthfully, "Yeah ... I've thought about suicide a few times. Usually in long spells of loneliness. Boundaries make a mighty wall, and anything can happen when isolation gets out of balance. So I keep that escape route in my back pocket as a trump card, but when push comes to shove, I now know I won't do it. Part of me sees it as a romantic notion – it would end the pain, my problems would disappear, or maybe to prove a point. But, energy is energy. If I want to experience life differently, I have to *do* something different - not just eliminate my body, because the energy still remains. That's like when Hitler killed himself – it didn't end his energy of destruction, it just passed on to other people who were willing to pick up where he left off.[43] Imagine if he would have gone into seclusion, figured out where he lost the path of the heart, and explained it to his followers?[44] Energy needs to be transmuted into something that resonates at a higher vibration for the suffering to stop.[45] So - why do you ask? Are you considering it?"

"Me? No! I'm a dad. I need to be here for my peeps. But it's happening way too much with the soldiers out there.[46] I think it's because our world is so fucked up.[47] It's like everyone is telling us to be calm and keep on, but on some level we know that carrying on isn't going to cut it for much longer."

"I agree. Social order is ultimately dependant on the natural order of the Earth, and if we're punching holes in her and pouring in toxic chemicals, that's a hard-hitting dead end! Even the Spiritual Elders of the Earth have released a Council Statement saying that 'powerful technologies are out of control and are threatening the future of all life.'"[48]

"See – that makes it official then. Spiritual Elders sound like leaders who aren't trying to gain money from the Earth, just take care of it. And I need it improved so my little peeps have something worthwhile to inherit. They think I'm superman, you know? Those are some big shoes to fill ... so whatever you can share, I'm listening."

"I know a lot of people have varying opinions on the food supply, but personally, I'm very mindful of anything I ingest or put onto my body – most people in the U.S. have calcified pineal glands[49] and I don't want to be one of them because then I'd lose my connection to higher intelligence[50] and possibly my short-term memory. If you want your kids to be smarter than average, let them grow their own food and connect with the plants. At the

59

least, choose the highest quality food from local farmers. Avoid putting artificial crap into the body. And for those times that you don't have a choice, then know that humans are able to bless food with a loving state of mind, transmuting any poison or projection of fear that people extend to each other or to the Earth, because of a fear within them. There are stories of monks changing gruel into nutritious food during the Inquisition.[51] Love always wins over fear. I know it seems crazy right now, but growth is happening from this. Speaking of which, want to hear something really bizarre that happened?"

"I *love* the bizarre!" J says, leaning forward.

"Okay. There was this one relationship I was in, that fell apart many years back. I was actually grateful when we did break up, because I knew we weren't a good match. So three months go by, and I still haven't found anyone I want to be with. I start missing my old flame, and then, it progresses to agonizing over the loss. Then, I fall into this depression that sucked the life out of me and I start contemplating suicide. The thoughts kept getting worse to the point where I started planning the best way to do it. But in a moment of clarity - I was like, what the hell?! Why am I crumbling over a person that I didn't even want to be with? So, I gathered all my energy into the center of my body, and pushed out really fast and really strong. It was powerful, like a bomb exploding from the inside, and I actually *felt something*

60

leave my body! After that, I felt just fine - like my usual self again. No more whispers of death or anything!"

"Yeah, that is bizarre!" J agrees.

"I'm not done yet. So, I go to my lifelong chiropractor, who's also an energy worker, and she starts going through the check list and says in a concerned voice '*What did you do*?!' And, I'm like 'what'? She said I blew a hole in my ozone layer!"

"Humans have ozone layers?!"

"That's exactly my words to her! I'd never heard that before, but I have heard the saying 'as above, so below' so I guess it makes sense. But yeah, she could see I had done something, so I told her about the entity that kept whispering for me to kill myself until I got sick of it and blew it out of my body. She replies all nonchalant that next time I need to blow something out, remember to close up the hole afterwards, otherwise I leave myself unprotected and something else could get in!"

"Crazy!"

"I know! There's so much that we aren't taught. I just try to stay open to all possibilities."

In response, J opens up as well, "Back when I was in my 20's, I got into hard core drugs. One time, when I was all fucked up, I watched this guy weighing out grams on a scale, and I swear I saw demons flying around the drugs and then disappearing *into* them. Freaked me the fuck out. There was no way I was going to be involved with that shit after that. It was the last time I ever used anything hard core. I figured those little devils could gain access to my brain from going up my nose."

"What did they look like?" I ask uneasily.

"Like bats with long legs and beady eyes, but not really bats – just that sort of shape in a vacuum of darkness – but with eyes."

"Whoa … I'm glad I've never seen them … I prefer the whisperers to be invisible."

"Whisperers?" J asks, pulling back a little and scrunching up his forehead. It's amazing how many folds can be seen on a forehead when it's not covered by bangs.

Re-focusing on his eyes, I answer, "Just a cute name to reduce their creepiness, but I picture the little devil on the shoulder that whispers in my ear things I shouldn't do. But, crafty as they are, they whisper things that aren't really clear cut wrong, just things that will lead me on a dead end further down the road. That's why it's so important to know myself, so I can track my thinking to ensure I'm heading in the direction I really want."

"I don't get it - what do you mean?" J asks.

"We make choices based on love or fear. Personally, I've never seen the fear choices work out. Never. Plus, the fear can be fabricated. So - by making choices based on whatever feels the most loving, I ascend to a higher vibration.[52] Decisions from fear, obviously take me lower. And if I know myself, then I won't become confused when opposing truths present themselves. I've examined my beliefs and aspirations and I'm at peace with them."

"I know what I believe in - my little peeps! They have knowledge far beyond what I knew at their age. I see my future through them. But with all that's going wrong in the world, will there even be a future? I don't know what to do and it really pisses me off sometime!"

"You do realize that the entire media conglomeration is owned by a select handful, don't you?"[53] I offer to point out that things aren't as bad as they are sensationalized to be.

"I know about that – but there's still a shitload of things going wrong – even without their hype."

"Yeah … I suppose. I suspect the media hype[54] contributes to the apathy[55] of the majority, and now a lot of the population is suffering from a combination of cognitive dissonance[56] and post traumatic stress disorder.[57] Until that's dealt with, they are overloaded. Grounding will help.[58] I consciously ground all the time. And since I had to heal from childhood PTSD,[59] I've untangled from that web and can take action. But I keep my focus narrowed down to the solutions concerning the

63

essentials of life - clean air, water and food. Once those get worked out, I can expand to other subjects. But I *had* to start with fixing myself first."

J nods, "And that's one of the things bothering me - clean air and water - like that fracking[60] bullshit that's going on. I hear about it from some bros in the field and they're making big money, but they're draining water basins left and right.[61] It reminds me of a t-shirt I once saw about not being able to eat money.[62] I mean, this is people's *water* and it's gone – *permanently!* Then, those big wigs are exporting the natural gas[63] and tar sand crude[64] so that means America gets screwed at both ends! And my buddy? He has lung problems because of the methane gas and the docs say there's nothing they can do. He's going to be the richest man in the graveyard," J says with mix of aggravation and concern. "And he's not the only one I'm worried about. Of course the planet's going to heat up when you've got gigantic lighters burning all day and night. They have satellites photos showing the frack sites glowing like a goddamn city[65] from all those flares burning.[66] They reached carbon emissions equal to a million cars in just one year - from just *one* location[67] and there are locations all over the world!"[68]

I respond, "I'm sorry to hear about your buddy's health problem. I really hope things change before anyone else makes such a worthless sacrifice. I've also done research on those fracking sites and discovered they mix large volumes of hazardous chemicals[69] in open pits, which means the solvents are evaporating into the air. If there's something I know, it's solvents! Ever walk into a paint booth after leaving a quart of thinner open? And that's a drop compared to the toxic lake at those frack sites. When I cross referenced the chemicals listed on the hydraulic fracturing chemical registry,[70] against the Center for Disease Control's website,[71] guess what I read? The chemicals are classified as *extremely hazardous to life and health,* and these are being pumped *into* the Earth![72] It doesn't make sense that I have to follow all sorts of regulations and pay money for hazmat[73] handling to prevent even a tiny bit of *my* shop chemicals from spilling onto the ground[74] while here they are *pouring* it into the ground, thousands of gallons at a time."

"My buddy said those companies are exempt[75] because of some loophole[76] that Cheney[77] set in place, way back when. So if this reaches all the way to the presidency, what the hell can I do to stop it?" The frustration at feeling powerless is heard in his voice.

"Don't put toxic chemicals in your own body. The macrocosm reflects the microcosm."[78] I respond logically.

He jokes, "I'm not drinking any lacquer thinner! But I guess there are some poisons I could stop pouring into my body.

65

But what do we do about the government when it makes the decisions it does?"

"There are good people everywhere, encourage and support those representatives, especially at the local level. Petitions[79] are another way of getting yourself heard, and the legal system is helping also. The highest court in New York State has ruled that towns can use zoning ordinances to ban fracking.[80] Other people are creating works of art that are stopping pipelines because they are copyrighted, which overrides eminent domain.[81] And people are realizing there's more than one way to get fresh drinking water."

"Like what?"

"If you have land, you can dig a hole with sloping sides, put in the proper plants, and produce a mini-ecosystem with water clean enough to drink.[82] And if you don't have land, there are ways to collect water from the dew and humidity.[83] Plus, more and more states have made it legal to grow industrial hemp again.[84] A field of hemp cleans the toxins from the soil and water, and reduces carbon dioxide[85]so that will help ease fears of climate change. Some say that hemp is the tree of life mentioned in Revelations because it has thousands of uses.[86] 'On either side of the river was the tree of life, bearing twelve kinds of fruit, yielding its fruit every month; and the leaves of the tree were for the healing of the nations.' [87]

"And you can get stoned from it too! Bwahahahaha!"

"J! I'm talking about *hemp*, not cannabis! You'll only get a headache if you smoke it. And I know you're a funny guy, but if we laugh off the benefits, then how will anyone take it serious?"

"All right. I know it played a major part in the victory of World War II.[88] I just like to make others laugh – but I'll stop ripping on the plant."

"Thanks. Those tiny seeds might be the answer to correct the imbalances of the Earth. Then no one will have to work for companies they don't believe in. Instead, they can hop on the hemp gravy train because it's just starting to gain steam, and it's only going to keep on growing!"

"How so?"

"Because anyone can grow it! Ha! You don't need special equipment or schooling to drill it or mine it from the Earth. You can be your own boss with just a little bit of land. It grows in 4 months[89] and will feed you too, because the seeds are a super-food.[90] Hemp composite is 10 times stronger and 1/3rd lighter than steel, and 7 times stronger than concrete. It can be made into any building material[91] as well as a *biodegradable* plastic composite which is tougher than steel!"[92]

"Now that's groovy! I was wondering how we were going to deal with those massive islands of plastic floating around in the oceans!"[93]

"The kids being born will have many more solutions, and people *are* listening to them.[94] At least those who aren't falling for the propaganda and division techniques devised to make us fight amongst ourselves and debate what the truth is. When you polarize issues, you get emotional responses that can be predicted in advance to manipulate people and keep them stuck or keep them from looking behind the curtain. I mean seriously – when a problem comes up at home you don't debate with your loved ones, you compromise because you love them and want their best. Again, making decisions based on love and not fear. Then you can put the energy into creating solutions. I don't know why so many people don't see that …."

"Because they're still plugged in to the matrix!" J says with force.

The push of his words makes me stop.

Noticing, he continues with a softer tone, "Well, it's just what you were saying earlier. Most people still sit in front of the boob tube or listen to the corporate owned radio stations all day, so they're getting programmed even when they think they're not. My little girl has a special needs friend who can hear when the music has the subliminal tones in the background."[95]

68

"True – there *were* all those experiments during the holocaust, I can't image a controlling personality letting that go to waste - but it's easy enough to turn it all off. I haven't watched TV in over 12 years."

J nods his approval. "Right on. It's been 3 years since the wife and I got rid of ours. The young ones whined a bit, but my job is to keep my little peeps safe and they're not wise enough to see this bull for themselves. And since I tossed the tube, everything in our household has gotten better. The kids can focus and their imagination is improving. And when we go to the park, it's like nature becomes our TV, but it's interactive! Feeding a critter a peanut gives my little peeps more smiles than any cartoon ever did. I also buy musical doodads when I come across them. Before, my peeps would start fights with each other when they were bored but now, they start drumming out a rhythm and its great how quickly the others will hear and join in. We're a regular Partridge Family![96] Bwahahahahaha!"

"How many kids do you have?" I ask, switching the massaging to my right foot.

"Three - ages 12, 7 and 6. My kids saved my life. I've got to save theirs. Tell me about more self-sufficiency things like that personal pond. I really like that and I've got a friend with a backhoe that I'm going to talk with when I get home."

"I don't know if you'll consider this self-sufficiency, but I

69

stopped putting chemicals on my lawn. Clover and Creeping Charlie started growing and both of them are edible, and the bees love the clean source of pollen. Now a young girl in the neighborhood has started a hive, and she sells me back the honey at a very reasonable price!"

"Yeah but, my yard is a source of pride for me. What if I want to grow grass?"

"Then grow grass. You can't eat it, but I'm not going to tell you what to do. I'm just saying I'm letting mine go natural."

"What about Dandelions?"

"Yeah, those pop up twice a year - also great for humans to eat because they clean the blood.[97] Then, I have an aquaponic[98] gardening system combined with square foot gardening methods[99] because it uses a fraction of the water and grows a lot of food in a small space. Natural sunlight and soil make a huge improvement in the taste. Depending on climate, the Naturhus[100] – a green house built around the existing home, is also an option. Then, I'm saving up my dollars for a solar powered energy system[101] combined with hot water tubes.[102] But, in the meantime, there's a DIY solar system on youtube that's made from pop cans which can be built for just a few bucks."[103]

"Right on. Do you think solar is the energy of the future?"

"They've created clear solar cells that can be used as

glass,[104] and the solar roadways[105] and bike paths would be super cool because any ice or snow can be melted off, and even sensors can be used so if an animal steps onto the surface up ahead, you can be alerted in time to avoid. So solar is great, but going large scale[106] zaps flocks of birds – we need energy to be individualized and free. Along those lines, I'm interested in seeing how the torus magnetic generator[107] comes along."

"What about over population – are you worried about that?"

"Worry is a form of fear, so nope, no reason for it. If everyone stood shoulder to shoulder, we'd all fit inside Los Angeles.[108] Besides, Japan is working on a habitat dome for under the ocean.[109] We have lots of oceans, so that's room for lots of people. Maybe people will stop throwing their trash in the water then!"

J bursts out, "Hey! That sparks another Navy story! There was this one time when our sub was pulled into South Carolina. Me and the boys had some leave coming. And out there, they'd keep the subs on the Cooper River, which has a bunch of swamp land all around. So, we're all ready to go drink at the local bar in town, and afterwards, on the way back to base, we're having trouble catching a ride. Now normally, hitching a ride back wasn't tough, but this particular night there just wasn't any traffic, and I'm talking about a good 7 mile hike too. So, we're walking along, and pretty soon, we all need to take a leak. So, we stand on the side of the road and start pissing on a log that's lying at the bottom of the ditch. I remember thinking to myself that it seemed strange for there to be a log out here when there weren't any trees. And wouldn't you know it, the log fricking moves! It was a freaking alligator! Oh my god, it was so funny if you would have seen us, we're all stumbling backwards, piss streams crossing in the air, three grown men screaming in the moonlight with their wangers hanging out! Bwahahahahahaha!"

"Hahahahaha!" We both laugh and fall back onto the grass. "Hahahahahaha!"

Chapter 3: **Miracles**

J sighs happily, then looks at me quizzically and asks, "So why are you here by yourself?"

"I wasn't supposed to be, but yesterday I went to Deadwood with my friend Darlene. She upholstered the bike seat. She did a really good job with the inlaid suede graphics."

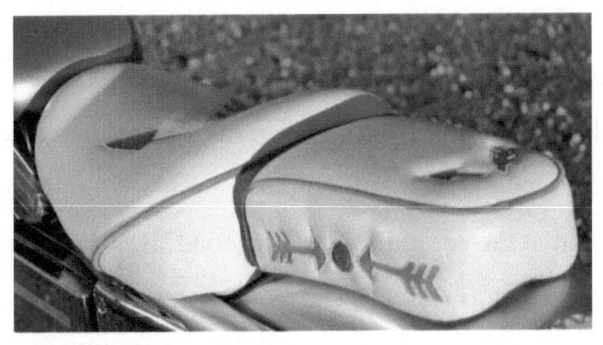

"What do the symbols mean?"

"A broken arrow stands for peace, and the two arrows pointing inward to a center circle - that wards off evil spirits."

"Too bad I didn't know about that symbol back in the day." J muses. "So, does it work?"

"The engine went back into the frame really smooth and no little nicks during any portion of reassembly. So, I'd say, so far so good."

→ ● ←

A couple more bikes rumble by. Among them is a torque series Indian heading over to the antique section. I make a mental note to take a closer look at that bike.

"Did Darlene die in Deadwood?" J pauses for a moment, and then lets out a "Bwahahahaha!" Apparently he's amused with his choice of words. I didn't really find it funny, but I chuckle, simply because I don't want to snub him.

"No, but she did start gambling and didn't want to stop. I kept telling her we had to leave, and she kept saying she wanted to play for another hour. And then another hour went by, and then another. Then it got dark and I *had* to leave because I still needed to get the bike ready for today. I was planning on taking 14A Eastbound back to I-90, but just at the edge of town I see this flashing road construction sign saying to use caution, they had just tarred and rocked the road. Really?! There was no way I was going to ride my show bike on that!"

"Where were you trying to get to?"

"Piedmont. We're camping on some private land."

"So what did you do?"

"I had to go through the black hills. Froze my ass off too. Earlier that morning when we hit the road, all I thought to wear was a t-shirt. I didn't bring a jacket, because it was so hot when we left, and we were only going to Deadwood to see Wild Bill Hickok and Calamity Jane's tombstones.[110] I had expected to be

74

→ ● ←

home well before dark, and had expected to just hop on the freeway back through Sturgis. Instead, I had to take 385 south to Nemo road, then just before Rapid City, I turned north on 79. The experience sucked. There were times when I was so cold I wasn't sure if I was going to make it."

"That's right - you don't have bags on your bike to carry anything."

"The fender struts have been integrated into the frame. No windshield either. I was totally unprepared for how cold it got in the higher elevations. Every place I could stop, I did. I'd slam coffee and buy sweatshirts and pile on the layers … that helped a little, but the air still got through. It was rough going there for a while."

"So, where's your friend now?"

"Don't know. She never returned to camp last night and there's been no word from her. But, it's not like she was mountain climbing or anything! She was just drinking and gambling. She's an adult - so there ya go. People are gonna do what people are gonna do and it's not my responsibility because I don't have the ability to respond. She wanted to come along for the ride, so I said sure. And she helped pay for gas which was cool, because the van sucks it up.[111] But, what she does while we're here is totally her deal." I shrug with resignation. "But, I do hope she shows up some time today to see the bike in the show. She really is a good egg and I'd like for you to meet her."

"I hope to meet her too! I think it's cool that ladies are in these fields. I like the idea of a woman working on my ride!"

"I was one of those kids who would watch other people do things, and whatever someone else did - I knew I could do it too. We all leap frog each other into greater things."

So how did you get into painting?"

"A miracle."

"Serious?"

"Totally. I had been driving cab for a couple years after I got out of the Navy and hit a point where I knew it was time to think about a different career path. I mean, the money was good, but working 12-hour shifts and the amount of partying I was doing ... I just knew I was heading toward a dead end. So, one day, I'm standing in the living room and I happen to say out loud, I wonder what career I should do next? To my amazement, a disembodied voice replied, "**Auto body**."

"Disembodied?" J asks.

"A voice with no body. I heard the words, but no one was there."

"Strange ..." J says softly. Then he bursts out, "Bwahahahaha! You had an auto body experience! Get it?! Out of body?! Bwahahahahaha!"

76

"Hahahaha! You are a goof-ball, groovy dude!" I laugh with him. "But yeah, it was strange, yet I figured it was my guardian angel or something, so I should probably follow the advice. I called the local college and asked if they had an auto body program and sure enough they did, and it was starting in a week. I signed up. I continued to drive cab to pay for living expenses, but switched to the airport line. It felt good being around planes again, although this time I was on the pavement. I'd sit in the long cab lines for hours until it was my turn to pick up a fare, which allowed me the opportunity to get my homework done. I took it serious and graduated top of the class. Then I also took additional classes in airbrush, pinstripe, sign design & layout, and welding. I *love* welding - the whole idea of pushing a bubble around seems very meditative to me." I pause for a sip of water, "While in school, my instructor told me that I'd have to find a body shop that does specialty work because I was so extremely detail-oriented that I'd never make it in a production shop, where it's all about speed. That was the best advice he ever gave me, because otherwise I would have gotten stuck working at a job that makes money off other people's misfortune. Having paid money for my education, I might have blind spots in seeing what my choices were doing to my karma. But, it all worked out. I took his advice, searched on line, and found a place on the other side of the city that does truck and conversion van graphics. I

77

went and applied, but they weren't hiring. I kept trying every week, but nope." I shake my head. "So, after a month of trying, I asked to talk to the owner. I told him I'd work for $5 an hour if he'd just give me a chance. Well, he knew a good deal when he saw it, so he hired me. At first, I was trained on fiberglass truck visors. I'd sand them with a DA - dual action sander, spray the sealer, color and clear. Every once in a while I'd get to spray one color, then lay out some basic graphics in fine line tape,[112] spray the second color, pull the tape revealing the first color graphics, and clear. Only bummer was they never told me what fiberglass dust does to bare skin. My forearms were breaking out in a rash something awful before I figured out it would be a good idea to wear a long sleeved shirt!"

"Yeah, you think they could have mentioned that, right?"

"It would have been nice," I say with a little attitude, and then continue. "I tried schooling them a little from the things I'd

78

learned in auto body, since most of the guys working there were more self-proclaimed painters than trained auto body technicians. There was this one kid, probably in his mid 20's, and he'd always work in cut-off shorts and no shirt - which is no big deal except that he would spray clear coat with all that bare skin exposed. Skin is our biggest organ and it absorbs chemicals.[113] That wasn't such a concern in the old days when paint was lacquer, or from before then, when it was made from hemp seed oil.[114] In fact, there are old Hebrew bibles offering an ancient recipe[115] for holy anointing oil, [116] which contains quite a bit of kaneh bosom[117] - cannabis. This oil is poured over the body and is absorbed through the skin for healing. And I recently read how molecular biologist Dr. Christina Sanchez at Compultense University in Madrid, Spain has scientifically proven that THC does, in fact, kill cancer cells.[118] But the paint and clear we spray now? We learned in auto body class that isocyanates are only a couple chemical compounds away from nerve gas."[119]

"That's fucked up."

"Yeah, I need to wear a full paint suit when spraying, complete with positive air flow. And now, truck manufacturers in the U.S. are increasing production with aluminum.[120] That's not good for my fellow technicians on many levels![121] Why can't they follow Canada's lead and make the panels out of hemp composite if they want to reduce weight?[122] It would further the healing of the planet. And that kid I worked with? There were days when he wouldn't even put on a charcoal mask to protect his lungs. Just crazy."

"Damn, not the brightest bulb was he?!"

"No, and I told him about his lungs hardening and the chemicals being absorbed through his skin and eyes, but he didn't seem to care. He was young and invincible. But he was a good worker – I have to give him props for that. He said the trick was to drink a lot of Mountain Dew.[123] So, being the newbie, I gave it a try. I drank Dew for three months - about two liters a day - and quickly became addicted, but yeah, I had more energy to work faster. Then, one day when I was at the blood bank …"

"Why were you at a blood bank?"

"Remember - I was making $5 an hour and that's not enough to live on, so I'd donate plasma to make money for groceries."

"Oh, sorry."

"Me too. Anyway, there was a physician there that would check everyone over to make sure we were healthy enough to donate. And, he discovered a nodule on my throat. Now, this hadn't been there when I had my discharge physical from the Navy and now it was? That had me wondering, so I did a little research and learned that Mountain Dew contains both corn syrup[124] and brominated vegetable oil,[125] which accumulates in the thyroid and is banned in Europe, India, and Japan."

"Vegetable oil doesn't sound like something bad ..."

"It's the brominated part ... think fire retardant chemicals."[126]

"Serious?!"

"Yeah ... and I'm thinking that's what caused this ..." I tilt my chin up and rub a significant lump in my throat. "It makes me look like I have an Adam's apple - which sucks for a female. So, I switched to drinking spring water after that and it's been my beverage of choice ever since. But, the lump still hasn't gone away and it's been twenty years."

J cocks his head horizontal and squints, "Wait – what twenty? I know I'm not supposed to ask the ages of a lady but, how old are you?" J looks confused.

"Over fifty." I reply indifferently.

"No way! I never would have guessed. I thought you were younger than me!" J takes a moment to really look at my healthy, wrinkle free skin. Then, he glances at my hair which doesn't show any gray at all. I know that there are half a dozen silver ones up there, but I see no reason to point this out to him.

He keeps staring at me, to the point where I feel myself becoming self-conscious. I'm about to ask him to stop when he says, "Okay, how is it possible that you're not aging?"

I smile gently and shrug, "I am, but differently than you. Our mind has influence over our body. If I wake up with sore muscles, I don't attribute it to years passing, but recognize that I've been skipping my yoga stretches and need to get back into the routine! Plus, everyone knows what's healthy and what's not. I choose the healthiest options and don't eat fake food;[127] thereby my body has the proper nutrients to continuously rebuild itself. Even when I went through my change of life, the only time I'd get a hot flash is if I ate conventionally. It seemed like my body was burning up the toxins, like when you get the flu. Lastly, the book series, *The Life and Teachings of the Masters of the Far East*[128] offers a nightly affirmation that I've been doing since I was thirty-two along with smelling high frequency essential oils.[129] Words have power."

"But words don't keep wrinkles away. Do you smear those creams all over your face like my wife does?"

"I don't use a cream, but coconut skin lotion.[130] I once met an old timer who was in World War II. He had his face burned during a firebombing and the doctor told him to moisturize every morning and night with high quality natural oils. He followed the advice and looked twenty-five years younger than his real age. He said if he ever missed a day, he could feel his skin tightening. I saw the wisdom in his words so I started doing the same. I don't use anything that harms the skin[131] and I drink pristine spring water which is another reason I'm concerned with fracking.[132] Hazardous chemicals that affect the human hormonal system are found in rivers near fracking sites, like the Colorado River.[133] They want to start fracking the Ohio River,[134] and an illegal pipeline was pushed through at the Mississippi headwaters.[135] Every one of these rivers is a drinking source. In fact, the latest U.S. studies out of Boston and Harvard University suggest that there are toxic chemicals in the drinking water for six million Americans[136] and we're what…60% water?"[137]

"I think it's 75%"

"Okay, so we're *mostly* water. I think protecting the water and making sure it's pristine should be the number one concern of every individual on this planet. Does that make sense?"

"Yeah – but most people just filter their tap water[138] and call it good."

"Not good under a microscope.[139] From traveling through miles of metal and plastic pipes, the water is dead by the time it reaches the faucet[140] so it will dehydrate people instead of restoring our cells like it's supposed to. People can bless their water and repair it, but a filter won't return it to pristine condition. Plus, science has warned us that we are depleting our ground water faster than nature can replenish it, and this affects half the U.S. population and 97% of rural residents.[141] Yet, here comes fracking, and it uses *millions* of gallons of water for *each* frack site.[142] So is natural gas worth more than our water?"

"Don't dive in to save me girl, 'cause I'm already standing on the beach next to you!" Then, he points with his chin at my neck and asks, "That lump - is it cancerous?"

"Luckily, no," I reply with sincere gratitude.

"Good. And what happened to the boy you worked with?"

"Don't know. I didn't stay there long enough to find out. At my six month review, the owner called me into his office and said how pleased he was with my work, and that he would give me a 50 cent raise an hour. I was like, really - I get to make $5.50 an hour … oh lucky me." I say this with a sarcastic tone and a shrug of the shoulders. "I don't know, I guess I thought that he'd bump me up into a livable wage after he saw how hard working I was. But, he didn't. So, instead, I gave my two week notice."

"His loss. But, so you know, as a business owner, I sometimes want the new kids to pay their dues before I start paying them good money."

"So, you want them to suffer? To not be able to pay their bills or eat decent food?"

"No, not *suffer*! Don't be dramatic. It's more like, I had to work hard and pay my dues so they should too."

"J - Not having basic needs met *is* suffering. I didn't donate blood as a fun afternoon on the town! You haven't heard

84

of people before profit? I believe people's needs are much more important than time, money, or keeping things even. I thought you would get that with your whole learning curve theory."

"That was for *my kids* - not my employees." He says with a little irritation.

I stop for a moment to think about his words. That was for my kids, not someone else's kids. I'm not sure how to reply to that. Why do his kids matter more than someone else's? It seems we see from different perspectives here so I reply gently, "Mitakuye Oyasin - that's Native American for All My Relations[143]... we're all related."

We look at each other. J is quiet. We hear talking in the distance, a laugh among friends. Then J says, "I thought you were telling me about your first job out of auto body."

"Yeah, okay ... I didn't want to work for peanuts so I quit that place and started my own business. I'd do the prep in my garage, and then lease out a paint booth for spraying. That was sufficient, but not ideal. The shop owner always wanted me to pull my fresh parts out of the booth so they could get the next job in. One time, I got jostled and a freshly painted fender hit the ground and ruined the candy cobalt finish. I was shocked, staring at the beautiful fender with a baseball sized dent in it. The shop owner saw what had happened and asked if I was going to cry. I said no - defensively. But, I was pissed. That was the day I

85

started searching for a new location of my own, but real estate was priced out of my range. The idea of having to make a few thousand just to cover expenses before paying myself wasn't very appealing. So, after spending a year searching out locations, I got the insight to go down to the city zoning office and ask them if there were any urban houses that were both industrial *and* residentially zoned. There was! So, I copied down the information and went to take a look. The first location was next to an electrical transfer station - I passed on it because I didn't want to deal with EMFs[144] because they disrupt the body – mind communication.[145] The other location was a short block of ten houses, and the corner house was for sale!"

"Imagine that!"

"I know!" I nod my agreement. "So, I made an appointment to view the house and it fit the bill. The garage was a pieced together rickety old thing, which was fine, because it brought the value down and I was going to tear it out anyway to build the paint shop."

"Right on!"

"Yes! So, I had a $7,000 budget. A good friend of mine from my cab driving days had carpentry skills and he agreed to help out as long as his needs were met …" I pause long enough to exaggerate a wink at J, "and all the food he could eat - which meant we had lots of spaghetti! So, with a hammer, cats-paw, and

Sawzall,[146] the two of us started demo. We did this very methodically, saving as much of the lumber as we could. Then we framed a new cement slab, and for the actual pouring, I found a cement guy with a Honda that needed paint and we did a trade with the agreement that I would paint his bike once I was operational. Then, more friends helped out, contributing leftover wiring, some fixtures, and some labor, whatever they could. Whatever I didn't know how to do, I'd go to the library and check out books on that subject and the corresponding city code. Then, I went to different salvage yards for fluorescent fixtures, windows, doors, heater, etc. The guys at the permit office made me hire a ventilation contractor for the exhaust system. Then I insulated, dry walled, shingled, and was ready to start taking jobs within 4 months. The first job being a scallop design on that Honda for the cement guy."

"But of course." J says.

I can't find any more knots or sore spots on my feet, so I put my socks and boots back on. J is looking at me expectantly, so I resume my story. "I started painting people's bikes and word spread rather quickly how good I was, especially since in the beginning, I would paint a set for $400. This probably worked out to less than $10 bucks an hour, but I was trying to get my name out there, and it doubled my income." I pour a little water into my hands to cleanse them, and finish with a wipe on the grass.

"That's still not your rate, is it?"

"Oh lord no! As word got out, I got to do some really cool paint jobs, so the more elaborate the paint job, the more money I received, and the more everyone knew that I had the skills to create whatever they needed on a high-end professional level. By the second year that my shop was open, my customers' bikes were taking awards at all the major bike shows, so it wasn't long until I was making a *very* livable wage. That allowed me to purchase the best equipment on the market and reinvest in my shop. I have separate HVLP[147] spray guns for the solids, metallics, primers, and clear coat. A couple touch-up guns and two Iwata airbrushes.[148] My entire air system is top of the line with a three-stage desiccant drier to ensure the paint flows on perfectly. I put a lot of effort into building my paint booth and business. I really worked some long hours. But, I was taught that self-worth is based on accomplishments, so I proceeded accordingly and really pushed some excellent paint jobs through the door. This went on for a few years until someone mentioned that I was totally living the American Dream. I was my own boss with low overhead, my days were my own, and I was an artist. I rode a custom painted bike that looked awesome. I must feel like I had it made. I was surprised when I heard this - and it made me stop and *really think* about what he had said … and I realized that even though I *should* have been happy, even though I had everything set up in a way that most people would envy, I wasn't happy at all. It's like what Jim Carrey said about hoping everybody could have everything they've ever dreamed of, so they know it's not the answer.[149] That was so true. I felt like I was some plastic person wearing a mask of happiness. In truth, I was angry. I was drinking and even having blackouts from time to time. My muscles ached at the end of the day. The food that I was eating wasn't nourishing my body, and I didn't really care. So even though I was living the American Dream, I was heading for another dead-end, so time for another change. It had nothing to do with my career or home life, so I finally had to do it - I had to take a good look at *myself* and really take inventory of who I was and how I went through the world each day. I was ready to find *real* happiness and know what it felt like to actually give a shit if I lived or died."

→ ● ←

Chapter 4*: **Madness**

The ensuing content contains strong writing or images which may trigger or unsettle some individuals. If you are sensitive, please skip ahead to Chapter 5.

"So how many bikes do you paint each year?" Groovy J asks.

"When it was about the money, fifty or so, but now … maybe a dozen? Dozen and a half? I don't know … that's not my gauge of success anymore. I pursue happiness, which means, I do my inner work, paint enough to cover living expenses, and enjoy life and gardening. "

"Only one bike a month? That's it?!"

I can tell from his expression of incredulity that the business man in him is balking at the idea of not reaching full earning potential.

Smiling, I explain. "J, I don't think you grasp how upside-down I used to be. There were days when just getting out of bed was an accomplishment. Life held no joy, so work was a low priority. I would write poetry like 'Blood screams through my boiling head, waiting for the words that need to be said.'"

His expression hasn't changed.

→ ● ←

"Here - look at my forearm…" I show the inside of my left arm so he can see the scar of letters carved into the skin.

F T W

Finally replying, he says, "FTW – Fuck the World. You don't seem like the type to be into scarification."

"I'm not really 'into it', but I'll admit that I've done it a few times. The first was when I was 9 years old and read 'The Exorcist'.[150] There was this part where the possessed girl had the words 'Help Me' appear on her stomach from the inside. That seemed like a reasonable thing to do, considering my mindset as a child,[151] so I used a razor blade and cut 'Help Me' into my stomach."

"Do you still have those scars?"

"They faded. I was so young that I didn't do it very deep. But, it's only an indication of the amount of pain I was in. Pain and anger. All those years without healthy touch, all the rejection, all the confusion and betrayal, even self-abandonment."[152] I let out a heavy sigh, "I used to hate this world so much … hated everyone in it too. I had so much anger radiating out of me that I'd walk through a biker bar and overhear guys say, 'I'd hate to get in a fight with her!' That would make me stand tall with false pride. I felt protected, because no one would come near me. But, waking up the next day after an evening of fighting off the world, I found myself depressed. All the effort and energy that went into warding off those who might harm me was exhausting. I'd lie in bed, not wanting to move, not wanting to eat, and just praying I would die."

"And this was because of your psychopathic foster brother?"

"I'm not going to push the blame on anyone." I shrug. "He was a messed up kid too, so it was just the life we were handed. But it was more than being sexualized as a child; I was put up for adoption upon birth. Adopted kids tend to have rejection issues and other insecurities.[153] But then, I didn't bond with my adoptive mom. My new father ... well ... something happened there so he set me aside at the age of five. Third time's the charm, right? All these rejections did some sort of programming in my head saying that's how life was – so I grew up repeating the behavior and choosing psycho people to be with who ultimately rejected me for one reason or another. It didn't matter how much time passed either – during high school, during the Navy, driving cab – I could find them anywhere! Ha! It's crazy the way it all plays out, but we repeat our childhood until it's healed."

Looking at me through a squinty eye, "Now, that doesn't make sense to me. I always thought adopted kids were lucky because the parents *chose* to have the kid – not like in a family where the pregnancy was a mistake."

"Interesting. I've read that before conception, the child's soul chooses the parents that they want to be with, in order to accomplish what they came into this life to do – so that would mean there are no mistakes for anyone.[154] And since I've told you so much already, I guess I can share more with you. When my parents picked me up from the adoptive agency, my mom dressed me in a cute little outfit that she got from my father's wholesale clothing company. The dress was one that had been used as a sample, so it had lots of straight pins used to keep it orderly in the showroom. As she was taking out the pins, she missed a few. As she put the outfit on my tiny body, the rogue pins poked and scratched me the entire ride home, so naturally I screamed and cried something awful. She kept trying to soothe me and would change my position – this was before car seats - but that just made it worse. My new mom became all upset and took it personal. She assumed that I didn't like *her,* and consequently rejected me back. Interestingly, she had an issue with her own mother not wanting her, so those pins could have been unconsciously missed in order to repeat a cycle, because it had never been consciously cleared. And I was already associating 'the mother figure' with abandonment, so even at one week old, I began a pattern that took a long time to correct."

"How long?" J asks.

"I kept my distance from her until I was in my 30's. I was pissed that she allowed *her father* to babysit me as a child, and also because she never did her inner work and cleared her issues. Wait – let me rephrase that - because *I* hadn't done my *own* inner work as an adult, I projected that onto *her* and was angry at her for not doing *her* inner work. But, once I started learning, and then forgiving myself, then I could forgive her also. Once that happened, our relationship had a chance to begin and the energy between us cleared. She no longer felt the need to put up her guard around me, and I learned how to love her despite her faults. [155] Families *need* to forgive, and everyone is family."

"Okay." J nods his head, and then asks, "What about your dad?"

"Father took care of me until I was 5." I answer.

"And then what? You instantly became independent? Or did he go off and do his own thing?" J guesses my answer, based on his own experience.

"No – the age of 5 was when my foster brother took a fascination with my private parts." Out of embarrassment, I turn away from J and instead gaze at the lifeless machines that are incapable of passing judgment. I continue, "One evening, after my father returned home from work, he was holding me on his lap. Apparently - according to the story my mom told - I rubbed my crotch back and forth on my father's leg. It was shocking to

94

both my parents and it was probably my way of saying something funky was going on down there. Father didn't know what to do so he looked to mom for help. She, because of her own childhood issues, told him with fear in her eyes and force behind the words - *put her down!* He did, and he never really picked me up again. I was filled with shame, thinking I had done something wrong. I still remember crying at a friend's house while listening to Wayne Newton's song 'Daddy Don't You Walk So Fast'[156] over and over."

J places his hand on my shoulder and my emotions rush to the surface. I know that crying will help release the pain of rejection, but I don't want to cry – not right now. I silently promise my inner child that I will revisit this memory when I'm alone tonight, and then I can release the tears and do some inner work. After a couple of blinks, my eyes are clear again. I turn and smile graciously at him in gratitude for his compassionate gesture.

Sensing that the tender moment has passed, he releases his touch and confides, "As a dad, I can say that something like that would freak me out a bit too. If only parenting came with a how-to manual, right? You do your best, but life … well, it iz what it iz."

I nod and repeat his words, "It iz what it iz. But I'm not sharing this as a boo-hoo - that's not the point of exploring our childhoods. Rather, it's to bring awareness into our adult lives. From this experience, I began a pattern of returning to toxic relationships with a false belief that no one else wanted me. With this realization, I can observe my actions and if I see myself falling into unconscious conditioning, I will take action and put a halt to it. Therein lies the gift! Plus, I snuck back into father's life when I was old enough to work at the family business." I smile conspiratorially. "Good memories there, especially having breakfast together. I'd get to witness my father interacting with strangers, and he was always kind and generous. Then we'd ride the elevator up to the 3rd floor and begin the work day. He would head into the main office and I'd clock in, pick up a work order, and head into the back where rows upon rows of items were stacked and numbered."

"What was your job?"

"I filled orders, my father ran the company, his brother was in sales, my cousins packaged the orders for shipping, and then they hired outside help to fill the rest of the positions. The hired help were all good people – at least that's what we thought – but later we discovered that they were stealing. Clothes, office supplies, toilet paper, but the worst was when the accountant forged the ledgers and stole a significant amount of money. Ultimately, theft killed the company. That really hurt my father's heart. I felt so sad for him, but I was only a kid. Now, I could

96

explain that what they did wasn't personal, it was a reflection of who *they* were and an expression of not receiving what they really needed."

"What did they really need?"

"Joyful connection."

"How do you get that at work?"

"That's an individual answer. I connect through nature. The company was located in a big city, but during my lunch break I'd carefully climb out the large double hung window and sun bathe on the ten inch wide cement window sill. One time my co-worker, a model who also filled orders, saw me napping and gasped! Her fear startled me and almost made me lose my balance! It was the only time I came close to falling to the city street below.

"Anyway, from working in those dusty conditions, running around a maze for numbers corresponding to stuff that people ordered, I now intentionally shop small scale to support individuals, not corporations or conglomerates. Purchasing through ebay and Etsy helps families provide for themselves, and then they can set up their work conditions so they have joyful connection in their life. Shopping at super-stores may save a couple bucks, but in the long run it encourages people to be slaves to other people. My dollars are my way to vote for the future I want, so I spend them intentionally."

"It sounds like it." J nods in understanding, then returns to his inquiry about my childhood, "And now for the infamous foster brother – will you tell me what he was like?"

"Exhausting! When he was around, I'd go through the day with all my senses on full alert – never sure where he was or what he was going to do."

"That's what it's like in war – the enemy might be right next to you and you have no idea," J recalls.

"Then, you know what I'm talking about – or as a veteran friend used to say, we've eaten the same dirt. Being on alert for such a long time did something to me, it fragmented my emotional body. One aspect was nervous, jittery, looking for any clues that an attack might be coming so I could avoid the unfolding situation and have a way out. The other aspect was calm, cool, and very methodical. I could do whatever I needed to protect myself, like I had an inner dragon whose body I could slip into. This was how my child brain protected itself from what was happening, I was simply too young to do anything else. As time went by, I would notice little quirks about how I interacted with people compared to how others acted in similar situations, which made me think I was crazy - so I learned how to hide my quirks and project a mask of being the perfect child. But, physical signs showed up that were beyond my control. I

98

developed warts all over my body and a speech problem, but hey, I survived."

"I can't believe your parents didn't notice any of this!"

"You can't see in someone else what you can't even look at in your own life. Plus, this was at the same time that Catholic Charities[157] called my parents saying they had an infant girl available - were they interested? They were, so while they busied themselves with my newly adopted little sister, my foster brother busied himself with me."

"Harsh! But, you must have made peace with your past, I feel calm just sitting here with you."

"I have." I smile with pride.

"So, what's a psychopath like?"

"Ha – you could ask Ron Paul! I remember when he used the phrase 'psychopathic authoritarians' in his farewell speech to Congress.[158] That made me sit up and take notice of politics for a short while! Ha!"

"You don't want to stay informed of what's happening in our government?"

"Not the stuff they want us to focus on! Plus, I do not require governing. And if one of their own says they are like my foster brother was? No. The day he arrived in our household was my oldest brother's birthday. He took a pocket knife to the tent my brother got as a present, and sliced it with a glare in his eye.

Just to show who was in charge. They never got along after that. Then say my parents left the car keys on the counter; he'd grab them and say it was their fault for leaving them within reach. Then he'd go for a joy ride and trash the car, along with any other cars that were in the way, because he was too young to reach the pedals and see over the dashboard at the same time. There was a lot of destruction - punching holes in walls, throwing rocks through windows, smashing things. He would jam a firecracker up a frog's ass, light it on fire, and throw it into the air to watch it explode. As a little girl I'd have frog parts raining down on me as he'd laugh and laugh." I quietly add, "A psychopath would have no remorse over blowing up buildings or trains, the lost lives would be considered irrelevant.[159]

"Another time, he took a baseball bat to the bee hive in the neighbor's back yard. The bees freaked and stung me so many times that I almost died. Luckily, the neighborhood nurse lived next door and she saw the unfolding situation and came running with a blanket and an epinephrine shot. She saved me, that day. As time went on, I became desensitized to what I would experience and see. I became selfish, because my true needs were not being met and he became my mentor instead of my tormenter. We would play skill games like throwing a switchblade between the other's bare feet. You start with your legs spread shoulder width, and decrease the open space after each throw. I have scars from the times I would win. I wouldn't complain. He was my only friend, and he liked me best when I was badass. I got good at hiding the *real me* beneath personas and bravado. The Latin word persona, refers to the mask that an actor would hold in front of their face, to represent the role they were portraying.[160] And these personas don't fade as we go through life, they accumulate - different ones for the family, for friends, for school, and for work. If anyone challenged one of my personas, I would get angry to the point of eruption; because I had come to depend upon my mask for my very survival, and because that's what he taught me, through example. But the problem with having a persona, is that I couldn't manifest a better life for myself, because the *real me* was still stagnant from unresolved issues. Life was same shit, different day. As for my foster brother, the constant disobedience and consequent punishment, he became ruthlessly conniving.[161] He learned to plan things out and people were simply pawns for his self-gratification. He didn't care how his actions affected anyone else. He'd steal stuff just to add it to his collection. One day he proudly called me into his room to show me his newly acquired set of 'thief tools' complete with glass cutter and suction cup. I just stared in shock and kept my mouth shut. Many years later, after I'd returned from being stationed in Spain, he ripped *me* off and stole a bunch of stuff including my prized CD collection and

101

high-end receiver that I had saved months for, and purchased at the Navy Exchange. I never confronted him on that.

"When the cops caught him stealing when I was eight years old, that was when he was sent away for the first time. Somehow, I thought I had done something wrong, suffering silently and awaiting his return. That turned into a conditioned response that I repeated with several relationships in my adult years, until I worked through it and stopped setting the stage to replay a part that was not in alignment with my soul."

J responds, "Wow. A lot of heavy things there. I know a thing or two about shame … can I share a secret with you?"

"Absolutely. Someone once told me that we're only as sick as the secrets we keep. Becoming transparent releases stuck energy - as long as it doesn't get turned into someone's permanent story, it's a good thing to get the old crap into the open."

J nods and begins, "When pop was gone on assignment, ma would rule the household with an iron fist. She said she needed to stay ahead of me, because I was getting so big she didn't want to lose the upper hand. So if I did anything wrong, she'd hit me with whatever was close - a cord, spoon, or frying pan. Just like in the cartoons. Sometimes, it was a backhand and her wedding ring would slice me. When she wasn't hitting, she'd use shame. I could take it, but I felt sorry for my lil' sis' because ma would tease her mercilessly about the way she talked and now my sis' seems always tense. She reminds me of a little dog – ready to snap at anyone who might look at her wrong. Some days I want to touch her nose and say 'no bark - go lay down,' but I'd probably get bit! Guess I'll just be patient for the day when our heart's touch. Maybe then we can talk about what happened."

I respond, "I'm sorry you both had to have that as part of your inheritance."

"Well, I'm okay now. But my lil' sis' – I still worry about her. I hope she has found happiness in her life."

"I hope the same for my foster brother. You know, he wasn't always a terror. I saw kindness in his eyes from time to time."

J interjects, "I've heard that psychopaths don't feel anything at all."[162]

"I've read that too, but I disagree. Sure, if he became threatened, there was a shift in him. I always noticed the personality changes from his regular self into the conniving self. Then, he was capable of anything … absolutely anything. I'd hide from him whenever I felt his heart go cold. But then, he'd show up when I was at a friend's house, a huge grin on his face and a stolen Chevelle Super Sport. He'd smoke the tires until he got me to smile, and then drive away laughing. He became attractive in his mid teens … like James Franco in Freaks N

Geeks[163]… so he had lots of girlfriends … he'd use them to meet his needs –he'd use everybody – but, since *his* only purpose for being born was so his birth mom could receive welfare money, it's logical that using others became programmed into his head as the norm. Sometimes, it was mesmerizing to watch how easily he could convince people to do his bidding. Maybe that's why I can see the propaganda people are being fed today. I got to see a young manipulator at work, so these spins and distractions don't ensnare me very often. There are so many good, trusting folks in this world who think that everyone is just as balanced mentally as they are, and it just isn't so. When abuse happens to some people, they break, and then *they* do some really horrific things. I mean, the heart is closed – *they don't care.*[164] But, as a child, I wasn't allowed to speak. My brother would threaten to kill me if I didn't keep his secrets. I was just the little sister, so I observed. It taught me not to trust anything people said, but to *feel* who someone was. As an adult, I've extended that to researching companies to know their source and track record before supporting them with my dollars and encouraging their growth. Luckily, websites and apps like The Better World Shopper[165] are available to make this easy. But I got to tell you that lately, from all the different mind games going on, I'm feeling a lot of fragmented people walking around and it's not from childhood abuse or combat, but from those damn TV's."

"Zombies. Totally mindless and wanting to eat everyone else's brain too." J says with finality while crossing his arms across his chest.

"Ha! Maybe … humans can certainly wreak havoc in the world and not be fully conscious of what they're doing. There are always clues, but if they don't have the courage to enter the unknown and figure it out, well … we get a fucked up world as a result."

"And speaking of fucked up … did your foster brother, well, did he still want to 'do it' with you when you were older?"

"He returned to our home when I was in fifth grade. He didn't try to do it with me, but he began having sexual relations with the family dog. The dog became depressed. She wouldn't want to eat. Days would go by without her taking a bite. So, seeing she was so unhappy, I'd play a food game with her where I'd feed her one piece of dry dog food at a time. Sometimes flicking the food across the floor and she'd catch it like a goalie. But on the days when she would just lay there, I'd get her to eat by soaking the food in my mouth first. Mind you, I was only ten."

"I don't know if I should laugh or cry." J says in shock.

"Cry. My foster brother was lost in addiction, living according to his pleasures.[166] He was so clueless in fact, that one

105

time he wanted to show the neighbor boy what you can do with a dog."

"He didn't...."

"Yeah, he did. He had sex with the neighbor boy's dog. The kid was grossed out and told all the other kids. How embarrassing. More shame I had to process out."

"That's like that top official lady from the Center for Disease Control who was arrested for getting her freak on with kids and animals![167] That's when I decided I wasn't going to allow the government to make decisions on my peep's health anymore. I'm the dad. I'll do the research."[168]

"Oh! My heart goes out to that poor woman! I'd like to know her story, to understand how she got into that position. I really hope she's able to heal from whatever her past was."

J gives me a strange glance.

I ask him, "What?"

"Nothing." He shakes his head and continues questioning. "What about your siblings – were you guys close growing up?"

"No - when everything is shrouded in secrets there's no deep intimacy. It's corny, but I bonded with Rudolph the Red Nosed Reindeer.[169] I felt like such a misfit that it was best to become independent at an early age. At school, I kept making friends, then moving on, like I was searching for a fit that I couldn't seem to find. Until one day, when I was at an assembly

106

in the gym, someone finally clicked. The song 'Cherokee People'[170] was being performed by some of the students. I still love that song – and its message. I think it would be so cool if their Nation returned!"

J gets it and agrees, "Right on!" giving me a knuckle bump.

I grin back at him. "So I'm at the school function, and while the next act was getting ready, I was looking at the different kids' faces. My eyes locked on this one girl and I didn't want to look away … she seemed really familiar. I gathered my courage and went and sat by her. We introduced ourselves and I learned that her name was Susita. But, when she found out who my foster brother was, she didn't want to be around me. I asked her why, and she said that when she was walking home with a freshly bought pizza, he ambushed her from the tall weeds and stole it. I laughed. She punched me in the arm. Then, we both laughed and I apologized for him. I assured her that I wasn't anything like him. She agreed to try out our friendship on a trial basis, and we soon became inseparable. Her parents were heavy alcoholics and always seemed to be fighting, but they'd leave us alone. We'd sit in her bedroom after school, smoke cigarettes, and listen to the radio. She had this clock radio with an LED design that made a flower pattern. We would puff and watch it go around and around. Above the clock was a poster that said, 'If you love something set it free. If it comes back to you, it's yours. If it doesn't, it never was.' The poster was yellow from all the smoke and incense we'd burn – thinking we were camouflaging the smell. That was our entertainment, and we were fine with it. As abused kids, it doesn't take much to satisfy; just the feeling of being safe and not alone, is enough. Although sometimes, we would sneak beer from her parent's downstairs stash. This one time, while her parents were watching TV in the upstairs living room, we tucked a bottle of beer into each of our socks, and while going up the stairs Susita hit the metal railing and the bottle broke. She started laughing because the beer was fizzing and leaking out of her sock – so we both started laughing and almost got caught! But, there were other times when her mom would ask us to skip school and she'd *give us* beer because she didn't want to drink alone. That made her mom cool to us. Her mom's eyes were yellow for as long as I can remember, but she lived a long time. When she did finally die, she only had one-fourth of a lung and her skin was completely yellow, including the nails. She was both pickled and bitter. Her husband had divorced her many years before.

"There were things that I didn't like about Susita – she would leave me stranded if her boyfriend called and she would bully other kids. But, I wasn't perfect either. One time while skiing, I pushed her down a huge hill before teaching her how to stop! The bottom of the course curved upward, slowing her enough so she didn't get hurt, but I still got punched for that one! She even got in a fist fight, in Junior High, with a teacher. This happened in front of half the school, during lunch hour, and it embarrassed me. I moved a little further away, and that's when I found the Bible. The Bible told me how much Jesus loved me and since love was what I was *truly* looking for, I ate it up like a starving child. My mom noticed my interest and bought me a Children's Bible. The stories were great … Joseph and his coat of many colors, Noah's Ark, the birth and life of Jesus … although with Jesus, I never could grasp why the church had stations showing the abuse Jesus had endured instead of praising His ability to rise from the dead, which to me was much more remarkable. My mom volunteered to teach the catechism classes at our church. The two of us started to bond through the word of God. She loved to explain her version of what she thought everything meant, and I loved the attention I received from her. I'd even help out as a student teacher for her on weekend afternoons. For 2 years, I flourished. I continued working at my father's company after school. Then, we'd drive home together, sharing how the work day went, so I developed a love for work and driving. When father wasn't busy running the company, he was into music. So, I got involved with band at school and learned the clarinet, sax, bass sax, guitar, and bass guitar. I met friends through the church who were a good influence on me and we'd form jam bands. But, then the bottom dropped out, literally. I learned that the church considered gays and lesbians to be sinners and deserving of hell. My world just shattered … I held it together until I got home and then ran to my room and cried and cried. I couldn't believe that I was going to lose this beautiful world that I'd so recently found … where I had a mom, and a father, and a savior in Jesus Christ. And not just lose it, but be damned to hell besides."

"You're a lesbian?"

"I'm not really sure … it's a bit confusing for me so I skip the labels and just follow my heart."

"So being gay is a choice then?"

"Nope, there are gay animals and insects.[171] I think it's more like a bell curve where there are different degrees of orientation[172] which can change throughout our lives. That's why labels are so limiting. Even Native Americans, before the white man arrived, had three to five gender identifications within their tribe.[173] But because of my childhood, I didn't know what gender was right for me, only that everyone wanted sex and I had better boundaries with females than males, so girl friends were safer. But that meant I had another secret to keep, and be ashamed of."

"I don't think the church is still against gays, are they?"[174]

"Depends on which religion; mine was. So here I was a pre-teen struggling with self-esteem issues, rejection issues, and abuse. When I found the Bible, and consequently the church, I'd finally found the golden nectar of life - feeling like *I belonged somewhere and that someone loved me*, but I lost it all to doctrine. However, I wasn't willing to go down without a fight … I needed a plan that would let me talk this over with the priest. I believed that he would make an exception and fix everything if he only knew how devoted I was to God. But, the problem with approaching the priest was that everyone knew my mom was a teacher there, and I didn't dare embarrass the family. Then, an idea came – I could use the offering envelopes for communication. I would write the priest long letters explaining my situation, my confusion, and ask for his pardon. Then, I would stuff the pages into the small envelope used for tithing – always making sure to scribble out any identifying numbers. In these letters, I gave him instructions to tape his response to the underside of the shelf, located at the side entrance, where we usually came in from the parking lot. As my family entered church, I would lag behind and then snatch the letter from its hiding spot while no one was looking. It always said the same thing; he wanted to talk face to face. I simply couldn't do that. After I sent off the third pleading letter, and his response still requested a personal meeting, I gave up. I resigned myself to being a sinner and accepted hell as my fate. Years later, I found out that he was one of the priests in the news, who was abusing young kids."

"No shit! You're kidding, right?"

"I wish I was. But from all that I've learned since then, I reason that those little whisperers go after the devout more than anyone else, because if they can sever *that* bond, they'll lower the vibration of many. Even Pope Francis warns us to be aware of the reality of the devil.[175] But, as a young child, I was told by the church that I was the damned one and beyond the love of God – so I finally gave up and said fuck it. I closed my heart completely and stopped caring. I reasoned that I might as well do anything I pleased, since … you know … I was already damned. And how does programming tell kids to rebel? Smoke cigarettes[176] – which weakens your breath and breath is life, and drink alcohol – which is a slow poison. So, in effect, society encourages rebels to die young – and they accept this programming because it makes them feel good momentarily. How convenient, right?"

"I never thought of it like that."

"I have. Anyway, I reunited with Susita who was living the sex, drugs, and rock 'n' roll lifestyle, I dived in - but no needles; needles are freaky. The two of us did some crazy things and got ourselves into some sketchy situations - like one time

112

when we were hitch-hiking and a creep picked us up. He decided that he was going to bring us back to his place for his own style of partying, but once we recognized the direction his scene was heading, we silently motioned to the door. When the van slowed for a traffic light, we jumped out while it was still moving and rolled onto the asphalt. We emerged from the late 70's a bit battered and torn, but we both made it out. Not everyone did. And I learned from experimenting with a great deal of different drugs that the natural ones, when used correctly, took me on a spiritual journey that enhanced my perception and helped to heal my inner wounds."

"What about the not-so-natural ones?"

"The synthetic ones destroy your soul, sometimes your life."

∞

"Susita got pregnant at 15 and dropped out of school, so I lost my main partying buddy. It took a year, but I found another best friend who came from a broken home, liked to get stoned, and listened to rock. But then, one day her parents found her stash and sent her off to treatment. Alone again, I kept my grades up until graduation day, and then joined the Navy."

J asks, "How did your parents react to their church girl changing into the party girl?"

113

"Father was busy with his company. Mom, she never asked. However, as I was shifting back into the 'bad girl' persona, mom started telling me stories about how she used to be badass as a kid too. She said she used to stand on the corner with her friends, chains in hand and a switchblade in her pocket, protecting their 'hood. It's hard to say if that's true or not, but I took her words as encouragement, and started to smoke cigarettes in front of her. She was fine with it. She loved the rebel movies, and got me my first motorcycle; the Kawasaki 100 street legal dirt bike. It belonged to my grandpa, and when he died she claimed that bike for me, even though there were older boy brothers and cousins. The first time I sat on that bike I got a thrill of excitement! I could finally feel more than the monotony of a life devoid of emotion. I quickly mastered the controls, and motorcycles became my path to freedom - I've been riding ever since."

"I hear ya … I'm grateful to my father for giving me his old Knuckle.[177] It would have been nice if he would've wrenched with me, but, at least I've got something of his to remember him by."

"Did he die?"

"Yeah, it's been a while now. Cancer got him. He went the chemo route, even though I told him the successes rate was under 3%.[178] I wish he would have been willing to try some alternative therapies,[179] but secretly, I think he wanted to go. He never met his grandkids, so I share his military stories with them while we're re-building the bike. It's a family project and even my girls like getting their hands dirty. I hope that doesn't make them turn lesbo[180] though …"

Snapping my head to look at J, I find him grinning from ear to ear – ah, so he's joking with me, trying to get a reaction. I slap him with the back of my hand and call him a turd.

He continues to joke, "Although that might not be such a bad thing … I'm not all that sure if I want my little ladies to meet biker boys either, especially if they're anything like Hollywood. He's manageable, just horny as a dog. But, there is some pretty rough stock out there."

"There's rough stock in every social group, it doesn't matter what click they belong to. If they haven't worked through their shadow side, it will show up, especially now. It happens to the best of us."

"You say that like there's a story behind your words."

I nod yes. "There is – but keep in mind that this isn't who I am anymore."

"All right."

"One night when I'd been drinking, I had so much anger built up that I was standing outside in the front yard, just being a total asshole and yelling into the night. This is right after graduating from auto body school - when I was living across the street from the body shop. So, it's a commercial/industrial area on the rough side of town. The cars would be thumping and buzzing with hostile music. A little gangsta, and the neighbors walked around a little scared. I didn't walk around scared; I didn't care. And sometimes, I was the one who did scary things. Like this night, after yelling at a few passing cars and being ignored, I started throwing beer bottles at them. I wanted someone to stop and fight me. I had too much anger building inside and the heavy metal music wasn't releasing it like it usually did. The rage would come in waves, and I didn't know it at the time, but it was because my heart was closed. A closed heart feels no joy, which reduces life to surviving, and deep inside, I knew this wasn't how it was supposed to be, yet I had no idea how to change it. I felt trapped and unhappy … and when the wave of hatred reached its peak, it came out physically. So I slammed another beer down and whipped the bottle with all my force. By some fluke, the glass didn't break - it landed on the opposite sidewalk, slid a little, and then jangled quickly into the grass. I analyzed the throw and made adjustments to how much strength to use so I wouldn't miss again. The next car that went by was an older 4-door and the bottle caught the back of the bumper, bounced off, then shattered on the street. Just like my foster brother taught me, I liked the sound of breaking glass …

brown shards scattering outward with little points that could pop tires resulting in visible damage. The brake lights came on as the car came to a halt; I was ready. As the driver's door opened, I saw a child's face turn and look out the back window; her eyes were large with fright. I locked eyes with her and froze. I hadn't thought about a kid being in the car. Looking at her was like having my child self looking at the 'me' that I'd become, and I hated myself. The driver saw the shocked look on my face from looking at his daughter, and then got back in his car and drove away. I didn't want another drink. I went inside and put Poison's Greatest Hits CD on, and played 'Something to Believe In' [181] at full volume. It was a request to the Universe. I was ready for things to change."

The sound of a distant helicopter grows. Out of habit, I turn and quickly scan the horizon and settle in on the aircraft. I'm expecting to see some logo for a touring company with this being Bike Week, but instead see the familiar USAF roundel of a star with bars. It's a Bell Huey[182] amongst a pattern of chemtrail stripes.[183] J follows my glare. I sense him looking and I turn to look at him. There is tension around his eyes, which makes me notice that my own facial muscles are tight. I concentrate on the muscles underneath my skin and consciously relax them. As I feel the release, I notice how his eyes regain their twinkle, their vibrant blue, simultaneously piercing and laughing.

I continue, "I know that everyone's got some sort of shit in their past. Some is worse than others and I don't personally know anyone who came through childhood unscathed. There was this one girl I'd met who had parents that were into power and ritual with a closed heart, in other words - black magic." My voice goes into a whisper, because words are powerful vibrations[184] and I want the next few to make as small of a ripple as possible. "Actually, it was *really* messed up what they made her do." I pause and pick up a piece of grass to play with. The feeling of something natural in my hands helps me balance the memory of what she told me. "They made her take part in a satanic rape ceremony when she was barely a teenager, which I'm not going to describe because it was way too sick. But, the end result was her getting pregnant. Then, when her baby was born, they made her *eat* it."

J's body flinches a little. "That's the most disgusting thing I've ever heard."

"Yeah … I know. That really fucked up her head. Only they know what their real intention was … anyway - I met her years after this and she still couldn't do much except stay drunk." The piece of grass shreds quickly, so I drop it and select another one that is a little thicker. "It disheartens me when I hear people bitch about those on welfare or panhandling. Shit like this is how people end up not being able to cope. Can you imagine what a

118

trigger must be like for her? I can't - that's just too far out there. Then, some haters say, 'Get a job' to those who need help. Yeah right. Like getting a job is at the top of their priority list after their parents' do something designed to break them. How can haters judge another's pain? I just don't get it."

"They're just ignorant of what the world is like for some people. There are some downright evil mother-fuckers out there." J says with contempt.

"Evil. 'Live' spelled in reverse." I say musing. "I was once afraid of evil, you know."

"How did you get back to good?"

"I examined it logically. Fear releases the hormone adrenaline.[185] People get addicted to adrenaline and manifest accordingly. Instead of using proven techniques to release the chemical,[186] they assume a stance of resistance. Closing their hearts and shutting down the emotions, they become numb to the rollercoaster of life and call themselves badass. Then, there are those who see the face of evil and want to prove how much they can handle while maintaining a 'fuck it' attitude. That was more my style, pre-healing. Nothing really mattered, just a smattering of thrills and pleasures that never satisfied. I'd drink beer to feel happy or get a tattoo to feel pain. But that wasn't enough. I wanted to *really feel joy*, which meant I had to be willing to feel sorrow without hiding from it. If someone hurt my feelings, I had

119

to experience that pain without striking back. Then, instead of reacting, I act and discover the insecurity that allowed them to affect me. This is part of the journey, which led me to discover that I still had fear about my own shadow side. I didn't know what she … I … was capable of doing, because of all the abuse I had endured and shoved into a dark corner of my soul. Sure, the childhood coloring[187] and magic mushrooms of my teenage years had cleared out some of the debris,[188] because these are healing plants found in nature, but there was a deeper level waiting to be examined. So rather than continuing to live in reverse, I make a commitment to change, and events began taking place to uphold my decision.

"Now, as far as other people being scary in the world, I see them as needing help because they are very *fragmented*. When trauma occurs, bonding is replaced by boundaries, which creates isolation. The experience also distorts the brain's ability to process sin and purity. The world becomes threatening and poisonous. The individual's brain can shift between viewing their own actions as being saint-like, and projecting any sinful thoughts outward and seeing evil reflect all around them, which requires even more isolation or aggression in an attempt to feel safe. In minor cases, they become indignant and offended. In major, or if they have access to power, their inner war is expressed by outer violence or they send people off to fight for them. Yet, what is really needed in all cases, is an empathic, nurturing community in which to assist them in healing their frightened and confused child within. So, as dark as humans descend, the opposite is also true – that's how brilliant we can become! Did you know that there's no word for 'evil' in the original Bible - not that I'm a Bible thumper or anything. But, a closer translation would have been the word *'unripe'*. And the word 'sin'? That's from archery - it means *'missing the mark'*. So, even those who do majorly messed-up shit - they're simply someone unripe who's missed the mark. BUT, once they reach the point of realizing what got them off track, it *is* their responsibility to get their life together and start atoning. They, and their family line, deserve forgiveness and a chance for a better future too."

"Well … I don't know if I can be as forgiving."

"I hope you learn. Forgiveness is what's needed now, more than anything. The new children being born know this. Anything that can't or won't accept unity consciousness will break down, including humans. Part of the evolution process. So hold a vision of these children, actually all children, as Divine beings and keep their systems pure. They will lead us into the Golden Age!"

I watch as his face becomes serious once again. He huffs each word louder than the next, "Evolving … unity … forgiveness

... what the fuck! Those are fluffy new age words, but the reality is - there are jokers out there who are carrying out an agenda to turn water into their next big money maker,[189] and the majority of people are being manipulated into acting like rats running a fucking maze! Bickering with each other over fabricated, bullshit media crap!" J says with disgust, adding, "During my Navy days traveling the world, I was blown away to see how many other countries *hate* the U.S. They see our government as this huge bully who manipulates for our own gain,[190] and keeps us busy being the world's biggest pigs. We make slaves out of third world countries, polluting their homes and using up all their resources.[191] And not everyone is as smart as you are with shopping - most prance from one shopping mall to the next, oblivious about what they're doing to the rest of the world."[192]

Seeing the struggle that J was going through, I speak gently to his vulnerable side, "I hear what you're saying, and yes, people have gotten into the habit of breaking apart our beautiful Earth in order to transform her into pieces of junk that are thrown away a short time later. I've also seen industries give their buddies millions of dollars to slow down production and create job insecurity, when they are trying to swing public opinion to their favor. But in all of these instances, there is an equal amount of voices rising for a more conscious way of doing things. And words like unity may be fluffy new age stuff, but that's just a judgment - your judgment. There are other people who hear these words, and say 'yes'! That's the world I want!

"Remember the disembodied voice that told me to go into auto body? It also told me, **Judgments Create Frustration**."

"Well, yeah – I feel frustrated, all right!" J punches the ground. "But hey, hearing voices - isn't that a sign of being crazy?"

"Another judgment?" Humorously, I look at him sideways. "In tribal communities, it's common for the medicine person[193] to talk with spirits to bring healing to the tribe.[194] Not everyone is capable of, or would want to do this. A healthy clan requires diversity of skills. There needs to be hunters, food preparers, and care givers. But if the hunter doesn't talk to spirits, that doesn't mean the healer should be called crazy simply because they can. That would be a judgment based on fear of a skill that the hunter doesn't understand. Should the connected person be afraid of the hunter that can lure a beast into a trap? Of course not! Each is thankful for the services the other provides. Now, in our western society, if conscious people shout out that we're harming the Earth with deforestation,[195] taking the tops off of mountains,[196] and altering the food supply[197] – you'd think they'd be listened to. But propaganda is used and dollars are dangled, resulting in our spaceship Earth being stripped of her minerals and fluids.[198] Chop something too far, and you end up with a basket case that nobody wants to put back together."

J calms down and exhales loudly. "Okay, so just a different set of skills – but then what's the difference between a medicine person and one who uses ritualistic magic? And how do you know which voices are positive and which are the dark whisperers?"

"A medicine person, or shaman, strives to be as hollow as a reed, so that the Great Mystery can work *through* them. Someone who uses magic has an idea, or is following someone else's idea, of what should happen. So control switches to an ego, with its limited sight. As far as which inner voice to follow, examine the path into the future before following it. For instance, if one voice tells me to stop making judgments and the other tells me to be afraid – it becomes obvious what the end result will be with a little introspection. One acronym for fear is False Evidence Appearing Real."

"But there ARE things to be afraid of! Do you know George Orwell's book, *1984*? In it he talks about Big Brother and surveillance - there are cameras set up everywhere!"

"Groovy J – when approaching a curve on your bike, where do you look?"

"Through the curve to where I want to go. Why?"

— • ←

"Exactly. Don't focus on what you don't want – that's target fixation.[199] If you want the cameras removed and have that ability, then fine, do it. If you can't do anything about it, then *look where it is you really want to go*. Notice the things that make you happy, expand them in your reality, look upward. If you're unable to find true happiness, then heal whatever is preventing it. We can't heal the world if we're out of balance. Even Einstein said, 'We shall require a substantially new manner of thinking if mankind is to survive.'[200] I wanted not only to survive, but to thrive[201] - so I buckled down and made a healing commitment, stayed on track, and guess what – *it worked*. Quieting my mind empowered me, analyzing brought me clarity, and opening my heart once again, brought joy into my life. If the heart isn't open, we stay in lower levels that bounce between survival, sex, and power. It's time to move up a level on the playing field! Plus, the mind can never be as intelligent as the heart. Try to *feel* my words, and ask yourself if they feel true. We have everything we need within us to overcome every challenge that we face, because it was put there in the very beginning by our Creator. We can pray for this healing - and have it accomplished in a second - but only if we believe it's possible. If we don't believe in a higher power, then we can still accomplish complete healing by overcoming limitations within, which will then project as no limitations in our outer world. As far as those

125

→ • ←

who oppose our healing choices – they will fade away. Justice comes from within, but it requires a fully functioning personal system, which we – through our choices – can attain."

J quietly mulls over my words. I sense his dilemma at feeling powerless with the threats society currently faces. I also know that nothing I say will convince him to begin his inner journey - that's his decision. I only hope that all will consider self-exploration as a viable path.

J clears his throat, "Somehow, I knew it would come to this – but I thought I could wait until retirement. With all of the shit I'm hearing these days, it seems like the time is now. When the student is ready, the teacher will appear, right? Are you my teacher?"

"The children are our teachers, especially the child within. I'm just a person in the transportation field. First, I was an air traffic controller, then a cab driver, and now a motorcycle painter - the 3rd time's the charm, right?" I wink at J.

He's calm again. "Right on. So where do you see us heading?"

"Into a future where energy is free and non-invasive, products are made to last, and inventions are able to come to market without being squashed by those with money and an agenda. The propaganda used to influence people's decisions will be so transparent that no one will pay it any mind and we'll stop being manipulated. Tones and vibrations are going to make a huge leap in our evolution,[202] and pollution will be cleaned up.[203] Food will be nutritious and plentiful - like it is naturally, without anyone owning the 'rights' to it. Ever notice how many seeds are in a fruit or vegetable? Abundance is the way it's supposed to be, receiving a bounty and then sharing with one another - gardeners know this already.[204] Nature will be *revered* as the Great Mystery's perfect creation and the air will smell of flowers everywhere - not just in the rich neighborhoods. The butterflies and bees will return[205] and pollinate with joy. Water will be clean from the stream and we can eat fish without contaminants once again."[206]

I watch as J takes in this vision that I offer, not sure if he is at the place of believing just yet.

He looks up from his musing, "You think this will happen in our lifetime?"

"I see it already happening. Those who are healed are creating sacred space around them, which merges with each newly healed individual ... and so on, and so on. As far as the Earth, a soil scientist[207] said a 2% increase in the carbon content of the planet's soil could offset 100% of all greenhouse gas emissions.[208] That's do-able, right? I know it's a complex situation and there are many working on it, but divesting from fossil fuels,[209] leaving the rainforest intact,[210] and planting a whole lot of hemp seems like a logical start. Then, the next generation can take it from there - allowing us to reincarnate into something better."

J tilts his head and says with a smile, "Okay, I like your vision of the future better than mine. It sounds groovy like an old time movie!"

Chapter 5: **PTSD**

"So, how familiar are you with post traumatic stress disorder?" I ask Groovy J.

"I saw someone lose it on the sub - that might have been PTSD. His name was Larry, not like you'd know him or anything. Normally, he was a great guy. We'd play cards from time to time and I considered him a friend. He was a good worker and kept his bunk and personal items all ship shape. Then, after we were out at sea for a while, he started getting ornery. Nothing major, just not as fun to be around. Then, he started bad mouthing other guys for the littlest thing and he'd try to talk the rest of us into joining forces against whoever it was that had pissed him off. Then, more and more people seemed to piss him off, so the list of enemies grew and allies dwindled. I tried talking sense to him, trying to get him to ease back on the bad mouthing, but I couldn't get through - it's like he was stuck in anger mode and it escalated the longer we were at sea. Then, he started thinking I'd been cheating him at cards – which I'd never do – groovy guys don't cheat. But, he wouldn't let it go … he'd rehash old situations and shift them to look like he had a

129

mountain of evidence against me, so I had to avoid him, as well. It progressed to where he was walking around angry and suspicious of *everyone*, saying we were plotting to harm him. And then, walking past him one day, he slammed into me so hard that I got knocked backward into some equipment." J turned and lifted up the back of his shirt so I could see the scar. It was a 4-inch long backward L, and a bit puffy. It looked even more out of place on J's back because the rest of the skin was smooth and perfectly sculpted from body building. The healer side of my brain recognized how the scar was Larry's initial backward, signifying the shadow side, but I didn't mention this to J. Instead, I listened as he continued with his story.

"After he shoved me, I didn't know if he was going to come at me again, so I knocked him out. When he came-to, we both went to the infirmary, and they wrote up the infraction. We got called into the Senior Chief's office where I explained how everything had gone down. I was dismissed right away, but Larry had to stay in the Senior Chief's office quite a while longer. Later that evening after lights out, Larry started screaming and scratching deep gouges into his arms with his fingernails. It was messed up. The medics were called in, and they gave him something to calm him down. The next day after the drugs wore off, he started gouging his arms again, and again the day after that - until they finally had to bring the sub into port so he could get professional help."

"It sounds like he went into a full blown manic attack. Did he ever return to the sub?"

"Yes, he came back to process out. We ran into each other and I tried to talk to him, but he was out of it. They had him pretty drugged up. I hope they can help the guy, and not just keep him in a doped state, but I'm still pissed about the scar he gave me."

"Can you forgive him?"

"I really got hurt." J takes on the appearance of a young boy for a moment.

"I see that – but, he was fighting some very hard battle that had nothing to do with you. If you went into a manic state and couldn't do anything to stop it – wouldn't you want to be forgiven?"

"What's a manic state?"

"The way my therapist explained it to me, is that there's an injured portion of your brain which contains the trauma, and it's not communicating with the overall brain. When someone gets triggered back to the time of trauma, they activate and live from that separate brain area. Faces can shift, landscapes can change, and the person will experience things from the time of impact. Once the manic state has passed, they may not remember

131

anything that occurred because now they're operating from a totally different area of the brain. So, do you get mad at Larry? Or do you blame the person who traumatized him? Or punish the person that hurt the perpetrator, making it possible for them to traumatize another? How far back in history do we place the blame, or does it finally make sense to forgive? Look through their madness and see the good person they once were, helping them to re-member also!"

J remains quiet.

Finally I ask, "Remember those demons you saw?"

"Yeah, what about them?" He responds belligerently.

"When we don't forgive people – or ourselves – it's like a dark space within us that can serve as an ego cave for the little demons to take hold."

"How so?" He asks a little less defensive.

"By disallowing the light to heal what happened, that darkness will attract more darkness to it."

"I'll think about it. I want to decide for myself what I'm going to do."

"Fair enough." I answer.

"But let me ask you this – what *were* those demons?"

"That's a huge question, and for those I've found that entertaining opposing truths at the same time, works best for me. For instance, are they *real* or not? Again, Pope Francis says yes, and many religions speak of devils. Then, some of these groups go on to help cure those who believe they have been possessed. So for these people, they are real entities that can help or hinder our lives. But for those who say they're imaginary, it's suggested that angels and devils are thought forms based on theology from the person's past. Therefore, the individual is creating the interaction with directed thoughts. So this goes to show just how powerful people's thinking can be. Were you raised with a religious background that had contrasts such as heaven and hell?"

"Yeah – my sis and I went to Sunday school."

"Okay, so either living entities or thought forms, you knew by ingesting hard drugs you were causing damage and it was forbidden, therefore your manifestation took shape according to childhood memories because by lowering your vibration into a darker dimension, you descended into a reality where you could see or imagine them. Have you seen anything of the sort since?"

"No."

"There you go - you raised your vibration, so you left them in hell."

"Have you ever seen an angel or devil?"

"Better than seen, I snapped a few photos of angels!"

"In real life?"

"Cloud angels, but it was amazing! I had sent up a prayer one morning asking for clarity, because over the course of a year,

133

I felt guided to break off a long-term relationship, enter another relationship, and then that didn't work out as I'd hoped. I was truly surprised and thought perhaps I misled myself, so before pondering further, I appealed to the Great Mystery to send me a sign and let me know if I'd been acting on Divine Will or out of my ego. I received guidance to stay near home. Early evening came and while enjoying a fire with the neighbors, in an otherwise cloudless sky, two angels floated over the peak of the house. Our jaws dropped! Then it clicked – my sign! I grabbed both a film and digital camera, and snapped several photos as the upper angel danced away from the strong, sturdy angel underneath. And because the cloud angels separated from each other, I interpreted that the relationship had run its course, but yes, I had followed God's will in my actions. Whew!"

135

"That's really groovy sister! I don't suppose you have a devil photo, do you?"

"No – but I did find a way of getting rid of pesky demons! By calling in an ancient Truth that before duality, all was One; therefore darkness is illusion because there is only Light. Poof, they were gone!"

"Right on! But what about the whisperers, where do they fit in all this?" J asks.

"Are we going with the idea that whisperers are mystical entities or humans?"

"If they are angels, devils or guides we've already covered that. Plus, I've seen enough ghost chaser shows in my day. Let's go with whisperers being human."

"All right, the easiest explanations would be that it's a very strong memory of a voice from our past, or it's our own ego, trying to keep us from rising into our full potential as a Divine Being, which would require the complete release of egoic thoughts – according to most spiritual texts."

"And if it's coming from outside ourselves?"

"Psychopathic authoritarians who have kept occult knowledge[211] to themselves, tops my list. We have proof that the government uses illegal programs such as MKUltra[212] where they manipulate people's mental state and alter brain function using horrific techniques. Next, there are United States Patents for the

136

manipulation of human's nervous systems through computer monitors and televisions.[213] What if all the holy wars were started from whisperers pretending to be God, and had something to gain from the fighting? The bottom line is that a skilled, controlling personality with an agenda can target certain individuals, if those people are lax with their thinking. That's why it's of the upmost importance to have a quiet mind. Then we have the power to truly be ourselves. Even those who aren't skilled can create anxiety in others by thinking directed negative thoughts. That's why gossip is so harmful. Luckily, the reverse is also true – we can uplift each other by thinking positive thoughts … also known as prayer.

"Then, I have also read in multiple resources that every thought that has ever occurred, is still floating around in the ether. So there's all these thoughts, and since like attracts like, you end up with rivers of thought that are similar. Start thinking that the world is going to hell and you'll tap into a river of thought that corresponds, drawing to yourself continuing evidence to support your theory. Believe that we're living in a heaven on Earth, and guess what –you're going to notice the beauty of life and see where improvements are occurring. That's why those of us who have seen a lot of crap need to clean house and revert our thinking back to a state of innocence, hence, the southern position on the medicine wheel, also known as learning

137

from the child within. Children see the world through innocent eyes and believe what they're told. It's important to always speak age-appropriate truth to them, and see them as *Divine Beings*, and then they will live their life accordingly, and we *will* have heaven on Earth within a generation. Every choice is ours, because every thought, or absence of thought, is under our control. We create the world around us by our thoughts and then share them with others, affecting their thinking. There are so many beautiful people … and so many people ready to be beautiful. A shift in perception is all it takes – gentle thoughts about ourselves and each other. So back to your friend Larry – if you can forgive him and visualize him going forward with a happy life, you are going to help him AND yourself, by raising both of your vibrations."

"I just think positive thoughts about Larry and he'll get fixed?"

"He won't be dealing with anxiety coming from your direction, that's for sure. Then there are some good trauma therapists out there using new techniques like Sensorimotor Psychotherapy,[214] TIR – Traumatic Incident Reduction,[215] and EMDR - Eye Movement Desensitization and Reprocessing[216] that don't require medication in many cases. There are also healers who use shamanic techniques that are effective,[217] as well as other techniques I've probably never heard of. But the first two steps in dealing with PTSD are to get the person into a safe environment and then help them come to terms with the past traumatic event. This could be a trained professional, a loving community that is willing to listen to the stories that need releasing, or a great healer who reconnects the brain, illuminating and balancing all quadrants."

"Do you think childhood trauma caused Larry's behavior?"

"Maybe, I see it that way, because that's how it was for me, so it's *my reflection*. It could be as simple as a poor diet[218], genetics, or environmental factors."

"Well, whatever set him off - I know throwing a knockout wasn't the best way of handling it, but I didn't want him coming at me again."

"If knocking him out was your instinctive response, then that was the right thing to do. But I have been creating a set of guidelines and I use them to maintain my own sense of self … in fact … I just so happen …" I reach into my back pocket for the piece of folded paper that I'd grabbed out of the glove box earlier and hand the page to J.

oo

A Road That Doesn't Suck

* Some People Are Assholes – Forgive Them *
Once you know someone's back story, you'd get it.
Give them the benefit of the doubt, forgive them now.
Give second chances but increase communication, getting counseling if needed.
If you push everyone away that does you wrong, you will be alone.
Of course, don't allow dangerous situations! And take breaks to honor your own feelings.
But, sometimes, what looks like offensive behavior,
is a projection that *you* are creating in order to clear the past.

* Find the Balance between Being Alone and Being in Community *
When abuse is part of the past, then it feels safer to be alone.
But that's when it's time to be truly great, heal the past, and find your soul group.
They're out there, looking for you too. Joyful connections begin with other people.
Yet, at the same time, being alone allows the space for deep, inner connection and reflection.
Don't be afraid to hear your own thoughts. They aren't the *real* you, but they will give you clues
to what you're attracting, and offer ways of improvement. Find the balance.

* Judgments Create Frustration *
Some judgments are associations, so it's bringing the past into the present.
Some judgments are passed down, be original, start anew.
No matter what's happening in the outside world, keep working on your inner world,
as is reflected by the thoughts you think.
That's where your power is, that's where you create your future.
When you get to the point of no thought, you are Universal.

* If Not Today, Then Tomorrow *
Don't give up. Keep going. Set goals. Make changes. Allow old habits to fall away gracefully.
Keep gentle thoughts. It will get easier the higher in vibration you rise.

* Let Your Word Be Your Bond *
If you say it, then keep it. The Great Mystery can set events in motion to assist you.
Life becomes magical this way. Personal power and pride grow with integrity.

* Pursue Peace *
Anything that doesn't bring peace, is from the ego – let it go.
The experiences and connections that touch an open heart,
matter much more than a pocket with some gold.
At the end of the road, wipe off the bugs, and turn the key with a smile on your face.

oooooooooooooooooooooooooooooooooooooooooooooooooooooooooooooooooooooooooooooooooooooooooooooooooooo

I watch as J reads through the list. He turns it over, making sure nothing's written on the back, so I mention, "I've watched tons of movies on personal justice and revenge, but now I recognize those flicks as being created from a lower vibration and certainly not a lasting solution. A heart free of anger can feel compassion, and compassion leads to forgiveness. So, what do you think?"

"This one – Let Your Word Be Your Bond – I have a patch on my leathers that's very similar. I hold true to this. A man, or woman, is only as good as the words that they speak."

"Good for you, integrity matters. The more you keep your word, the more your personal power will increase."

"Personal power?"

"Personal power is control over yourself and, as that grows; it extends to power over your immediate world, that's when you start to approach *em*powerment. But, that's not to be confused with power *over* someone else – that's a trap of the ego – therefore transient."

"I'm pretty damn strong physically, how do I increase it personally?" J asks.

"Many ways, I increase mine by having control over my thoughts, taking all of my energy and directing it into one passionate endeavor - like changing my Sporty into a show bike, or by closing my holes and stopping the energy leak from old issues and insecurities."

"Closing holes from leaking energy? What are you talking about?"

"You have a body, but there's a larger part of you that's not visible to most people. This is your energy field. A hole would be a tear or actual hole in the auric or energetic field[219] around the body. Scientifically speaking, it would mean nervous system damage. Post traumatic stress is something that rips a major hole in the field. Whatever happened to Larry, it was a large enough hole to drain his energy so that he dropped into a lower dimension where his vision shifted to seeing everyone else in a low vibration as well. He became paranoid and violent because he was filled with fear."

"I can forgive him for being afraid." J says in a fatherly tone.

"That's worthy of praise then. A lot of forgiveness is needed these days because many people are acting out, based on fear, because they have continuous daily stress - and situations are sometimes manufactured to create stress holes. A large number of people's hearts can be closed by strategically airing shocking or traumatic stories. If their hearts are closed, they can easily be controlled because they will feel vulnerable and require a savior. But remember, it's only their thinking that creates this, it's *not real*. Plus, if you keep people fearful and angry, they won't notice what's behind the curtain. They'll be so energy depleted jumping from one escape route to the next that they'll be too exhausted to do anything beyond the very basics for survival. Some people steal energy to replace what's been leaked out - like a vampire. The book 'Celestine Prophecy'[220] shares good information about energy exchanges, and how to correct them, I highly recommend all the books written by James Redfield."

"People really like those vampire stories." J muses.

"I'm sure they do. They recognize what's going on, even if it's something subconscious. Lovers will steal energy from each other, parents from their children, and I found clues in my own life that I was stealing energy."

"Who did you take it from?"

"Total strangers. It would be a glance that was sexually charged. It only lasted a second or two, but I discovered that I was trying to replace the sexual energy that was stolen from me as a child. I would do it if I was insecure or if I gave too much of myself to a person or endeavor, because I'm still learning the whole boundary thing.[221] But I'm aware of it, so change has already started. I don't want to mentally separate someone's spiritual body from their physical just because they're attractive. Plus, I can see how a sexual innuendo creates an opportunity for

143

ego based thoughts in other people, therefore confusion - and I don't want to hold anyone back from their own ascension. I'd like to see us *all* rise in vibration. Now, I know not everyone cares about stuff like this. They think they've got it made as they go into the energy of entitlement and use those around them as their personal slaves. Or think that they don't have to play by the same rules as the rest. I hear people talk about bosses who expect more and more out of their employees. They put profits before people, and it's stressing their workers out. The bosses think they're getting more bang for their buck, but they're actually making life worse for everyone by lowering the vibration of the planet while incurring negative karma for themselves. I mean, if some people are overworked and others are underemployed … it would just take a little tweaking to get that back into balance!"

J holds his hand up to stop me from talking, "I get it! I'll crunch some numbers when I get home from vacation." I high-five his raised hand! "But I'm only one boss out of millions. There's a lot that still needs to be dealt with."

"And it will be dealt with, as people become aware of their holes."

"How do I know if I have any?" J asks.

"In the Toolbox I mentioned earlier, there's a questionnaire[222] and a chart that can help determine where your holes might be. The chart and questionnaire have the word chakras in them, but don't let that throw you. Chakras are just the name given to the body's energy centers to identify what body area is being referred to.[223] Like the throat chakra for speaking difficulties. Do you want me to email you my Toolbox when I get home?"

"I've heard of chakras before - no big deal and yes, I'll give you my email address. Here – enter it in your cell …"

"Can't."

"Why not?"

"I'm not plugged in. I only have an old flip phone in my van for emergencies. I knew a guy who had one of the very first cell phones ever made. A year later, doctors found a brain tumor in his head on the same side as he'd use his cell. He said he *knew* the tumor was caused by his phone. There is even a similar case in Italy that was upheld in court.[224] But, most importantly, I tossed mine because it reduces intelligence."

"Because of the radiation?"[225]

"I don't know anything about that – I was referring to having my friend's phone numbers memorized, if I store them in the cell, I don't need to memorize them anymore, so I stop exercising that muscle. I'd rather *strengthen* my abilities of memory and intuition. Learn my city, rather than be directed around by a GPS. Learn to communicate with my loved ones through telepathy, rather than texting. Human beings have many

145

undiscovered skills which we won't unveil unless we set aside technology in favor of curiosity of the unknown."

"But, how do you run your business without a cell?"

"Divine timing. You'll understand when you do. Remember, those screens are designed to entrap.[226] I've seen people become *lost* when their cell is taken away – no thanks, I'll keep my freedom."

"Well, alrighty then, I'll get you my address before the day is done. Tell me more about this Toolbox - like, how did you heal the holes from your trauma - did you see a therapist?"

"Yes, a therapist was great for explaining how text-book my thinking was in relation to my ordeal.[227] I also saw energy healers and used alternative techniques,[228] which I enjoyed very much. But my career as an artist is therapy in itself, plus the freedom of being independent allowed me the opportunity to take care of things the moment I notice something was off. The trick is in the noticing – because truthfully, I had no clue I had PTSD - I just knew I was pissed off."

"Pissed off – yeah … that sounds like my friends that think plugging into media is the way to stay informed. Instead of knowing what's going on, they are misinformed and angry."

"More than misinformed – they become traumatized by fabricated systematic alerts and dangers that threaten daily survival, making them feel helpless. Because the bulk of my

146

abuse happened at such a young age, I felt like my only recourse was to surrender to it until I was old enough to live on my own. I also learned to hide my flaws - *even from myself.* But once I grew up, I realized how unhappy I was and started reading positive books. It was something immediate I could do to raise my vibration. *Way of the Peaceful Warrior*[229] was the first book. It's a book that changes lives; it says so on the cover and yes, it changed mine for the better. Then the Neal Donald Walsh[230] series came after that, followed by many Deepak Chopra[231] books. These books answered my big questions on what life was all about, and all are extremely beneficial for someone who's ready to grow, but for the actual PTSD I came up with a technique that's a little different from most."

"What was it?"

"Well, first of all – being an artist gave me the perfect opportunity for self-reflection. Picture me working alone in my shop, behind the house, year after year. Sanding, painting, artwork, clearing, buffing, all activities that keep the hands busy but the mind free to wander. I noticed my mind was in continuous chatter mode, and usually about negative subjects, which lowered my vibration and turned me into an angry person. But, since I was alone, I couldn't blame my anger on anyone else – which is actually a good thing, because it made me finally take responsibility for my unhappiness, and since I owned it, that gave me the power to change it. Make sense?"

"Not sure – can you say it differently?"

"If I blamed my unhappiness on a customer, a friend, or past event, then I was powerless to change it. It's no longer in my control, because it's *their* fault, and that makes me powerless because I can't change them or the past. If I don't blame anyone, *for anything*, I am more powerful. Can you feel how that is true?"

"Yeah … I think so. If we blame – we lose our power. If we accept things as they are, we keep our power and then we can take action from a place of power instead of victimhood."

"You got it. Okay. So, if I recognized myself going into anger, I'd retrace my thoughts to see if the core situation was one where I needed to forgive someone or myself for something in the past. If so, I'd forgive, release, send in light to heal, congratulate myself, and get back to work. But if I couldn't easily identify the core, I'd sign off the job I was working on, and head into my meditation room. Then, I would sit on the west side of the room, which signifies introspection, smudge with sage to clear away any negative energy, and then start journaling about the thought that led me into anger. I'd use a technique whereby I ask a question with my regular hand and then let my inner-child-self answer with my opposite hand - my non-dominant hand. The response looked like a kid's chicken scratch, which is pretty cool,

148

and the slowness of trying to make it readable gives time for the answer to formulate clearly. I'm patient with my child-self because I want to gain self confidence. Well-being is worth more than time or perfection."

"Learning curve!"

"Yep." I give J a nod for his contribution, and then continue, "Once I discovered the root of the incorrect teaching that was pissing me off –either I would use forgiveness again, or a visualization technique where I yank out the root, or core issue, while seeing it leave from all aspects of my present life, past, and future lives."

"What if you can't find the root?"

"No worries – I'd use EFT - Emotional Freedom Technique[232] - to reprogram my brain, so I'd stop thinking in the old way."

"EFT?" J questions.

"EFT was created by Gary Craig and is tapping on meridian points to reprogram thinking from something negative to acceptance, then from acceptance to positive, using acupressure. He has a website that explains it in detail, [233] as well as videos online. I started with his technique, but because I didn't want to tap all the places that he says, especially if I'm in public, I reduced it to five points on my face, and I have a chart in the

Toolbox on this. Then to make up for the skipped points, I tap in front of a mirror and lock eyes with myself – *really intense!*"

"Give me an example?"

"… an example without a mirror - sure. First, I notice something I want to change about myself … you've heard the saying what you resist will persist? This is defusing that. No more hiding from embarrassing issues, I'm dragging them into the open and taking a good, hard look. Then I'll switch to feeling joy for myself, for being responsible." Enthusiastically, I shout, "I rock because I'm doing the work! Haha!"

J laughs.

I continue, "You don't really have to shout though! Then, even more than happy, I'll drop into a state of love for myself, because I am choosing to improve myself at *this very moment*. I put my hands on my heart until I can feel a heartbeat, sometimes visualizing bright green. Then I'll state what the new 'me' will be like. The new energy I'm choosing. So here goes … 'When looking over past failed relationships, my heart fills with sorrow.' – I feel that sorrow in my heart, and tap 7 times on the different meridian points. 'But I totally and completely, love and accept myself unconditionally!' Fill my heart with love for myself and tap 7 times. 'And I now realize that there was great joy in those relationships, so I am filled with gratitude of being able to experience love within this lifetime.' – feel gratitude and tap 7

150

times. Then, I record the EFT session in my journal so I can look back and see how far I've come, and have pride in myself all the more for the effort I am putting forth! I've filled up so many journals over the years that I'm now comfortable writing with both hands in cursive."

"They've stopped teaching cursive in my peep's school."

"Then teach them yourself – it's been proven to develop the mental processes of perception, memory, and reasoning.[234] Just like music is absolutely amazing for the intellect,[235] and drumming with both hands synchronizes the brain.[236] So all this healing is actually a lot of fun!

"Besides this technique, there are Bach flower essences[237] for help in shifting runaway emotions. 'Rescue Remedy' is great for stress, and there's one called 'Gorse' which is for people who have given up all hope, and have fallen into total despair. If you wouldn't have been able to see the value in my words earlier, and had willfully refused to believe that things will improve, then I would have suggested using Gorse in order to open your mind to new thinking."

"I didn't need it though."

"No, you didn't, which is good because I don't have any on me! Then there are essential oils to switch the brain back over to good.[238] These oils have been proven scientifically to raise our overall vibration.[239] And by psychoanalyzing myself on my own terms whenever I saw the need, I healed my PTSD. Even the medicine wheel teaches that introspection leads to illumination – sitting in the west, with Bear, eventually brought me to the east, Eagle, and Spirit."

"And what is north and south again?"

"Going to the north, Buffalo, I learn wisdom. Once I feel like I know the subject I'm studying, then I return to the south, Mouse, which is innocence. That was the end goal – to heal my inner child and return to innocence.[240] To regain the trust that I once had that the world was safe and the people in it are loving."

"But, I still don't think that's true." J replies.

"Depends on perspective. Remember, there are different truths, and what I expect to see, is what will be reflected back to me. Have you ever heard of the Peace Pilgrim?"[241]

He shakes his head no.

"She was a woman who started walking all over the United States at age 45 and continued for 28 years until her death. She took a vow to remain a wanderer until mankind learned the way of peace, walking until given shelter and fasting until given food. That means she would sleep on the side of the road, in bus shelters, and in strangers' homes. This woman has many stories of Divine Protection in her book 'Peace Pilgrim: Her Life and Work in Her Own Words.'[242] One time a man picked her up in his car and had ill intent, but once he saw her sleeping trustfully, he couldn't do it. Another time she defended a frail eight year old girl against a large man who was about to beat the child. The man chased down the girl and the old woman followed. She could see the girl cowering in terror in the corner, so she stood between the girl and the man. She just stood and looked at the poor, psychologically sick man with loving compassion. He came close and stopped. He looked at the woman for quite a while. Then, he turned and walked away and the girl was safe without a word having been spoken. The Peace Pilgrim states that we should never underestimate the power of God's love, because it transforms. It reaches the spark of good in the other person and the person is disarmed."[243]

I can tell from J's expression that he isn't convinced, in fact he says so. "But, maybe he didn't do anything because she's an old woman? She might have reminded him of his mother. It's different when guys interact with other guys."

I decide to offer another example. "Okay, then, there was one time when I had the same dream three nights in a row. In it, I was on my motorcycle at a stop sign. Twice I had a passenger, once I was alone, but in every dream there was a guy that would be running at me all crazy. I would quickly take off and he would lunge at the bike and either tackle me or pull off my passenger. Then, the day after the third dream, I'm coming home from a softball game and stopped at a light. I'm wearing my leathers,

153

clear goggles, and a bandana, so I look masculine. There's a drunk pissing against a building about 100 feet to my right. His left hand is supporting his weight, his right hand is directing his stream, and his head is swiveling left and right telling invisible people to fuck off and leave him alone. He finishes, tucks away, and turns around and sees me on the bike. He approaches and slowly his strides lengthen into a run and he starts coming at me full-bore. The light turns green. I recognize this scenario from my dream and hold my ground. When he's about 10 feet away, I point my finger at him, lock eyes, and order STOP! He skids to a halt and gives a little shake of his head, like clearing away cobwebs. Then, he replies, I wasn't gonna do nothin'. I calmly said *good* – and slowly let out the clutch, driving away."

The silence between us is comfortable. In the distance, some pipes are heard accelerating. I smile at the coincidence.

J is thinking, and then he asks, "Did you call the cops on him?"

"Naw, justice comes from within. I'll let him deal with his karma. No harm, no foul."

"You think that karma is real then?"

"Yes, but once you move through karma, you enter grace. Grace is amazing. It's like, you make mistakes in life, but once you realize where you went wrong, I mean, really *feel* remorse, and the tears come releasing the devastation that's been brought

154

→ ● ←

to your awareness … then after, this light, this forgiveness which can only be described as Divine, floods your entire body. It's like being totally filled from the inside, or maybe from above, but it feels so wonderful. It's better than anything imaginable. It's worth doing the work, it's worth changing *everything* for. That's why we need to keep clearing the old while following the Golden Rule in the present – 'Do onto others as you would have them do onto you.'[244]

"Does this feeling last?"

"Depends … it felt like the light leaked out my holes, because I still had quite a few issues. But from that amazing Grace, it propelled me to continue closing holes and reaching for the light to fill me again. And it has … and it leaked … but slower the next time, which is why it's like a hole in a bucket. So, I continue healing. But more than that, this experience taught me to trust in something other than myself. I touched the Divine, so I know it's real. That means I don't need to be a badass anymore to protect myself, I've got something Great watching my back. I can open my heart and regain my childlike trust, my innocence and assurance that I am safe, and I will walk as a child into heaven. Yeah … follow the Golden Rule into the Golden Age."

"But not everyone follows the Golden Rule anymore – how do you deal with those people?"

155

→ ● ←

"Forgiveness."

"That's what you said to do if they have PTSD – that's one person. What if it's *many* people doing asshole type stuff and the PTSD doesn't have anything to do with it?" J says pointedly.

"There was a time in my life when everything I touched, turned to shit. Everything I read seemed dismal and tainted, and I was really concerned about the direction the world was heading. Because I saw enemies 'out there' - I attracted two associates who threatened me with unfounded lawsuits, and then two customers wanted me to fix their paint problems that weren't my fault. I started feeling persecuted and went into a personal hell, because I no longer had hope."

"What did you do?"

"I not only forgave them, but I learned how to surrender - literally and figuratively. I bought a bottle of essential oil designed for this purpose and would breathe it in, saturating my lungs. I prayed, and went into meditation. From that place, I was able to see my experience wasn't all that bad in comparison to what others were experiencing around the world. I stopped feeling sorry for myself, and that raised my vibration. From the higher vibration, I was able to remember that where God is, love is, and if I can stay in a place of love, then it will invite the Goddess to work miracles in my life to take care of the current struggles I was facing. Then, I prayed for those who wanted to take me to court, and within two weeks, the disputes dissolved. For those who wanted me to repair paint flaws caused by them, I agreed to repair the work at half cost, although I did grumble to a friend about the money that I lost. She kindly reminded me not go into victimhood, and instead gift that money to the Universe for future karma, so I could remain empowered with a positive and conscious thought process. The situation turned into a growth opportunity for me, and by looking around at what I was doing, I saw my error in finding fault and blame and returned to having a fun life. If I would have fought these people in court, I would have been strengthening the energy of opposition and lost precious time. So I blessed them, which advances all of humanity. If enough people bless, pray, and forgive[245]…well, that's a road that doesn't suck!"

J responds with agitation, "But, what if *I* don't believe in prayer? I mean – you *really* think that there's some Guy hanging out in the clouds listening? What about babies that are thrown away in garbage cans?"

"There's no *nature* around a garbage can. How would the Divine have access? But there *are* stories about babies surviving in the woods, with apes or wolves taking care of them."

"But Zora, even if a few people pray – then some invisible Guy is going to fix everything? And if so, then why

157

didn't He help during the Holocaust and other similar tragedies that have occurred over time?"

"Well, I don't imagine myself praying to a single entity – that's why I minimize the use of the word God, because that suggests something individualized. I view the Great Mystery more as a blanket over everything, something that permeates the entire universe. Science has suggested that this force may look like little strings everywhere that vibrate at different rates.[246] When I'm praying, I'm going off the experience of previous miracles – so I have confidence in my words. The little cluster of strings that make up the 'me' that you see, are lighting up with the knowledge that I can lighten up more little strings – both mine and in my vicinity - with perfect vibration and thought. When I invite someone else to pray with me, a bigger glow will be established by the little strings that surround the both of us – and the stronger our confidence, the stronger the glow. Get enough people directing their little strings toward light and healing, and you're going to get a big glow. Miracles happen with these big glows because the strings are influenced by thought – quantum physics and the observer effect.[247] So, as to your question of why didn't this work for those who were killed during the Holocaust – there weren't enough strings lighting up with good thoughts. From what I've read, propaganda and mind games were used to make one group of people hate another group. Then, those that hated were rewarded with receiving the material items of the eliminated group. Where were those bright strings that could have turned the tide?"

"So everyone should just sit around praying all day?"

"What everyone does is their statement to the Universe about *who they are*. I don't care what anyone else does, as long as they don't cause harm."

"And what if I do cause harm?"

"Then you're harming yourself. We're all connected, so be good to yourself and others. The Golden Rule."

"What if I do something on accident?"

"Become conscious, and you won't do anything on accident."

"How do I become conscious?"

"Discipline!"

Chapter 6: **Silence**

"Have you ever tried meditation, J?"[248] I ask. "If you can hear the sound of silence, it makes it easier to be conscious in your daily life."

"You enjoy giving advice, don't you?" Groovy J responds.

"Haha! I guess I do. I have an uncle that was an advisor to the President, so I guess it's in my blood. We can stop here."

"No! I'm not … that's not what I meant." He stammers a little. "I'm learning things. I don't know how much will stick in my brain, but I want to take advantage of this afternoon together. So no, I've never meditated before. How do I start?"

"Rest the tip of your tongue on the roof of the mouth which activates chi, or Universal energy."[249]

"Like this?" He opens his mouth to let me see in.

"That's right. Now, relax your jaw. Allow your mouth to rest in a slightly open, comfortable manner. Over the years, this has become my normal mouth stance, which relieves tension and allows for easy breathing. Next, consciously focus on your breath … inhalation and exhalation. In the beginning, I'd achieve silence for a few seconds, but then catch myself thinking about something I'd heard or seen earlier in the day - mental noise. That's when I became proactive and turned off ALL external information sources like TV, movies, radio, and video games. After that, it became easier to stay in silence because my brain wasn't trying to analyze the input from earlier. So I kept the outside noise turned off. And because I work alone, I kept it quiet in the shop too. My circumstances gave me a unique opportunity to travel this path to see if it was worth it, and then report back, knowing not everyone has a situation like mine."

"Like an Indian scout."

"Yeah! So with external noises eliminated, I slowly started to make progress. It was like zeroing out a scale before adding things back on. And I was practicing breathing at every opportunity. Breath is so important. Without breath, there is no life. So I breathed. I had notes all over, reminding me of my mission. If a friend came over, we'd sit in silence and practice together - in front of a fire or by the water, just watching the sun sparkle on the surface. And eventually, with persistence, silence was heard."

J shares his own comparison, "That's similar to when I'm 50 miles into a ride and I really settle into my machine and everything quiets down in my brain."

"If only we could ride all the time, right? Although truth be told, that doesn't always work either. I did a paint job for a vet who, after returning from Vietnam, got on his motorcycle and rode all over the United States, Canada, and into Alaska. He said there were sections of road in Alaska that were such deep tire tracks that he couldn't get his bike out of them, so he just kept going, sometimes riding for days on end. The concentration kept his mind from returning to thoughts of the war and seeing his mates being reduced to chunks of meat before his eyes. But, after ten years, he stopped riding and went home. The nightmares came back. He tried sleeping pills but woke up in the psych ward. Apparently, they contribute to both sleep walking and even worse nightmares where he dreamed he was murdering everyone and had no control to stop himself – and this doesn't just happen to vets, even children are experiencing this!"[250]

"Real fucking zombies!" J exclaims.

"Yeah!" Agreeing, I continue. "So now, he ingests cannabis daily to ease his trauma.[251] The human brain has cannabinoid receptors[252] and is designed to accept cannabinoids, so he has been relatively okay since choosing this ancient healing path.[253]

"As for me, I prefer meditation. I knew from a past life that achieving a quiet mind was not only possible, but necessary. So, I focused on the breath. If a thought does come up, I just let it

162

go and don't try to call it back. Not engaging it at all, because silence is the goal and I know it's a muscle that needs to be strengthened. Concentrating on the silence between thoughts, the mind becomes silent, at peace."

"Wait, hold on a minute, are you saying that you stopped the mental noise completely?" J asks.

"Not *absolutely* completely, but for long enough periods of time so I now notice when the mind chatter starts to creep in again. Then I look at whatever is causing the chatter, and make peace. Unless it's music playing - sometimes I'll let a soundtrack continue to play, ha! But yes, once the muscle is strong enough, the brain becomes silent."

"How long did all that this take to accomplish?"

"Does it matter?"

"No, I guess it doesn't. But, say a guy wants to fast track it - would it work to go into total seclusion to get it done faster?"

"I've read that three days in a completely natural setting without any electronic device can restore us to *proper thinking*, but have never come across a time frame for the absence of thought. That might take a bit longer ... but, it all depends on how developed the muscle is already and how strong your willpower. I could ask the same thing of you - how long did it take to develop those guns you're packing right there?" I reference his biceps.

163

J proudly does a couple of impressive poses, "This is several years' worth of work. But, okay, I get what you're saying."

I continue explaining, "So now that the goal of silence was met, I could track any remaining thoughts that were incorrect. And of course, I found more crap that had been incorrectly programmed into my brain. Since *negative thoughts create holes too,* it was back to EFT to transmute them.

"But the good thing is that a quiet mind drastically improved my driving! Before, I had a bit of road rage. The way road construction is planned and my inner commentary on how other people were driving, I wasn't helping the situation! But now with a quiet mind and Rescue Remedy[254] at my side just in case, I cruise along all serene and watch others' driving and laugh! It really can be funny! I no longer take anything anyone else is doing personally because I can sense what they're going to do ahead of time by watching traffic flow. So, instead of bitching at other drivers, I do an eight-count breathing exercise."

"Why eight and not seven or nine?"

"Well, you could do seven or nine if you'd like. I'm sure if you research online you'd find many different teachings, and some will be opposing, that's why the teacher *within* is the one that's right for you. For me, I know that eight is the number for infinity, while seven is completion, and nine is ego. Six or less is too short of a breath for me, and anything ten or more feels like a stretch, so I go with eight."

"Okay, just curious. As you were."

"So I breathe in for the count of eight, hold for eight, exhale for eight, hold for eight. That's one of the eight, so then seven more times. I worked out a system of counting on my fingers so I really don't have to pay attention to what number I'm on. Instead I focus on *nature and trees* while breathing on the road and that *gives* me energy instead of depleting it – because nature is the Creator's handiwork, therefore it nourishes naturally! And by seeing the natural beauty wherever I go, I reflect more beauty into the world. I've also stopped reading the billboards and focus on the landscape in terms of color groupings. Very cool! Rush-hour used to make me feel trapped, now it is an opportunity to practice my breath work and mindfulness. And then, with my mind quiet, I began to heal any remaining fragmentation."[255]

Groovy J raises his hand and asks, "What's fragmentation again?"

"As a newborn infant, we know that we are Divine and so is everyone around us. The first few times we experience abuse in our life – we are so shocked, that a piece of our soul breaks off and hides in order to keep ourselves from totally shutting down. This is called soul fragmentation, and it's like a fuse that gets blown to protect the main circuit. When we lived more tribal based, the medicine man, woman, or shaman would attend to the injured person, facilitate healing of the abuse, and then call back the missing soul pieces; although people can do it themselves through prayer. They just need to remember to do it. Get it? Re-member. Ha! Anyway … by becoming silent, I was able to become a witness to myself and watch how I went through my day. I could *see* where improvements were needed because there wasn't any mind chatter trying to defend myself. I could pick up on the clues that my subconscious was leaving and use it as opportunities to clear even more."

"Bwahahahaha! You found a groovy way to get those loose screws tightened up!"

"Hahahahaha!" His laugh is so infectious! Then I mention between giggles, "You'd love Laughter Yoga, you know that?!"[256]

"Oh yeah? You want to see me wear those little tights, is that it?! Bwahahahaha!"

"You don't wear tights in laughter yoga! You wear normal clothes and do exercises that use the same muscles as in real laughing!"

"Well, in that case I could be the instructor!

"You really could! I'd go to your class! To see a big, badass, biker like you helping others laugh their way to greater health – that would totally rock!"[257]

As the mirth settles, I confide, "Now – there's another clue I deciphered that goes along with this - how I learned to love myself again. But if you're getting tired of all this talk we can go look at bikes."

"No, no, not at all! I'm lovin' this real talk we've got going on here. It's all good! *Please*, continue …" And J sits up all prim and proper, and makes a motion like he's straightening an invisible tie.

I smile at his antics. He continues to beam at me, so I continue, "In order to learn to love myself, I had to figure out where I learned to *not* love myself. What I discovered was that in my childhood, from being rejected by the first people that came into my life, I was pulling in rejection as something that I was asking for." I pause to look at J again to see if he really wants me to continue. He raises his eyebrows as if to say 'go on'.

"As a kid, I experienced separation, rejection, and abuse. So then I made a decision that this was how the world was - and that's how I saw it from that point on. See, life doesn't happen to us, it responds to us. That's the way it's set up. Remember the whole 'ask and it shall be given'?[258] Yeah, except the asking isn't just by words or prayer - it's also by whatever I focus on longest

167

\- thoughts and emotions. That's why I needed to quiet my thoughts. I couldn't think positive ones because I was still being influenced from childhood. And life is neutral to what it thinks I'm asking for … helpful people, creepy people, good job, suck job, a car, or a bike … whatever. It's like, you know when you're researching a truck to buy, and the one model that you like best - you start seeing it everywhere? It seems to catch your eye while you're driving around or pulling into parking lots?"

"Yeah, I've experienced that."

"Well, that's it simplified, but it works the same way. You see what you're looking for. Since I expected people to try to screw or reject me, I pulled those people into my life and they did just that. So, even though my parents gave us kids' very comfortable lives, those first few years dictated how the rest of my relationships were going to unfold, thereby influencing the quality of joyful connections I would experience. That's why I became a seeker, I wasn't willing to ignore – be ignorant – of my off-behavior. Ninety-five percent of our life is controlled by our subconscious[259] and from birth to 6 years old - we're simply downloading information. This is called the hypnagogic state.[260] I've heard people say kids don't remember anything under a certain age. That's a lie – not only do they remember, but it becomes their unconscious navigational system and it's also what *the dark side uses to exploit* in us."

168

"Explain further."

"This is getting deep, but I can offer two ways that I've experienced. One, is our own shadow self messing up our lives, which is a personal journey to be explored so the hidden can be healed. The second is when other people's shadow sides impact us – for example, let's say that there's someone in a position of power who experienced trauma but never healed from it. They will notice some quirks here and there, and learn how to hide them. This requires maintaining a delicate balance, so they become ultra controlling of themselves in order to hide their brokenness. This will be reflected by feeling the need to control their outer world, as well. But since fear of discovery is their guiding force, they will make decisions based on fear, which means two things. Everything they try to establish will dissolve in time, and they will be projecting fear into those they are trying to control."

"What does that look like?"

"Manipulation techniques that mimic the same ones installed by parents, unconsciously, because then it will trigger emotional responses. For example, favoritism – give one group of people something and not another, so jealousy results. Or scarcity – sorry little guy, there's just not enough for all of us, which makes the man greedy because of a false belief that he'd better get his before it's all gone."

169

"But sometimes there's *not* enough."

"Perhaps in a world governed by man-made laws, but not true in nature's world. Ask an organic gardener how many seeds one broccoli plant will produce – I'd guess a thousand from growing my own. So if natural law is one plant becomes a thousand, how can scarcity be a truth? Sure, someone might think they don't have enough money, but we can't eat money and what is it that we really need to live?"

"Clean air, water, and food. So how do we fix this?" J asks with growing understanding.

"The same way we fix every imbalance - with a loving community to enfold the broken person in, until they feel safe enough to release the old conditioning and let new light shine. Imagine if the vets coming home had a tiny house community to return to? One centered on a community garden or walipini in colder climates. Diversify that with kids who can't afford the rising rental rates and perhaps some refugees, and you'll create a microcosm society that bonds over nourishing and healing food. Remember, you don't want the vets eating crap food, because that will worsen any mental imbalance.[261] Add in an art center, since I can attest art transforms tragedy into triumph, and you'll truly be helping those who have given to their country! Caring about others is the solution in every spiritual book I've ever read, and also what worked in my own life. I bonded with my birth mom, and was healed by her acceptance and love."

"How did you find her?"

"Actually, she found me. The day I turned 18, I received a letter from Catholic Charities saying she wanted contact. We took our time getting to know each other via mail since I was in Spain, and then one day I asked the big 'why'. Long story short, she fell in love with this guy who was 17, she was 20 and still living at home. They slept together, I was conceived, but he went to Vietnam when he turned 18 and her parents said that she couldn't keep the baby and live under their roof. So she went to Catholic Charity's home for pregnant girls with the intention of handing me over for adoption. I was born in the home's hospital and their policy was to take me immediately after I popped out. She *really* begged them to let her hold me, and finally, they agreed with the condition that she not breastfeed me, because apparently that creates a bond between mother and child. She promised, and they walked out of the room to clean up.

"She told me how she held me, and then almost as if in a dream state, she offered me her nipple and I nursed. Now, she never told them that she ignored their demand, but I'm glad she did, because I read in *The Ringing Cedars* that the feeding ritual is necessary to transfer the mother's knowledge to the child. The newborn baby needs the nutrients found in breast milk[262] – not formula - plus some formulas contain corn syrup,[263] which I consider to be poison. What would be nice is if new mothers pumped as much breast milk as they could, and then sent that with the adopted child. Anyway, she fed me and we bonded. When the staff returned to the room, I was sleeping peacefully on her chest and she informed them that she had changed her mind, she couldn't let me go. They huffed and puffed, and then the nurse looked at her chart and replied that if my birth mom didn't give me up, they would charge her with a felony. The father was underage at the time of conception and that was considered statutory rape. So basically, they forced her into handing me over. I woke up as I was being passed to the nurse, which as you can imagine, was a traumatic experience for my birth mother. I was programmed at birth to associate the emotion of love, with heart wrenching anguish and loss."

While I was talking I wasn't looking at J, so I take a moment to study his response. He's listening intently without any judgment showing on his features, and his return gaze is consistent with both eyes focused equally.[264] I explain, "Unconsciously, I repeated the programming. Then, I would choose partners similar to my foster brother and family members.[265] Every relationship I tried, failed because I believed love leads to rejection. A belief like that hurts - but instead of living from my emotions and crying it out as a child would, I

172

lived from my head. I had all sorts of ideas on how to improve my life, the world, my business, and my love life. These ideas ate up my days, weeks, and years - always cycling through patterns of self-abandonment.[266] Instead of being with people, I chose thinking instead of loving. The heart is where we make connections with others, but that's not where I lived - I was too busy. Even after learning meditation, I'd still think up activities and see them through to completion, and sure, I'd have a quiet mind throughout the process, but I still wasn't living in my heart.

"Finally, *finally*, I could see my pattern and stopped. I learned to simplify. Eat good food and exercise. To discover those activities that brought me joyful connection. To feel which people in my life made my heart expand and sing. I finally learned to love myself."

J says proudly, "That's really good to hear. If you can overcome, so will others. And did you ever talk to your birth dad?"

"No, but I did learn that he served one and a half tours in Vietnam, 18 months total. He had served the extra to make sure he had money for a brand new car when he got home. He bought a '68 Plymouth Roadrunner. Unfortunately, a month after returning stateside he was out drinking with friends when he ran the stop sign at a crossroads and hit another car at about 2:30 a.m. Two people were killed; my birth father was one of them."

173

"Sorry to hear, Zora."

"It's okay - he became my guardian angel. We repeat our parent patterns as well, until cleared. I was stationed in Millington Tennessee for radar school, and I went into Memphis to party. Driving home about 2:30 a.m., I started to fall asleep. I woke up from a loud CLAP! I felt his presence inside the car and knew who it was immediately even though we had never met. He may not have been around for my life, but he gave me the gift of living, twice."

Chapter 7: **Love is Alive**

"Can I ask you something J?"

"Shoot."

"Do you cry around your kids?"

"The father is strong – he's the rock that the family is built upon. Why would I want to appear weak? It might scare them."

"It won't scare them, it will make them powerful. Kids need to learn how to release grief and pain, since chances are that it's going to happen eventually in life. Grief is a wonderful teacher. It allows us to see our shadow side clearly. The feelings of loneliness, abandonment, terror, anger and rejection all come to the surface in times of grief. With tears, we flush these old wounds out of our system, so we can move forward and manifest the life we truly desire."

"You've got a lot of new words for me today – so now, what's manifesting?"

"Another word for creating the life you want. Have you ever seen a human cell under a powerful microscope? Our cells are busy creating more cells, which means even at the most microscopic level, we are creators."

"So, you're saying I have to cry like a baby to get the sort of life I want?! Bwahahahaha!" J jokes.

"Yes, for a more magical life, then yes." I know he's kidding, but I'm serious. "Back in the 70's, when I was growing up, emotions were said to be a weakness – but they're not – just the opposite is true. You lose your power when you stuff everything down, and you lose the skills of psychically navigating. Plus, the latest research shows how tears are a critical aspect of the human emotional makeup and that they carry stress-related toxins out of the body. So, if I didn't relearn how to cry when it was needed, then I might develop an illness like ulcers or colitis."[267]

"My father had ulcers." J ponders.

"So did mine. I don't know if you've ever closed your heart during your life, but I did. And those in the manic phase of PTSD, they display classic characteristics associated with a closed heart."

"Like what?"

"Being cynical, anxious, and suspicious. Arguing with others …"

"That was Larry, my mate on the sub that went manic!" J bellows with recognition.

176

I continue, "Betraying someone and not giving a shit, receiving delight in hurting others or watching someone get hurt."

"Yep – that too!"

I nod and add, "When the heart is closed, the mind-body communication is shut down so people react in negative ways."

"How did you get your heart to reopen?"

"I made a pact with myself that the next time an opportunity arose, I would allow myself to cry – something I hadn't done for more than a decade. Well, we get what we ask for, so I didn't have to wait too long. I still remember that day … another relationship had fallen apart and I was sitting on the floor. The tears simply streamed out of my eyes without a sound, no pushing and no holding back, just a steady flow of tears. I thought to myself, so this is what emotions are like - not that big of a deal, I can do this. It just felt like a tear duct cleansing. Then, as other opportunities arose and I became more comfortable with the crying experience, I incorporated sounds which helped me to go deeper. I'd throw a blanket over my head and really go at it, pulling up and clearing anything that was still hiding under layers of forgotten memories. This helped me to forgive each person who had hurt my heart and to wipe out caves of darkness within me. But, I did learn an important difference – it's one thing to cry because I was feeling like a victim, and another to cry out of

177

compassion for having to go through a rough experience. The crying out of compassion made me feel clear and clean - the crying out of victimhood made me feel weak and vulnerable. So, no pity parties! Ha! Then, because I was working with my breath, that allowed my heart to return to a calm state faster, which allowed me to see the humor of living, which led to feeling joy again, and that helped me feel safe enough to open my heart to those around me!"

"And, that's how you learned to forgive?" J asks.

I respond sincerely, "Yes. Plus, I learned in the book *Chakra Mirror Math*[268] which includes the Forgiveness Method,[269] that people did things to hurt my heart because *their* hearts were closed and *they* couldn't feel joy. Had their heart been open at the time, it never would have happened. Plus, a particle of the Creator is in everyone, so they'll bring on their own judgment day when the time is right - so what's the sense in holding a grudge? I benefit more by just going ahead and forgiving as soon as possible, then getting on with my life. Same with the reflection; I did things I'm not proud of while *my* heart was closed - I'm hoping those people can find it within themselves to forgive me too."

J takes in a large breath of air, exhales, and then asks, "How did you clear guilt? I still have some things that I'm not very proud of doing. Whenever I think about them, I feel like I'm going to puke."

"That's a clear signal that something is ready to be released! There's a technique from Hawaii called Ho'oponopono[270] that I use to clear bad energy. *I pardon myself* - instead of giving someone else the power to clear sins for me. The proper intention is vital, so whenever I do it, I have to be *very sincere* with my words. The simple method is saying, 'I'm sorry, please forgive me, I love you, thank you.' Sometimes I feel the old energy shift to the good, other times I hold the belief that things will improve and give it time."

"That's it? You don't even have to be face-to-face?"

"Face to face is best, because then you have the opportunity for feedback, which eliminates assumptions. So yes, if you have two-way communications available, then by all means engage it. But, if that option isn't available, then intention will set the stage. Energetically we're all connected, so just by saying these words and really meaning them, old disputes begin to heal, because words are very powerful when the aim is true. And then, if for some reason I don't feel like this technique was strong enough to undo the mistake, there is another prayer that I read in *A Course in Miracles*[271] that invokes the Holy Spirit. I've memorized this direct quote from the book, 'The first step in the undoing is to recognize that you actively decided wrongly, but can as actively decide otherwise. Be very firm with yourself in this, and keep yourself fully aware that the undoing process, which does not come from you, is nevertheless within you because God placed it there. Your part is merely to return your thinking to the point at which the error was made, and give it over to the Atonement in peace. Say this to yourself as sincerely as you can, remembering that the Holy Spirit will respond fully to your slightest invitation: I must have decided wrongly, because I am not at peace. I made the decision myself, but I can also decide otherwise. I want to decide otherwise, because I want to be at peace. I do not feel guilty, because the Holy Spirit will undo all consequences of my wrong decision if I will let Him. I choose to let Him, by allowing Him to decide for God for me.'

"So, I went through my life and cleared everything that I could think of, and then I reached the point where I thought I'd gotten everything. That's when it happened - apparently I reached a certain level in my purity in thought[272] because God, or as I like to say, the Great Mystery, was kind enough to remind me of *past* sins that I'd completely forgotten about, so I could clear them too. These impressions weren't coming from me - I know that for a fact - it was something mystical and really cool, even if I *was* being reprimanded. As I followed the lead, and cleared everything that was shown to me, I experienced spiritual bliss as a reward! It's an amazing feeling to be acknowledged by

180

the Great Mystery! It let me know that I found a path that wasn't a dead-end. That's why I now have a spiritual foundation based on experience, not faith. And with an open heart, I feel love. And love keeps me safe. Love is my armor. Get it? Armor – amor?[273] And then, because I am safe and happy, I'm able to call home any remaining lost soul parts of myself and they want to return!"

The sun, which had been hiding behind a cluster of clouds, started shining as if on cue. Both J and I look up to the light and smile, laughing at the synchronicity. He says to the heavens, "Okay, that was done perfectly! Well played groovy Big Guy!"

After a couple beats, I continue, "Something else happened right after that, which was also a miracle. I had been searching for a new receiver for my home stereo system. I couldn't afford high quality, but I still wanted high-end - so I decided on vintage. It turned out a friend of mine who drives a city bus for a living, gets off work every day and visits local thrift stores looking for high-end components. So the two of us connect and I go to his house with $150 in my pocket. We chat for a while, and he ends up selling me a $300-valued Onyko receiver for half price. I'm stoked and head home to set it up. As I'm connecting wires, I start to feel déjà vu … this receiver, now in my home, was *the receiver* stolen by my foster brother when I returned home from the military!"

"No way!"

"Yes way!"

J laughingly rubs his forearms, "I've got tingles all over! Bwahahahahaha! That means, what your foster brother once stole from you, was returned!"

"I know! Justice really does come from within! Hahahahaha!"

Chapter 8: **Making Sense**

We sit quietly and feel the breeze become stronger against our skin. It reminds me of where I am. I look at the rows of exquisitely fine motorcycles displayed in front of us. Over to the left, a group of Christian riders are gathered together in fellowship. Clouds continue to play with the sun to keep the temperature hot, but not baking. As I look around, I feel gratitude for the beautiful day spent in nature, sitting on the grass, and having an intelligent conversation with a new friend.

Groovy J slips off his riding boots and socks, while making some remark about his feet sweating. Within a moment or two, his hands start to massage his feet in an absent-minded sort of way. It makes me happy that he's willing to try something new.

"So what other books[274] have you read that are really groovy?" He asks.

"I know I've mentioned it already, but *The Ringing Cedars* book series[275] is quite amazing. It's based in Russia, where there are kids that cover an entire high-school math curriculum in one year and get Master degrees by the time they are seventeen.[276] They don't use memorization techniques, but teach *each other* the subjects which allows for intuiting new knowledge. Their skills include building their own homes and school without adult supervision. However, the series' main subject is Anastasia, an enlightened woman currently living in the world – like a Buddha or Christ. [277] Her family line stayed true to humanity's pristine origin and birthright by separating from civilization when it began to explore other paths. Therefore, she retains many skills that the rest of us have forgotten, out of deception or ignorance. She is familiar with the school, and also shares other ways on how to increase intelligence, from growing your own food[278] to studying one subject at a time so momentum is built up within the brain. In fact, they tested her and she's faster than a computer! She shares how to make living water, how to create sacred space, the beginnings of the Universe, when humans arrived, and how we got off track back in the days of Egypt."

"Wait a second – how does she know things before she was born? Is she a researcher or something?"

"No, it's because she's so pure. The great libraries of ancient history were burned with each conquering nation[279] so the new rulers could introduce their own agenda. She goes directly into the Akashic[280] records to get her knowledge. There are people all over the world who are able to do this,[281] perhaps without the same clarity, but as we clean up our lives, more and more will regain this skill. Anyway, Anastasia shares how to get back on track – which is the real focus, and how righteous it is if everyone creates spaces of love where they already live. I highly recommend reading the series; I think you'd get a lot out of it. One of my favorite stories is how the naturally connected Vedruss civilization lived peacefully for thousands of years without *anyone* governing them. Each family had their own land, about 2 ½ acres, which contained everything they needed for life – clean air, water, and food. They even defeated the Roman army when they showed up to overtake them, by sending bees to sting the elite Roman warriors! But, unfortunately, the Romans didn't stop there. They set up a new plan to infiltrate these trusting people with missionaries and whispered into the ears of those with insecurities, so the Vedruss did eventually fall. No worries though, that's the past and many of us are waking up once again, and reconnecting with the natural world."

"I'd like that for my peeps! Are there other books like this?"

"*The Life and Teachings of the Masters of the Far East*[282] by Baird T. Spalding comes to mind immediately."

"And what is that about?"

"Written in the early 1900's, it is the true account of a group of American scientists who heard about Spiritual Masters living in the Himalayans who don't age, who teleport across vast distances which is called 'God speed,' who use Divine energy for heat and lighting, who manifest their own food and money on an 'as needed' basis, who raise their vibration so high that they can walk through fire without getting burned, and who walk on water and do all the things that the Christ was reported to do. These scientists were skeptical but intrigued, so they traveled and lived with these Masters for years to prove or disprove what they had been hearing. They researched, tested, and took notes. In the end, those American scientists believed in the miracles and some of them even decided to stay with the Masters and continue learning and never returned to the United States. Luckily, the author did return to write the books. While reading this book series, I could feel healing taking place deep within me and I rose up in vibration at the joy of what is revealed. These Masters have no need for a nemesis. They don't draw their opposite to them, out of ego, and when they do encounter bad guys, they interact gracefully, recognizing that all require compassion."

"Right on! Any others?"

"*The Ancient Secret of the Flower of Life* by Drunvalo Melchizedek[283] is a book based on the workshop he gives." I draw an oval on the grass and where the blades bend over; a faint circle can be seen. "Our planet has a 26,000 year cycle, give or take, which is oval. NASA refers to this as the Great Year[284] or

Platonic Year. At the top of the oval is when we are closest to the galactic birthplace, where science has determined the Big Bang took place, and logic dictates this is where we would be closest to our original blueprint. As we move counter-clockwise on this oval, the point that is 1/3rd away from where we started, or from the top, we begin to fall asleep in our connection to the Great Mystery. In the ancient Hindu yugas,[285] this is referred to as Descending Satya.[286] I visualize this as being similar to the changes humanity underwent when transitioning from Ancient Greece with its philosophers, knowledge and sculpture based on sacred geometry[287] into the warlike Roman empire of conquest, oppression, and rape. Then, as a cross reference, I read in *The Ringing Cedars* about how 10,000 years ago our ancestors started to lose their contact with the Creator and no one knew why - which also equaled the 1/3rd point away from the Big Bang. In the *Cedars*, our ancestors built stone structures called dolmens and used them to keep their consciousness and knowledge preserved for future generations, but then the new generations that were born forgot what the dolmens were for, and they fell into disarray. Only now, the dolmens are starting to be re-discovered along with the ancient wisdom contained within. But, I digress - back to the oval. As we cycle around, we move away from the creation point, or Creator, and hit a point where we are farthest away, and then we begin the journey back towards our birth point. When the human race was farthest from the Creator, we did all sorts of cruel things and call that time the Dark Ages.[288] We, as a race, have been very unripe over the course of history, but now each generation is improving. On December 21, 2012, we passed the $1/3^{rd}$ mark on our return to the light, which also closed a major cycle. Indigenous cultures have prophesized this time as the Awakening, the Purification, or the Holy Quickening. That was the whole thing with the Mayan calendar ending on December 21st; it marked the closing of the Old World.[289] So time is not linear, it's circular. And present day, it seems like we're going from the warlike Roman times back into the wisdom of Greece, which means buildings and statues will be created using the principles of sacred geometry again, just like I do with my paint designs."

"You mentioned an awakening …."

"That will mean different things to different people, but to me the awakening is our realization of how interconnected we all are. I feel this is the time when the lion lies down with the lamb,[290] teaching us that we need to forgive our previous predators.[291] Others make reference to the pineal gland located in the center of the brain, which happens to look like an eyeball but faces upward. It's waiting to blink open and allow contact with the Divine; hence, the eye is awake. Most people in the United

States have pineal glands that are calcified, but that can be undone.[292]

"Then you might have heard the word apocalypse thrown around for the last few years – it's a Greek word meaning lifting of a veil.[293] We get to see what's happening, both in society and in ourselves - who *we really are*, shadow sides and all, in order for us to transmute and evolve into the next cycle."

"Is that why things are so weird now?"

"The better spelling is wyrd. Look it up, you'll find an ancient word meaning to draw in our personal fate or destiny. If we have some karma to clear, or grace to experience, life will create complex interactions of universal necessity for the clearing to take place, because the Divine loves us and wants to help us move onward and upward. We might hear or see something, later to find that the person never said or did it, but it resulted in an interaction where we can release a past miscreation. If we blow the opportunity, no worries, the sacred circle of life will make sure it gets wyrd for us again!"

"So back to it iz what it iz."

"Yes, and like the old Polish proverb, "Not my circus, not my monkeys" suggests, we need to resist pulling others into our wyrd-ness. Go within, don't make assumptions, and claim responsibility for everything we can – and we'll have the *ability* to *respond* and pardon ourselves that much faster. In the military,

189

they taught us that assume is the acronym for making an ass out of u and me. Ass – u – me. In this new cycle, no one wants to be the ass so by releasing the games of the ego and coming from a heart in balance, we can stop manifesting from the subconscious and shadow. The ego puts up a fight though – for some, it would prefer to go insane than to give up its power. But in the end, when we release the ego and its pettiness and criticism, which is really just insecurity, we open ourselves to universal knowledge and *true greatness*."

J responds, "True greatness … there's something pulling about that. *True greatness* … not just greatness, or strength, but the real deal." J weighs this new thought out loud. He begins to busy himself with putting on his socks and shoes, still pondering. When he speaks again, his voice is very quiet and even-toned, "I know I like to throw my muscle around every once in a while. There's nothing wrong with that, is there? Sometimes an asshole needs a good swift kick to give them proper perspective."

"But, you're trying to forcefully give them your perspective, and there are different truths. I don't expect you to agree with everything I say, should I punch you then? Ha! And really, no one can change anyone else. By seeing them as doing something wrong, they'll just dig their heels in even more and start avoiding you, thinking *you're* the ass. You know the serenity prayer, right?"[294]

"Yeah, accept the things I cannot change?"

"That's it. See, I was never able to change my foster brother. Neither were my parents or even the correctional facilities that he eventually ended up in. But, he did change - and that's because he met someone who stirred something within his heart. He found the person who made his life become more than just surviving and stealing. Of course, she would freak out every few months and run away with all their belongings and pawn them. That's the cycle of attachment followed by the inner protector rebelling and fleeing – again, something that can be helped with a good trauma therapist. Anyway, he would eventually find her and bring her back home. They'd get new stuff, and then she'd get triggered again, steal his shit, and disappear. So, not only did he change his heart, but he was clearing his past karma as well! The point being: Love is the great motivator for achieving lasting change, not fighting, shaming, or punishing. That only trains people to act in a certain way until they have distance from their persecutor. It's creating two unripe individuals. Love creates two ripe people. But, in order to love someone, we need to love ourselves first. After I reached that point, it was easy to forgive my foster brother for *everything,* because I was able to look at *his* life and find resolution. I mean, what if he became a fragmented psychopath because his mother was forced to eat one of his older siblings?

191

→ ● ←

She then closed her heart, stayed drunk, and had more kids as a way to survive in the welfare system? Sure, that may be a stretch, but *it may not be* – not with all the crazy stuff that happens in this world! So, heal and let it all go. Thoughts of forgiveness are felt by others even if you never see them again. That lightens their load and allows them to start healing because they're not defending their mind against negative thoughts.[295] So now, my True enemy is any insecurity that causes me to choose anything other than Love."

"So you're saying love is the answer. You sound like a song."

"It's true. Love is the only thing that's real. Everything else fades away with time. Love healed my brother. Love can heal all governments, until they are no longer necessary. Not to say we shouldn't jump in there and get some work done, but loving the work sure feels a whole lot better!"

"And those people who are assholes, or greedy, or who have been using black magic and manipulating people for eons - they get off the hook with no payback?"

"Black magic is conjured with the power of the ego. Anything created from the ego will always dissolve, because ultimately, it's only an illusion. To avoid the momentary traps, study the main chakras to see what they are trying to spin. Is fear of basic survival being pushed? Then they are trying to block your first chakra. Are you being seduced with a certain sexuality that results in guilt? That would be second. Being shamed or overpowered? That's the third. Those are the three basic traps of the lower dimensions. Rise into the heart, clear any grief, and you'll also rise into heaven on Earth. Make your choices with love as the deciding factor, and you'll be golden. As far as payback, we know that justice comes from within; give it time and it will all work out. And for those who are religious, the Bible talks about a lake of fire[296] – that would be some major payback. So, no worries – contain the dangerous[297] if necessary, and let the Great Mystery within them work out the details."

His voice rises in volume, "But that's the opposite of everything I've known!"

I mirror his energy, "But, the old cycle is *closed now*! Be truly great! It takes a hell of a lot more strength to forgive those who have wronged you than to just overpower someone by force! Have power *over* yourself! Otherwise a weaker man can always grab an 'equalizer,' right? Will it lead to a dead end? Eventually, yes. Why? Because when you're angry, you'll attract anger, and that leaves no room for miracles." I return to a gentler tone, "It takes courage to walk through this world with an open heart. For your kids - can you be strong enough to override your need to prove your physical strength and become a peaceful warrior?" And then I realize what I'm doing - "Ah … shit. I'm sorry. I just

193

told you what to do and that's not who I want to be. Do what you want."

I move to get up, but then think better of it, let out a deep exhale, and slowly sink back onto the ground saying, "Listen J, I rebuilt my life by doing my inner work and removing all the obstacles between Love and myself until I experienced enough Divine flow to firmly establish a foundation within me that knows, *absolutely knows*, that only love is real. Where love is, the Divine is. And the will of the Divine will never lead me to where Divine grace cannot protect me. With this as my foundation, I tell my mind to dismiss any obstacle in my path that does not correspond to this reality, and the obstacle dissolves. Then, I work my way up my chakra system, closing any holes I might find until I operate at peak performance. That allows me to fill with energy. By quieting my mind, I become a master of my own self, and my self-mastery goes out and impacts the world around me - drawing to me any need or desire I might have. I'm talking about *real* power ... *love* power. The power of love does not depend on money or engine size or owning your own corporation - all things that can be taken away. I have the freedom to choose how I want to spend every moment of time for myself. That's how I'm creating this life, and also what being an alpha means to me. I know you're an alpha also – I'm just hoping you make a similar commitment, because this world could use some hero's right about now."

→ ● ←

Chapter 9: **Heal!**

We had been sitting without talking for a while when J says, "I have a question about love …"

"Go ahead." I answer.

"Before my wife, I dated this one woman who I was totally in love with, but she never loved me back. Sex was more of a good workout to her, a two-person exercise routine. I put a lot of time and energy into moving our relationship from just occasional sex into something romantic and long term. Now, I consider myself to be a good looking guy with plenty of integrity so I *should* be able to manifest from what I hear you saying - but she never let it progress beyond sex. What's up with that?"

"Well first of all, everyone has free will. Then, in order to truly manifest, it's not just integrity with your words but also a balance between your masculine and feminine sides. Again, that means embracing tears, sensitivity, and emotions. I know guys are told to 'man up' and 'soldier on' – which is a waste of words because we all have a greater impact in the world when whole; we become more beautiful also.

→ ● ←

"Then, whenever I put forth a manifestation, I do so *with* the Great Mystery as my co-creator so I don't mess anything up. I'll say, 'If it's in my highest good,' when stating what I would like to experience. I overheard someone in Sedona Arizona tell that to another person, at a restaurant, and I've been using it ever since. I think of it as a failsafe. Then, I'm okay if something never happens. So, in answer to your question, if she didn't want to be with you, then maybe that relationship wasn't in your highest good. At least, that's how my reality works."

"But, you could just be saying that!" J argues.

"Does that make it any less true?"

"But, you got pissed with Hollywood. Did you manifest that?"

"Yes. Maybe not consciously, but yes I did. I even claimed responsibility for it earlier, remember? I said my anger was because I was mad at myself. I never became a victim of Hollywood's flirting; it just angered me that I couldn't say no in the moment. So maybe I pulled that event into my reality to work on my boundaries or response time. It sounds reasonable, doesn't it? Everything that happens in my world is always in Divine order, because there is nothing else I acknowledge except for the Divine. It's like a fish in the ocean. It doesn't see the water, but *we* know it's there because we are seeing it from a higher

197

consciousness than the fish. A shift in consciousness is all that's needed."

I stretch my arms up and feel some knots in my shoulder area. I use my fingers to massage those tight spots while consciously relaxing the muscles.

J watches me for a few moments then asks, "Well then …" He is unsure how to word his next question. "I don't want to piss you off – but I'd really like to ask something else."

"Go ahead."

"How did you – as a little child – manifest the sexual abuse?"

I exhale slowly and lower my arms. I can feel my body temperature rise a little at the question, but it's only fair that he ask what's on his mind. I respond, "I have thought about this … and I'd have to say that either I was an asshole in a past life and I'm clearing it now, or before being born, I volunteered for a healing mission so I could help others. I hope it's the latter! I can see how the Universe set me up in my own shop to get the job done, and by running as a lone wolf, I avoided getting lost in the illusion that's being spun present day.[298] Having distance from the constant stream of information, and focusing on strengthening my pineal gland,[299] I receive messages on how to stay healthy and what to safeguard. The human race was once proud, the people honorable, and the time has come to return to a noble way of living. We do this by making contact with our inner authority, the one who knows us best. I did this, and discovered that everything I experienced growing up, was actually an illusion because my True Self is perfect and beyond trauma. She also lives a very, very long time and this life is pretty short in comparison. Only my ego self can latch on to what I perceive as being done to me, and to pacify her, I must admit that I *like* who I am today, so I have to *gracefully accept the circumstances* that got her to be the person she – I - am."

"So you're saying that child abuse is a blessing?"

"No! Absolutely not! We can teach enlightenment without having such degrees of contrast! My childhood friend Susita? She's lived her life on Prozac, Xanax, and Atenolol to the tune of $100 bucks a month. For that price, you'd think she'd be cured, right? But traffic jams and store lines *still* send her into a panic because she equates getting trapped with being molested. And I know other women who still struggle as well. Some were abducted as children and some were defiled by men they knew. Male babysitters, karate instructors, school teachers, brothers, and fathers have all raped these fragile children and changed the direction of their lives permanently. Why? Did they twist the words of the Bible and believe women were made for men's pleasure? Were there whisperers urging them on? Maybe they were abused when they were kids, or maybe they had a closed

199

heart - I don't know, they do. But, whatever – it's out there and needs to be healed. And these children, from the perspective of their ego, are left with soul loss and false limiting beliefs like, I am a sex object; adults' sexual needs matter more than my own; sexual needs are uncontrollable; I am not in charge of my own body. I could go on, but you get the gist. Then these young girls interact in society with these skewed beliefs and they find plenty of men willing to take advantage of their incorrect thinking. These men feel like they are 'getting lucky' by having sex with these women, but instead, they are *adding to the trauma of the first violation.* Some girls get pregnant early, hide in their homes and have panic attacks about not being able to escape, so they need welfare to survive. I knew one woman who would go into panic mode if her house would creak – just normal settling sounds – but in her mind, it was her father sneaking down the hall in the middle of the night to rape her. Talk about a mind-fuck! Then, some of these women are drawn to men who end up abusing their kids and the cycle continues. Some answer an ad for a sex partner when their urges become too much to handle,[300] and find themselves taken hostage by a sex trafficking ring operating at the frack sites.[301] Some become the black widow spider types, figuratively eating their mates or using sex to climb social ladders. Get enough at the top[302] and their way of thinking will be shared[303] - perhaps accepted by society, even when the

200

thinking is so skewed. People have been driven insane – and I'm not talking about those forced into prostitution, I'm talking about the girl next door. There was this one lady who was a bartender, very beautiful, very sexy, probably an alcoholic. She had a reputation for being easy. She used to call our cab company around two-three in the morning and all the guy cabbies would race to win the dispatch call and take her home. Well, one time I got the call, because I was on the cab stand when it came in. So, I tap on the bar door, just to let her know I was waiting outside and she unlocks it and invites me in, saying that she still has one more till to count, would I like a beer on the house? I said sure, and one thing led to another, and pretty soon, we've had a couple beers and we're chatting like old friends. Out of the blue, she starts crying and tells me that she's aware of what people say about her. That most of those one-night-stands felt more like rapes. The guy would start touching her and she felt powerless to do anything about it. She felt like her entire life was a shitty movie where she was just a hole for men to make deposits in. She hated her life and that's why she stayed drunk all the time. She blamed it on her father, because he used to molest her and her little brother when they were kids. Her brother is a heroin addict and lives a crap life also. Well, I sympathized with her, and assured her that she's a wonderful person and all, then gave her a ride home for free. A few months later, I overheard some cabbies saying that she got majorly drunk at work one night and started dancing on a table. At first it created a few laughs but when she started doing a strip tease, her coworkers tried to get her down. She refused and started screaming about how everyone just wanted to fuck her. They ended up taking her to the psych ward and I never saw her again. You know the Pink Floyd lyrics about how it was well known that 'their fat and psychopathic wives would thrash them within inches of their lives'?[304] Abuse is how I think those women got that way."

I look at J to see if he has any response. He is silent, so I add, "You've got girls, so you know the fairy tales that they're raised on -destined for true love and living happily ever after. As they grow up, that little girl remains a part of the woman, watching every move with judging eyes. My therapist told me that every time someone has sex with someone they don't know, their child self is traumatized. And this goes for the little boy inside, as well. Children don't want to feel dirty, pushed aside, and worthless. Growing up with pain that's never been dealt with will lead to adults who don't care about anyone else's pain or even what happens to spaceship Earth! Both children and adults need to live with a heart wide open! Atonement with nature and all of life like the gods and goddesses we truly are. But it requires our adult self to take responsibility and get the healing done; otherwise, if everyone stays in a reduced egotistical and sexualized state, there'll be a hell of a lot of holes in a low frequency state, which leads to a leaky mess in a freaky world - another dead end."

Chapter 10: **Peace**

I'm completely surprised as Groovy J slams his back on the grass and starts to cry. He throws an arm over his eyes, and sobs shake his whole body. I'm not sure what to do. My first instinct is to withdraw, because being around a strong male makes me puff my chest a little more. But, then, I convince my inner toughness to assume an "at ease" position. I coax my softer side to come forth, the receptive side that everyone has. My heart opens gently to his pain but I'm still unsure how to comfort him. He's lying down so it's not like I can throw an arm around his shoulders … and I'm not going to crawl on the ground next to him! I opt to hold his foot and move it back and forth to let him know that I got his back … or actually, his foot. But then, I become concerned that he might think I'm trying to hurry him up and stop his tears - which I'm not! Knowing how important crying is, I whisper, "The degree to which you can feel sorrow now, will be equal to how much joy you can contain when its turn comes around again." To this, his crying becomes more convulsive. Whispering again, to give encouragement, "Good job buddy … let it all out."

Allowing him his privacy, I turn to watch the biker world. Almost in total opposition to the subject we had been discussing, four women walk by wearing the smallest bathing suits I have ever seen. Following them are two young guys on pocket bikes,[305] laughing and weaving, trying to engage the barely dressed ladies in conversation. All of this is done in clean fun, with no intention of abuse whatsoever. I recognize the disparity of how people interact in regard to sex and sexuality. My main concern is when relations occur with those who are too young to decide for themselves. That's when those people's tribe need to gather together and communicate, protect the children by ensuring all interactions are chaperoned, and facilitate healing for any damage that might have occurred. If the child has no tribe to call upon, then I'm grateful to organizations such as B.A.C.A. - Bikers Against Child Abuse[306] and Guardians of the Children.[307]

Softly, J says, "I'm fine Zora. Thanks. I just need a moment." And he continues lying on his back with his arm covering his eyes. I let go of his foot and decide to make the most of the silence. I sit in the lotus position[308] and start deep breathing. In … and out. Slower and deeper, with my tongue on the roof of my mouth. Feeling my lungs expand … pushing just a little more, stretching them. Starting to take on more air now, visualizing any dirt or toxins leaving with my exhale. A few more breaths and my head starts to tingle, full exhales, emptying the lungs and holding, one, two, three, and deep inhale through golden light, purifying and Holy, exhaling whatever needs to be released. Then I'm ready and I push out and have a golden ball of energy around me. From doing this over the years, I've noticed that some kids can see what I'm doing, but I figure no one at the bike show will notice. It just feels good to stop talking and be back in sacred space. To just *be* - with a mind that's quiet and a calm heart. I start to focus on my muscles, noticing what's tight so I can consciously relax them too. I tighten and release my shoulder muscles different ways until I feel the tension leave … then continue onto the rest of my body. I am fine-tuning my interior so even though I'm sitting perfectly still, I'm still being productive - which I like. I still enjoy accomplishments, and this is something I deem to be a high priority. Then I begin the 8 breath prayer - first for myself, then for J, to maintain balance between give and take. With half-open eyes, I gaze at the grounds, watching blurry figures moving this way and that. As I breathe, I imagine that by connecting the dots of how everyone is moving that a pattern is taking shape, visible from a higher vantage point. I notice one fuzzy shape that is heading in our direction. It keeps coming closer and starts to take on dimension. It's Mike. I open my eyes a little more.

"Yoda."[309] Mike deadpans.

Laughter bursts from my lips as I realize he probably means yoga![310]

J starts laughing also, "Bwahahahaha!" I feel him move to sit back up. "Damn! That was some intense shit, but it was worth it. I feel like my heart just got cracked open!" He says joyfully. "A heart-a-crack! Bwahahahahaha!"

Delighting, I offer him a hand and he grasps it strongly as I pull him into a seated position, using my own weight as a counter balance.

J turns and says, "Hey Mike! How's it going? Man - that was frigging fantastic! I feel like the Grinch[311] when his heart grows in size! What a clean feeling I've got right now! I could jump around and do somersaults, just like little Yoda in that one movie! Bwahahahaha!"

"Hahahaha!" I laugh with him picking up on the joy he is feeling. Mike looks like he hasn't got a clue.

J gets up surprisingly quick given how large he is, and then turns to help me up. With a flick of his wrist, he pulls me upward and into him. I suddenly feel like a dance partner, and we catch each other's thought and he starts to whirl me about. Hahahaha! It's wonderfully fun and I hold my hand out to Mike. He clasps his hands together in merriment but declines the invitation. Hahahaha! Imagine the odds, here we are, two bikers in steel-toed boots doing a quick tango at the Sturgis bike show.

When we feel the dance energy start to diminish we bow to each other then turn towards Mike. J asks him with an arm flourish, "What news do you come with, Sir Mike of Nottingham?"

I giggle at J's antics, but Mike simply replies, "The awards will be given out soon."

"Excellent, you shall be rewarded handsomely. Let us now go visit our horses!" J enjoys his portrayal of a knight in shining armor. I am simply happy. Yeah, crack a heart open anytime and let the sun shine in!

"Hey, is this a private threesome or can anyone join?" Hollywood comes walking up to us from behind. We turn to see him arm in arm with a large woman, who is Darlene!

"Darlene! How are you?!" I run to greet my friend.

"Good!" We give each other a hug, first on the left side, then on the right - always holding just a little bit longer on the right since we're meeting heart to heart.

Darlene says, "This handsome man found me over by your bike. I was waiting there for you – it's not like I can call you to check in! But I was a good girl… kinda … a little … okay, not really! Teeheehee! But, that's okay, because I made it here before the trophies so I get brownie points for that!"

"Of course you do!" I'm happy that Darlene is okay, but now I'm curious about why she was arm and arm with Hollywood. I lower my voice and ask her, "So are you into him?"

She slaps me good-naturedly and laughs, "Teeheeheehee - I wish!"

I glance at Hollywood and imagine what life must be like for him. Because of his extraordinary good looks, nearly every woman he meets flirts with him to some degree. I watch him survey the different ladies walking past and more than one return his gaze and flash him a smile of interest. With so much sexual energy directed his way, I can see how it would come to be expected, and could even turn into an addiction. Perhaps that was why he hit on me earlier, he might not know any other way of interacting with women. I find myself sending him a blessing, because even though many men would love to be in his position, it would also be very easy to manipulate him into a situation that could really get him into trouble. So while others envy his appearance, I hope he has the strength of character to stay in balance. Just then, a long haired beauty saunters over to him and they begin talking. A little laugh, a touch on the elbow, and the two of them slowly move away from our group to have a more private conversation.

J introduces himself to Darlene and draws my attention away from the couple, "And you must be the infamous Darlene

209

of Deadwood. I hope the ghosts of bank robbers past didn't clean you out too bad."

"Honey - let's just say I've had better days … but, I did win enough to treat you all to burgers! Anyone hungry?!" A cheer went up, which made Hollywood look back. He says a few words to the attractive lady he is interacting with, and returns to our group.

"Hey, what's going on?" He asks.

"Darlene's treating us to burgers! You coming with?" J responds.

"Sure!" And Hollywood resumes his former arm-and-arm position with Darlene and I take her other side. Then J joins in on my left and Mike does a shy look-away before giving in to joy and running over to Groovy J's open side. Together, we walk as a pack to the burger stand.

"Four buffalo burgers and one walnut burger please." Darlene orders from the vendor. Then, she says to us, "Is that good with everyone?"

We all look at each other and nod yes, except for Mike who asks, "Who eats the nutty burger?"

I raise my hand proudly.

While we're waiting for our food, J turns to Darlene and asks, "Why buffalo?"

210

"They roam freely![312] I met the guy who owns this stand and he uses organic products so I knew Zora would appreciate that." She turns to me and says, "I'm sorry about holding you up last night and I hope this makes up for it. Are we good?"

I recall my bitter cold experience that almost led to death, but that wasn't anything I was willing to blame her for. All she did was delay my leaving, the rest of the choices were my own. With firm completion, I answer, "Sure, we're good. Thanks for lunch! Order mine with lettuce and tomato, will you?"

The vendor overhears and says, "Lettuce and tomato on the walnut. Check. Anyone else want their burger dressed?"

Mike leans into the vendor's trailer and says, "No rabbit food for me."

We laugh as the vendor replies, "Organic rabbit food is like turbo charging the body buddy! But sure, I'll give it to you plain. We grow our own produce so we know the source of what we offer. We're not going to feed you guys anything we wouldn't eat ourselves. And that conventional food the other guys sell? That's like ethanol – made cheaply with corn products. You're not going to find us peddling that crap.[313] We've got biker pride!" And he pulls his head back into his food truck to whip up the order.

Darlene says to Mike all sassy, "Didn't your momma ever tell you that you are what you eat? I deserve the best because I am a goddess in human form!" And she twirls around with her head thrown back and her arms rise to the sky.

"Majestic!" Groovy J exclaims. "We were talking about stuff like that!"

I'm surprised to hear a new word come out of J's mouth. "Majestic? I thought you were a groovy type of guy?!"

"Right now - I'm feeling much more than groovy. I am feeling majestic like I've gone up a few notches. If having a good cry once in a while is what it takes to feel this good, then sign me up, cause I'm staying in *this* realm!"

The reaction to J's words varies on the different faces. Darlene looks at him with pride, and then she looks at me and gives a little wink. Mike looks puzzled, and Hollywood … well Hollywood looks sad, and kind of lost. The look on his face makes me think that he is feeling dejected and my heart goes out to him. I think about walking over and hugging him, but because of his sexual innuendos earlier, I don't feel he's a safe person to make contact with. Then that thought makes me sad. In the middle of this wonderful moment, there is a block between me and love. So I decide to find the balance between safety and compassion, and I walk over to Hollywood and put a hand on his shoulder.

"Everything all right?" I ask him.

"Hey, I'm sorry about earlier when I was annoying you. I could see what I was doing but I didn't feel like I could stop myself. I was on autopilot."

"Not being able to control yourself is a sign that something in your life has shaken you to the core. Are you okay?"

"Yeah - and something *has* happened recently."

"Like what?"

"Nothing. I don't want to talk about it."

"All right. Blessings then …."

"Order up!" The vendor announces happily. Mike and J grab their burgers and begin eating. Because J is a giant, he eats his burger in four bites.

Mike asks Darlene, "What do you do with non-organic food?"

"You have to bless the shit out of it, darlin'!"[314] And she shows the guys the center of her palm and explains that by visualizing and allowing energy to flow out of the hand, one can purify and heal with that energy. Then Darlene returns to the food vendor and passes me my burger and grabs one for her and Hollywood. J wipes his hands on a napkin and then pays for glass bottles of water to pass around and share.

"People are already gathered by the stage." Mike announces in between mouthfuls of burger.

213

"Shall we?" J says grandly with a flip-flip-flop of his raised hand into a bow with a sweeping motion of his arm.

I look at Hollywood; he is starting to eat his burger. I return to Darlene, who has her arm open to me.

"Let's go!" she says. We link arms and then grab J into our chain. Mike veers over to the parking lot while Hollywood walks quietly a few steps behind, eating. Our forward progress is halted about a third of the way to the stage by guys clamoring to see the entertainment already underway. All the trophy girls are dressed in beauty pageant, bathing suit competition style.

Darlene draws my attention, "So talk to me! What have you been doing while I was gone?"

"Talking with J here for the last … how many hours?" I look to J for an answer, since I don't wear a timepiece, but his eyes are fixed on the stage, sporting a huge grin. I laugh and turn back to Darlene, "I'm not going to get an answer out of him. Plus, I'm all talked out - you tell me how you made it back to Sturgis." I begin to eat my food.

"The owner of that burger stand gave me a ride in on his bike. We met at the casino and he's a great guy. He *really cares* about his fellow bikers. Again, I'm sorry about holding the whole show up."

"It's okay - we're good."

"Yay! Thank you! I wish he would have been working so I could have introduced you - he's a real hunk!" And she gives an exaggerated wink which I really have no idea how to interpret since I know she has a serious boyfriend back home. I shake my head in confusion. I'll never make sense of other people, only myself.

Darlene continues, "He was telling me that if you win today with your Harley - you will be invited to a bike show in Germany! Would you do it? Actually go over there and show your bike? And if so, can I come with?!"

"Hahahaha! Too funny Darlene!"

"Why? I would pay my own way!" She says in between bites of her own.

"I'd need a *team* to help me do that. Do they offer sponsorships so I could hire a crew?"

"Yeah ... I don't know. He never said anything about that."

"Well, unless a miracle happens, I won't be penciling that on the calendar."

"Well, I just thought I'd ask ..." Darlene gives a little pout then continues, "But if a miracle does come through, then can I go with?"

"Let's see how it unfolds, Darlene."

215

"Okay! I won't be in the way - and I'll market for you too. I just know you're going to win something here today!"

"I have won!" Lifting up my clean food in one hand, clean water in the other, and with a smile on my face I take a deep breath of clean air. "Let's be sure this is available for the next seven generations to come!"[315]

"You got it sweetie! That's the direction we're facing." And she squeezes my shoulder in a sisterly manner.

∞

The classic rock music coming over the loudspeaker is cut short for the winner's announcements. "Now listen up! When you hear your name and the model of your bike, come up here to receive your trophy from one of our lovely ladies, but before you leave the stage be sure to smile for the cameras. And yes, we need a smile out of you!" After a light smattering of chuckles, the awards begin to be announced.

"In the 1 to 1000cc class we have …" the announcer's voice blends into the background noise and I know Darlene is paying attention, so I don't feel the need to.

I feel a tap on my shoulder. I turn to see Mike … and it seems he's found himself a lady friend. "Hey Mike!"

"Yes ma'am. I have a friend here with a question. This is Julie."

"Nice to meet you, Julie." And I hold out my hand to a petite little lady with freckles and red hair.

"Hi, ummm … Mike says you paint bikes, is that true?"

"Yes, it is."

"Well, I have a bike with artwork on the tank and I was wondering if it's possible to remove the art without stripping it down and re-painting the entire tank?"

"Did they put clear coat over the artwork?"

"No, they did it here in Sturgis a couple years back, freehand - like a tattoo but now some of it is chipping in places. Do you want to see it?"

"That's not necessary, but what year and model is your bike?"

"1998 Softail Custom."

"Factory paint?"

She nods yes.

"Okay - since it's factory paint and not lacquer, you should be able to remove the graphics with Easy-Off Oven Cleaner[316] and it won't damage the rest of your paint. There might be a little discoloration where the sun has baked it though. Oh, and it's always good to test in a hidden area first." I give the disclaimer out of habit.

Julie looks very happy at the news, "Great - thanks a lot! I was hoping there would be an easier way, I can't afford a new paint job but I didn't want it looking the way it does, either!"

I return her smile, "I'm always happy to help out a fellow biker. We're all family."

She smiles and then turns toward Mike, and her smile becomes shy. They exchange eye language. Ah, young love … always a beautiful thing to see!

∞

"That bike has a toilet seat for the passenger!"

"Yeah! And a urinal cake as an air freshener!"

"Bwahahahahaha!" I overhear Hollywood and J laughing about a rat bike that took an award.

A few more awards are given out and then it's time for the Radical Sportster class. Both 5th and 4th place are handed out and I haven't heard my name, so far so good.

"In 3rd place, we have Ed Englemann with his 1975 Harley Sportster!"

Hollywood and J start debating, "That was the blue rigid digger."

"I saw it coming in, but he could have put that in the Antique Class, couldn't he?"

"Sssssh! Guys! I need to hear!" I quiet them.

218

"In 2nd place, we have Adam Hagen with his 2001 Harley Sportster!"

Oh my gawd! That was the Paughco rigid I knew would score well with the judges … and it took 2nd! What's with all these guys riding rigids? Do some people just like to suffer? But, that wasn't my chief concern … because that means … unless there was another bike that came in while we were talking …

"And 1st Place goes to Katarina Zora with her 1986 Harley Sportster!"

A cheer goes up in our group and everyone turns to smile at me! However, the act of so many people clapping me on the shoulder and congratulating me starts to overwhelm my sense of space. Nervousness races through my body and settles in my legs. Walking onto a raised stage is going to make me ultra visible, but I fight down the panic by focusing on my breath. I start my mantra of "everything is unfolding for my highest good" and focus on keeping my heart open. I weave through the crowd. I can feel my legs shake, but I refuse to give in … just a few more seconds and this will be over. I receive my trophy and then awkwardly smile at the cameras and pivot towards the side of the stage before feeling the relief of getting out of the spotlight. As I'm making my way back down the stairs another trophy girl intercepts me and brings me to a side table where I'm given a wall clock with the rat and cheese logo, and a matching wristwatch to boot. By this time, I can feel a trickle of sweat running down my back. One last congratulatory handshake and I'm free! Whew! I did it!

I return to the safety of my friends and they all take turns looking at my prizes and offering congratulations.

Darlene, who knows me, whispers, "Doin' okay there hon?"

"Yeah, but I really need to ride."

"I kind of thought so. You go enjoy, I'll take care of the van and meet you back at the campsite ... *I promise*."

"Okay, thanks. I'll wait until after J's class though." I smile appreciatively at her, knowing I'll be in the wind again soon.

A few more awards are announced and then it's J's class. His name was the first to be called - which is never a good thing because that means you only get a little mini-trophy for 5th Place. We all pat him on the back and offer congratulations anyway, and he takes the loss and shakes it off. He's in good humor as he walks up and opens his arms wide to the trophy girls - they love it! He gives a toothy smile to the camera then lifts both ladies off the ground in a one-armed squeeze for each girl. They squeal and he laughs, "Bwahahahahaha!"

I remember that I never got a chance to look at the torque series Indian, so I hand the trophy and timepieces to Darlene along with the van keys. I give her a quick kiss on her cheek, and head over to the antique section. The bike is sweet, a 426cc Scout which later became the Warrior, with a power increase to 500cc.

J finds me over by the bike, "I heard you're heading out – you sure you don't want to join us for a beer?"

"I'd rather go for a victory lap – feel some wind."

"Where you headed?"

"Spearfish. There's a natural food store there,[317] and I want to fill a backpack with munchies for later."

"Right on. Darlene is going to join us at the bar, that's cool, right? I'll help her watch the time on all those clocks you have her carrying! But - does she *really* think she's a goddess?"

"Of course! We're all Divine!" Looking down at the ground, I spy and pick up an acorn. "What will this acorn grow into?"

"A tree."

"Right, an Oak tree … not a bush or a flower, but a tree because that's what's encoded in its DNA, right?"

"Yeah."

"Well, if the Creator created humans in Her image, then what will *we* grow into?"

J tilts his head, thinking, then slowly breaks into a wide grin, "Groovy little lady, very groovy indeed!"

"Groovy like an old time movie?" I tease. We laugh and walk towards my bike. J throws an arm over my shoulder, and I put mine around his waist. Even with him towering a half foot over me, our stride is very smooth. I hesitate asking him something, but I'm curious and figure he can always sidestep the answer if he wants, "So - what made you cry earlier?"

"Oh, that." He stops walking. "That was about something ... something that I'm not very proud of."

I look at him questioningly, wondering if he will share. His eyes are on the ground, but then he returns my gaze, and with a sigh of resignation, begins to explain. "Remember earlier when you were talking about the shadow side?" I nod yes. "Well, I have a shadow side too. From what you told me about abused girls, I now realize that I ... well, even though I try my best ... I'm not always such a groovy guy. In fact, I've been an absolute a-hole to some women over the years. I'm not going to make excuses because I don't want to give my power away. I'm going to man up and make things right. That's why I cried – all the women I've wronged started flooding my brain. And what if that happens to my own girls[318] because of my karma, you know?" His eyes mist slightly. "I missed the mark. But now I'm going to be truly great. I am going to make it right, by really opening my heart, first to myself, and then to the women in my life."

His eyes reveal sincerity, so I return the gaze tenderly, knowing he will. I feel grateful for his effort, and my heart swells in forgiveness. "I believe you."

J continues, "I also realized something – how you claim to call your experiences to you? Well, there's a good chance that I am partly responsible for Larry slamming into me, and scarring my back. He never attacked anyone else on the sub, and I've often wondered, 'why me'? Now, with this new awareness, I can see how my ma would use violence to keep me below her, and Larry attacked me just as I was up for a promotion. It doesn't feel like a coincidence."

We begin to walk again, remaining silent. Upon reaching my bike he exclaims, "There she is - the big winner of the day!"

I laugh lightly, and with a bow of the head utter a gracious, "We're all winners, and thank you."

"So why was this bike in the Radical class?" J asks.

"Only because of the frame alterations. I know – it's not that radical to me either - but it's their show so I'm playing by their rules for today."

"Here, I wrote down my email – don't forget to send me the Toolbox, okay? And I mentioned a little of this to Hollywood. He'd like to take a look also - is that cool with you?"

223

I slip the piece of paper into my front pocket. "Absolutely! You have my permission to share with anyone receptive. Tell Hollywood to use whatever feels right and dismiss the rest. And for you J, when starting your journey, information can come from any direction, but use caution when interpreting 'signs' since that's making assumptions. Stay with logic and communication as much as practical. If you start to get overwhelmed by input, or you're not sure what to believe, use your imagination to change up the rules. Tell the Great Mystery you need to see something three times before you'll really sit up and take notice. You are the co-creator of your reality and Divinity is a particle within, so go for whatever makes you feel joyful, as long as it doesn't impede on anyone else's happiness. Even Einstein said, 'Imagination is everything. It is the preview of life's coming attractions.' In *The Ringing Cedars* this is called the 'Science of Imagery' and it is where we made leaps of progress - but when misused, it created the enslavement of humankind.[319] But now, it's time to catch that ball and get back on track."

"What do you mean?"

"Over time, we were persuaded to hand our life essentials to others whose main interest was ensuring their own intelligence, comfort, and profit – but now it's time to take that responsibility back. During one phase of my growth, I'd drop things. Keys, pens, travel mugs, books – nearly anything that went into my hands - was dropped. And I am not a clumsy person either, so this was strange! During that month, I was curious why it was happening, but I didn't put myself down or think any negative thoughts about what was occurring. Instead, I learned how to catch. I'd feel the item leave my fingers, and I developed the reflex of catching it again before it hit the ground. It started becoming a game of sorts. I knew that the Great Mystery was offering me a lesson and I didn't mess it up by becoming judgmental or defensive. I simply learned to catch. After that month was up, I went back to being able to pick up things like normal. My theory is that I was given a parable in life, that we all drop things but we need to catch them before they fall too far."

"Some say climate change has already gone too far, you know."

"As long as we're in the game, we can make that catch.[320] And I think you hit upon a great idea with extinguishing those massive methane torches at the fracking sites."

Groovy J is quiet again. Then, he says with deep meaning, "I'm going to miss you."

"Yeah … I'm going to miss you too, buddy."

He puts his glove-like hand on the back of my head and pulls me into his chest, squeezing tight ... a little too tight, actually. This guy doesn't know his own strength. My face is getting smashed into him and it feels rather awkward. J feels me squirm, so he releases. Not sure where to rest his hand next, he bounces his fist lightly on the motorcycle's handlebar grips while forming his next question. "You know, all this talk about miracles really touched something deep inside. Any last advice … I mean that you would give to yourself if I were you?"

"If you have a question, ask the Great Mystery for clarity. Then listen to what *you* say for the next few hours and you will tell yourself the answer when talking to someone else."

"I like it. I'll remember."

"Other than that, be kind, be grateful, and seek out joyful connections - something you do naturally!" And I smile at my beautiful, new friend with all the love in the world. And he beams love right back at me. The air around us glows with happiness. It is a golden color and the temperature is absolutely perfect. We continue to grin at each other until the outside world starts to make its way into our bubble.

A couple bikes roar past, so I take that as my cue to leave. I step away and swing my leg over the seat of my chopper - my tribute to the Four Directions that gives me something to believe in. I turn on the key, open the petcock, lift the choke lever, give the throttle two full turns, then hit the start button. The motorcycle roars to life with that wonderful sound of thunder. I look back at J. Putting on my sunglasses, I raise my hand in a salute. He salutes back. It's been a long time since I've done that - it still feels good. "I see who you are J, and it's a very groovy - and majestic - sight. Namaste' my friend."[321]

The sun twinkles in his beautiful blue eyes, "Keep it real, Katarina Zora."

We both smile. Then I close the choke and give a quick kick to the stand, nod, then eyes forward and I'm on my way to explore some sacred ground.

J watches as the bike pulls out of the parking lot, and catches a glimpse of the personalized license plate that reads, 'IMWHOLE'.

→ ● ←

→ ● ←

→ • ←

Author's Note

When I made the decision to write this book, a piece of paper flew out of an open school bus window, landing in my yard. Upon examination, it was a student's lesson on how to construct a proper sentence - ha! I believe I had Divine help from start to finish!

Originally, my intention was to publish under the pen name, Katarina Zora, to avoid impeding on my foster brother's life. But, then he died. So at the urging of my editor and other business associates, and with the blessing of my brother's daughter, I republished under my legal name so to be available for speaking opportunities.

Journaling helps me break down some of my dark experiences into tiny parts, thereby dissolving and releasing them ... many ways to heal the holes - the whole point of this. And also, an opportunity to bring awareness to things happening in society, with references, so that with awareness, change will occur and we will have clean air, water and food for the next seven generations ... and beyond.

I hope this book helps those who have experienced abuse and are stumbling through disorders such as

229

→ • ←

PTSD. There is a way out - many ways! Just don't give up.

I am also doing this because I feel for the customer service girl who works at the store for 12 hours and then exhausted, goes home to her baby who doesn't understand why mom wants to sleep and won't play with her.

I am doing this for the bike mechanic who's worked his entire life at the dealership. His hands ache with arthritis every night. He looks forward to retiring but has fear because there is no pension plan.

With open hearts, bosses will treat workers better.

I am doing this for my parents whom I watch eat GMO food and their body's react with inflammation and disease.[322] Then, they take the prescribed pills and become trapped by medications and lose their teeth.

With open hearts, corporations will sell items without harmful side effects.

I am doing this to honor my commitment to the Pachamama Alliance[323] where I read George Bernard Shaw's quote, "This is the true joy in life, the being used for a purpose recognized by yourself as a mighty one; the being a force of nature instead of a feverish, selfish little clod of ailments and grievances, complaining that the world will not devote itself to making you happy." - I did not want to be a selfish little clod.

I am doing this to hold Sacred Space for the new children who are so much more connected to the Creator, who can read minds and heal through touch.[324] The children who will recreate our Utopia so if I reincarnate - it will be so much better!

~ Rowan Glaser

Motorcycles, Madness & Miracles

Toolbox

Email from Zora to Groovy J:

Hey Groovy J!

Here's the Toolbox that I promised to send you!
I decided to make it a little more presentable that just a bunch of black and white pages, so I took a little time and added color and character – what else would you expect from a custom motorcycle painter, right?!
Be sure to check out your contribution of 'Learning Curve'!

You'll find tools of inspiration and encouragement, photos and stories of growth. There are products for health and well-being that are slowly coming into mainstream. Healing methods that have worked for me are included, and never overlook the basics, such as a rock.

This is my favorite massage rock – I use it to get rid of knots in my shoulder blades and back.
Here's my technique:
• I ask the rock if it's willing to help and then listen. Yeah – don't laugh buddy! A rock has a pulse of once a day. Plus, by listening it trains you to be more receptive.

• If yes (or silence) is the answer, I lie on my back and put the rock under a sore spot, knot, or trigger point. I relax my body onto the rock and allow it to gently apply pressure to the trigger point until it releases. This will allow blood flow to reach the muscle tissue once again. Toxins are released so drink plenty of spring water to flush them out of the body.
• Thank the rock, and place it in sea salt for cleaning or rinse with water. After it's cleansed, pray and re-energize it, or put in the sun for re-energizing.

Rocks can do amazing things: clear negative energy, heal, align chakras, bring abundance, bring the subconscious forward into the conscious and much more.

A great book on the mineral kingdom is 'Love is in the Earth' by Melody.[325]

Next, I'd like to share the inspiration for painting my Custom XLH Chopper. This Opening Prayer/Meditation by Lynn V. Andrews can be found in her book *"Teachings Around the Sacred Wheel: Finding the Soul of the Dreamtime"*[326] Used with permission.

Close your eyes. Let your body begin to relax into the vision and vibration of these words. Let your body deeply relax. Notice any places in your body where you feel tension, and feel free to move, to let the tension go.

Life is a circle. We are each unique and specific people, points on this circle. In using [this workbook], you will be forming a bond that will continue, possibly beyond the end of your life. Your work together with the work of others using this book will be to shine your individual uniqueness, to develop tools and ways to help your-self and others shine, while developing and strengthening your circle, the bond that is formed. This circle will radiate out into the world, a strong, sacred wheel made up of many shining crystals, many fine and important human beings, each with a journey, a journey to discover one's own enlightenment and to help heal our Mother Earth.

Imagine yourself at the ocean on the sand before a great sea. See yourself in a circle of many people, all the people whom you love, your circle, each of you joining hands, touching. Don't worry if you do not exactly see this vision; just feel this vision inside you.

Now call the powers of all the directions to be with you, to be with you at the edge of a great sea, which *is* where you are now – at the edge of a great sea, the sea of enlightened vision, new insight, the sea of your unknown, wild, unconscious life – a place where earth and water, conscious and unconscious, meet.

At this new place, I call the sacred powers of all directions to be with you now. Banish any energies that wish you ill will. Call the power of Mother Earth, symbolized by the Great Turtle, the slow one, the necessary one, the one who carries us on her shoulders, the earth spirit who teaches us patience, who teaches us to take one step at a time on our journey here, Powers of the Earth, come in! See the turtle in the middle of your circle, here to guide you in your earth learning.

Powers of the South, Sacred Mouse, come into the center of my circle. Sacred Mouse, Teacher of Trust and Innocence, come in. Teach me today to trust, to find again my innocent eyes, my fresh vision, my childlike wonder of the world. Teach me to see what is right in front of my eyes so that I may gather learning, gather trust, gather the power of touching others in gentle, healing ways. Powers of the South, the Mouse, come in!

Powers of the West, place of intuition, looking within, woman place inside all of us, home of the Great Bear, come into my circle here and now. Bear, bear with your sacred task of hibernation, of dreaming, come into my circle in order to teach

236

me better to go inside and listen. Teach me to go inside all the winter of my life, into the darkness, without fear, with excitement, with your great power, Sacred Bear. I pray that I will learn to be quiet, to hear my inner voice, to distinguish my voice of intuition from the false voices of fear, doubt, and indecision. Powers of the West, Sacred Intuition, Sacred Bear, come into my circle now!

Powers of the North, place of storms of wisdom, mountains of knowledge, home of the Buffalo, come in. Come in Buffalo, to my circle now. Teach me how to give away, to share what I have learned, to nourish others with the bounty of my beings. Teach me to face the cold, to stand alone when I must, to take care of others like a tribe, like a true circle. Buffalo, Sacred Provider, provide me with wisdom, with knowledge, and with the ability to share what I learn. Powers of the North, come into my circle now!

Powers of the East, come into my circle, be in the middle of my life now. East, place of illumination, light, visionary truth, and experience, home of the Eagle, bird that flies highest and sees farthest, come into the center of my circle and teach me now. Teach me how to rise up above my daily vision, my tired eyes, into new vistas of sight. Teach me to take my vision to my Higher Self. Teach me to let the vision of my Higher Self down into my daily mind and revitalize my life. Teach me to prey upon whatever does not feed my Higher purpose and to rid myself of false paths that do not serve me. Great Bird of Spirit, Sacred Eagle, Powers of the East, come into my circle now!

Powers of the Sky, Great Spirit, fill my circle now with your great light, as I envision my circle surrounded by infinitely bright yellow light. I am enveloped in your great light, touched deep inside by the power of your healing ways. I stand here in the center of my being and call to each of my brothers and sisters to the center of their being. May the Great Spirit, the One Who Carries Us, the True Guide, nourish our circle, allow the powers of the Earth, the south, west, north, and east to shine in and through us, enlightening our circle and teaching us peace, joy, and wisdom.

May all the powers of all directions guide us and keep us! Ho!

Two Wolves

A Cherokee Elder was teaching his grandchildren about life.
He said to them, "There is a fight going on inside of me.
It is a terrible fight between two wolves.
One wolf represents fear, anger, envy,
sorrow,regret, greed, arrogance, self-pity,
guilt, resentment, inferiority, lies,
false pride, and superiority.

The other stands for joy, peace, love, hope,
sharing, serenity, humility, kindness,
benevolence, friendship, empathy, generosity,
truth, compassion, and faith.

They thought about this for awhile,
and then asked, "Which one will win?"

The old man answered,
"The one you feed."

Native American Code of Ethics

Rise with the sun to pray. Pray alone. Pray often.
The Great Spirit will listen, if you only speak.
Be tolerant of those who are lost on their path.
Ignorance, conceit, anger, jealousy and greed
stem from a lost soul. Pray that they will find guidance.

Search for yourself, by yourself.
Do not allow others to make your path for you.
It is your road, and yours alone.
Others may walk it with you, but no one can walk it for you.

Treat the guests in your home with much consideration.
Serve them the best food, give them the best bed
and treat them with respect and honor.

Do not take what is not yours whether from a person,
a community, the wilderness or from a culture.
It was not earned nor given. It is not yours.

Respect all things that are placed upon this earth -
whether it be people or plant.

Honor other people's thoughts, wishes and words.
Never interrupt another or mock or rudely mimic them.
Allow each person the right to personal expression.
Never speak of others in a bad way.
The negative energy that you put out into the universe
will multiply when it returns to you.

All persons make mistakes.
And all mistakes can be forgiven.

Bad thoughts cause illness of the mind,
body and spirit. Practice optimism.

Nature is not FOR us, it is a PART of us.
They are part of your worldly family.

Children are the seeds of our future.
Plant love in their hearts and water them
with wisdom and life's lessons.
When they are grown, give them space to grow.

Avoid hurting the hearts of others.
The poison of your pain will return to you.

Be truthful at all times.
Honesty is the test of ones will within this universe.

Keep yourself balanced.
Your Mental self, Spiritual self, Emotional self, and Physical self -
all need to be strong, pure and healthy.
Work out the body to strengthen the mind.
Grow rich in spirit to cure emotional ails.
Make conscious decisions as to who you will be
and how you will react.
Be responsible for your own actions.

Respect the privacy and personal space of others.
Do not touch the personal property of others -
especially sacred and religious objects.
This is forbidden.

Be true to yourself first.
You cannot nurture and help others
if you cannot nurture and help yourself first.

Respect others religious beliefs.
Do not force your belief on others.
Share your good fortune with others.
Participate in charity.

~ This originally appeared in the "Inter-Tribal Times", October, 1994
© nativevillage.org Used by permission.

→ ● ←

THE EGO	THE SOUL
false self	true self
ME	WE
Attack	Accept
Separation	Unity
Blame	Understanding
Hostility	Friendliness
Resentment	Forgiveness
Pride	Love
Complain	Gratefulness
Jealousy	Co-happiness
Anger	Happiness
Power	Humble
Materialism	Spiritualism
Madness	Wisdom
War	Peace
Coldness	Sympathy
Past/future oriented	Now orientation
Intolerance	Tolerance
Self-importance	We-importance
Egoism	Altruism
Self-denial	Self-acceptance
Social intolerance	Social acceptance
Living up to this and that	Simplicity
Doing	Just be

→ ● ←

SEXUAL ATTITUDES

Sexual Abuse Mind-set *(Sex = Sexual Abuse*	*Healthy Sexual Attitudes* *(Sex = Positive Sexual Energy)*
Sex is uncontrollable energy.	Sex is controllable energy.
Sex is an obligation.	Sex is a choice.
Sex is addictive.	Sex is a natural drive.
Sex is hurtful.	Sex is nurturing, healing.
Sex is a condition for receiving love.	Sex is an expression of love.
Sex is "doing to" someone.	Sex is sharing with someone.
Sex is a commodity.	Sex is part of who I am.
Sex is void of communication.	Sex requires communication.
Sex is secretive.	Sex is private.
Sex is exploitive.	Sex is respectful.
Sex is deceitful.	Sex is honest.
Sex benefits one person.	Sex is mutual.
Sex is emotionally distant.	Sex is intimate.
Sex is irresponsible.	Sex is responsible.
Sex is unsafe.	Sex is safe.
Sex has no limits.	Sex has boundaries.
Sex is power over someone.	Sex is empowering.

From *The Sexual Healing Journey - A Guide for Survivors of Sexual Abuse*
by Wendy Maltz, who also wrote, *The Porn Trap.*
www.healthysex.com   Used by permission.

Motorcycles, Madness & Miracles
A Badass Journey to Empowerment
Foot Reflexology Chart

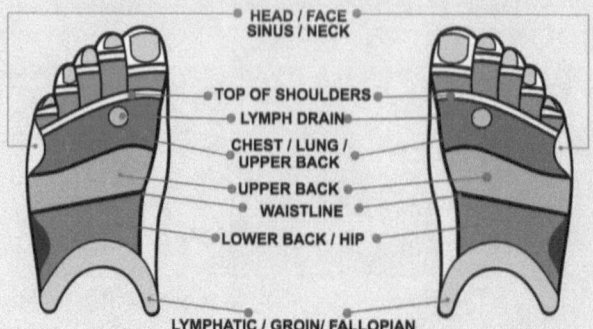

HEAD / FACE
SINUS / NECK

TOP OF SHOULDERS
LYMPH DRAIN
CHEST / LUNG /
UPPER BACK
UPPER BACK
WAISTLINE
LOWER BACK / HIP

LYMPHATIC / GROIN/ FALLOPIAN

TOP LEFT   **TOP RIGHT**

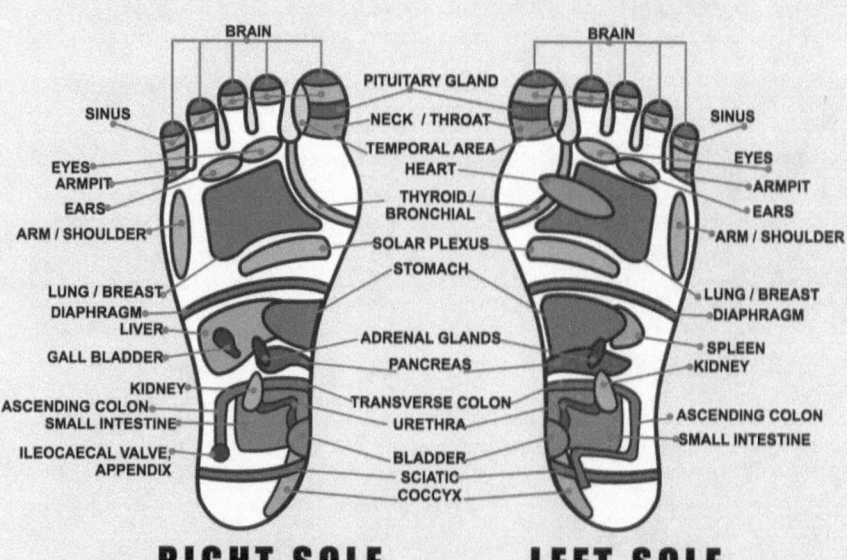

BRAIN   BRAIN
PITUITARY GLAND
SINUS   NECK / THROAT   SINUS
TEMPORAL AREA
EYES   HEART   EYES
ARMPIT   ARMPIT
EARS   THYROID /   EARS
BRONCHIAL
ARM / SHOULDER   SOLAR PLEXUS   ARM / SHOULDER
STOMACH
LUNG / BREAST   LUNG / BREAST
DIAPHRAGM   DIAPHRAGM
LIVER   ADRENAL GLANDS
GALL BLADDER   PANCREAS   SPLEEN
KIDNEY   KIDNEY
ASCENDING COLON   TRANSVERSE COLON   ASCENDING COLON
SMALL INTESTINE   URETHRA   SMALL INTESTINE
ILEOCAECAL VALVE   BLADDER
APPENDIX   SCIATIC
COCCYX

RIGHT SOLE   **LEFT SOLE**

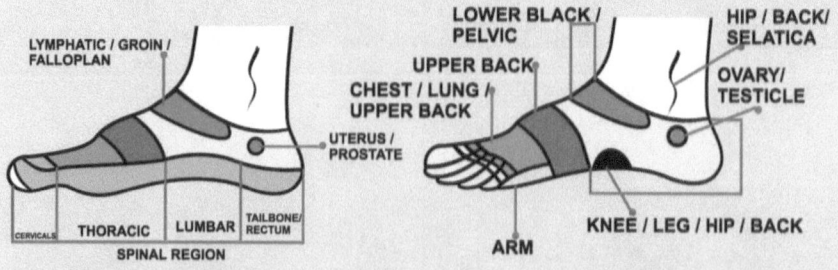

LYMPHATIC / GROIN /
FALLOPLAN

LOWER BLACK /   HIP / BACK/
PELVIC   SELATICA
UPPER BACK
CHEST / LUNG /   OVARY/
UPPER BACK   TESTICLE
UTERUS /
PROSTATE

CERVICALS THORACIC LUMBAR TAILBONE/
RECTUM
SPINAL REGION   KNEE / LEG / HIP / BACK
ARM

INSIDE RIGHT   **OUTSIDE LEFT**

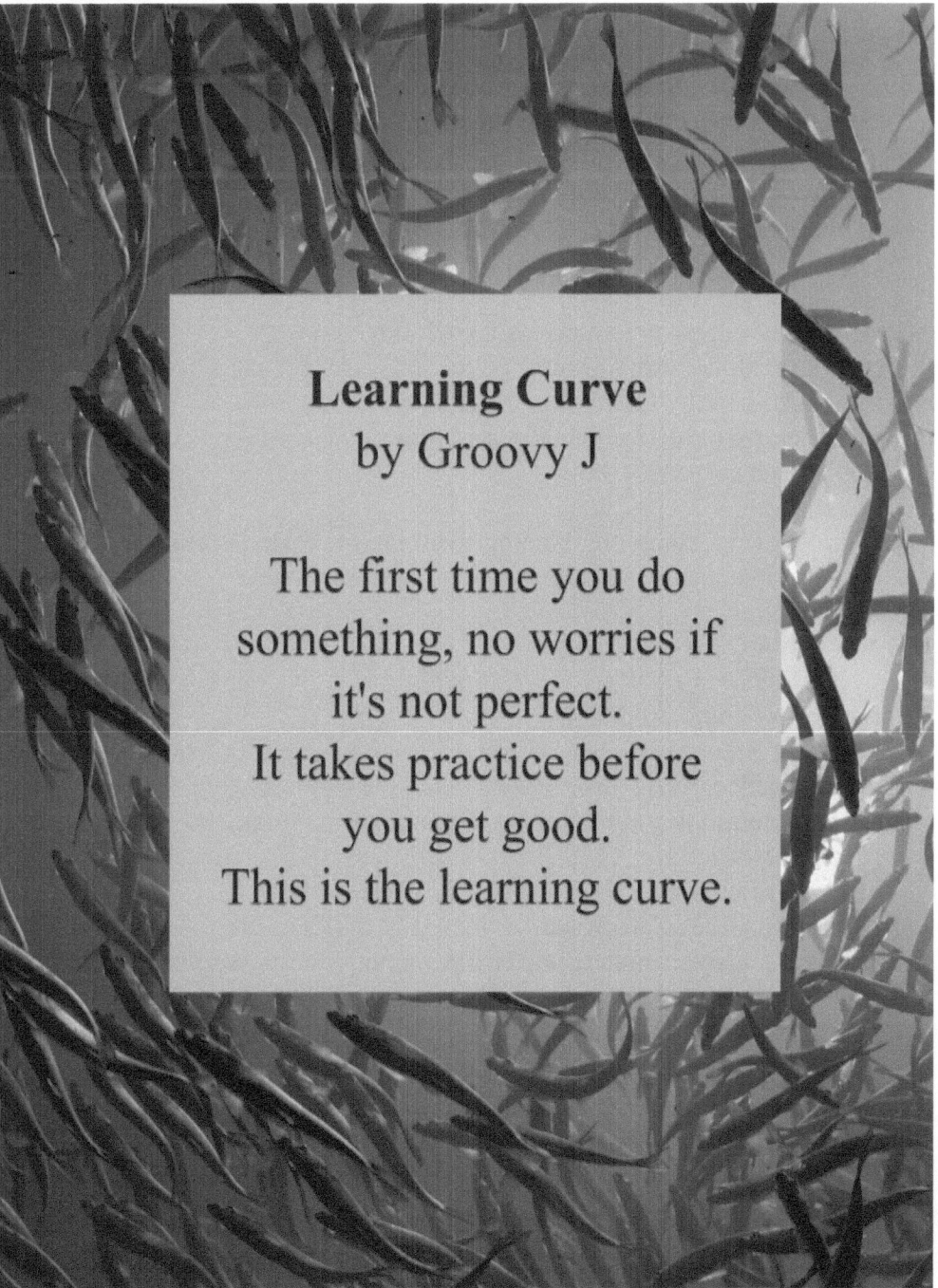

Learning Curve
by Groovy J

The first time you do
something, no worries if
it's not perfect.
It takes practice before
you get good.
This is the learning curve.

Heal Holes and Keeping the Aura Strong

Your aura is the energy field that both surrounds and protects you. Many indigenous cultures believe that illness first starts because of a hole or weakness in the aura. Maintaining a strong and healthy aura will keep you strong and healthy.

Sage and smudging
One hour in nature or natural light each day
Meditation alone or in a group
Fitness and healthy habits
Hydrotherapy (water) especially with sea salt
Rubbing sea salt on the body
Cold shower
Grounding (visualization, dancing, walking on Earth barefoot)
Reiki attunements or other energy healing modalities
Sound healing
Toning 'ohm'
Essential oils
Zero Point Global products
Crystals & Stones
Flower essences
Positive intentions and thoughts - if unable to maintain, go to **Inner Work** section.
Avoid or minimize alcohol (especially dead spirits)
Reduce exposure to electrical devices (EMF's) like the microwave, electric meter, power lines, compact fluorescent lighting, cell phones, etc. especially where you sleep - clock, electric blanket, night light, etc.

To determine amount of EMF's a device has, use an old AM radio tuned to static (between stations) and hold next to device when the device is turned off then when it's on, the louder the static, the more EMF's.

Article Written by Iah Ka Onge-Ja
for *Healthy Times Newspaper,* September 2012

Holes in the aura need to be repaired to maintain proper health.   The aura or auric field is the energy field that surrounds the body. This can be done by grounding yourself with the earth's metals, minerals and elements through meditation. Crystals often contain the elements needed. Or by taking the trace elements and minerals that you are deficient in, which you can purchase at a health food store.

When a hole is too strong to repair on your own, it is best to seek out a shaman as this is what they specialize in.   A shaman is a holistic healer with advanced skills on repairing the energy bodies of the soul. The main way a shaman repairs a hole in the auric field is by placing sacred geometrical patterns of the needed earth elements from the periodic table into the body while spinning the appropriate light wave frequencies and particle structures into the hole. This takes a high amount of skill.

Some indicators that you have holes in your aura:
Repeated injuries in the same location, popping or dislocations in the joints, burning sensations, sharp pains that don't go away, uncomfortable tingly vibrations, feeling of a rod-shaped hole in the body, parts of the body

that bruise easily, medical tests that show nothing physically wrong, feeling constantly weak, sudden tiredness out of nowhere, sudden nausea out of the blue, sudden feeling of being hit by a heavy thump, sudden illness or hospitalization when otherwise healthy, coma, and ALL migraines.

How does someone get a hole in their aura? This difficult challenge comes when someone is attacking you in some way with their emotional words, also known as psychic attack. This begins to tear a hole in the auric field. It does not matter if the attacker is in your presence or merely thinking harmful thoughts about you from a faraway distance. These thought forms have a life force of their own and actually can cause instant physical pain and illness. When others are attacking you, the incoming energy will look for a hole already in the auric field to enter into. If someone's thought form is strong and aggressive enough, it can create a new hole.

When you have repaired the holes in your aura AND released all of your anger towards your attacker, the energy is karmic bound. In other words, it gets sent back to the sender. It is not up to you to decide where it goes. It simply belongs to and is sent to its rightful owner. Sometimes it's returned instantly, or at a later time in life or even another lifetime when the person is ready to work on their harmful actions. There is no need for you to stay angry or want revenge for what someone has done to you. When you understand the laws of karma, your attacker will truly pay for their actions at some point in time, oftentimes in a worse way than you experienced.

An unfortunate circumstance that occurs to an innocent person who is caught having to listen to someone else's angry spew is that it can tear auric holes in the innocent listener as well and then rapidly drains that person's energy. A psychic attacker truly cares not who they are attacking, just as long as they have someone's energy to take.

But this goes both ways. You must know that if you are speaking angry, aggressive, or harmful thoughts to someone, whether it's directly to the person's face or behind their back, or even if it is only thoughts in your mind, you have now become the psychic attacker. It is best to recognize this action within yourself and learn to develop better coping mechanisms so you do not fall prey to your own vicious cycle. Don't let this be you. The true learning is to speak only from the heart with love and compassion.

→ ● ←

For shamanic healing to repair the holes in your aura,
contact Iah Ka Onge-Ja of Balanced
Energies, www.BalancedEnergies.com, *951-699-9010.*
Located in Temecula and Escondido, CA.
  Used with permission.

I have used the Emotional Freedom Technique or EFT to reprogram old beliefs and thoughts, which no longer work for me, for more than 18 years. It is one of the best tools I have. EFT is as useful as a screwdriver, but with the impact of a drill. And, because I don't have to wait for a therapy session to utilize it, it becomes the cordless drill with a fresh set of batteries! It is indispensable to my growth. There is information about it on-line and on Youtube but the best resource is where I learned it –
from the founder, Gary Craig. http://www.emofree.com/

After using Gary's approach for several years, I developed my own technique in front of a mirror. But for the beginner, Gary's approach is the place to start. He explains everything fully with much better examples and diagrams. But for those who just want the basics, I will include my technique here.

(Anything presented in this toolbox or online can be altered to suit individual needs.)

EFT involves tapping on the face's meridian points to reprogram the brain.
I use it when I notice something I want to change – i.e., 'I have a fear of public speaking.'
I sit in front of a mirror. I look at myself in the mirror, and see myself as I am.
I think gentle thoughts, and know that I am doing the best I can, at that moment.
I thank myself for taking steps that allow me to grow.

Then, I use the following three sequences:
- Part one - I ask myself on a scale of 1 to 10 how affected I am by this subject. For this example, I am at an 8 in discomfort, with 10 being the most uncomfortable.
  Next, I lock eyes with the 'me' in the mirror and tap each point on the face,
  numbered 1 through 5: the inside of the eyebrows, the outside of the eye, under the eye, under the nose, and on the chin. Each point is tapped 7 times while both saying out loud and feeling internally (truthful), what I have discovered about myself that no longer suits me. i.e., "I have a fear of public speaking."
- Part two - I soften my gaze toward myself and feel love. I look at myself like I would imagine a loved one might look at me. Then I tap each point 7 times and say, "But, I totally and completely, love and accept myself, unconditionally." (or whatever is appropriate)
- Part three - I again tap each point 7 times and with a happy heart, state my new reality and allow it to shift into place as my truth. "And, I now choose to experience excitement and joy, when speaking in front of the public!"

Then I just feel my body. If there is still significant resistance, I will go through the procedure again. If it has nearly dissolved, I might say it's good enough. Most times, these quick few exercises is all that's needed to remove old programming, so then I can just go forward and live my life until the next miscreation is noticed. And then I record it all in my journal so I can look back and see how far I've come.

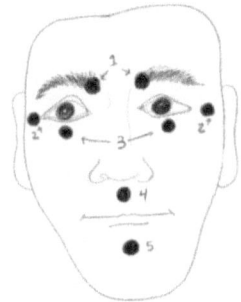

→ ● ←

Inner Work

Notice inner dialogue or writing it out on paper.
(keep in mind, I call all situations to me, because I am a creator - not a victim)

First - I stop myself from going numb or being angry to deflect having to do my work.
(This means resisting the urge to get drunk when the shit hits the proverbial fan.)

Next, I move into compassion for myself, making sure that personally, I do not take on the other person's words and behavior. (if this is something coming from another)

I allow sadness, heartache, helplessness, and sometimes loneliness over the action to be felt.
I place my hand on my heart.
(I feel, I cry, I dance, I pray, and I find a way to release that causes no ill will or bad karma)

I journal to gain understanding.
(This is done in a combination of dominant hand/non dominant hand writing or
continuously writing whatever words pop into my mind without analyzing.)
If nothing comes to me, I start by answering the following questions:
 • What is really going on, within me and my heart? Is my heart closed?
 • What am I trying to avoid?
 • Do I need to be 'right' or place blame?
 • What am I trying to control?
 • What am I fearful of?
 • Am I willing to forgive myself or another, for being less than perfect?

Lastly, I make peace and send myself or the originator, a blessing.
Journal to understand:
 • How can I view this as a blessing?
 • In what ways am I now stronger for having experienced this?
 • List the new ways that I am grateful

Release the energy.
(breath is sacred – blow it away, fire is sacred – burn words to ash, water is sacred – wash the spirit clean,
thoughts are sacred – hold ones that are pure for they are held in the ether)

Perhaps, the next interaction will be better … sometimes, alone time is best.
I release old visions, allowing the possibility of healthy interaction the next time we meet.

I become more conscious in the world and how my actions impact others.
(If I fail, this is how to apologize)
I admit that what I did was wrong, and that I feel badly for doing it.
I ask them if there is something I can do to make things better.
Sometimes, if it feels right, I will explain what caused my hurtful behavior. (I find this really important when
dealing with children. Kids are quick to forgive … and also just as quick to blame themselves.)

Everything I do is my choice. My choices will affect the next generation, and my next life.

→ ● ←

Ho'oponopono

Nothing beats face-to-face communication, but when that is not possible, there is a **Hawaiian technique, Ho'oponopono**, which allows for apologizing without having to be together. I pull up their image in my mind's eye, and say with all sincerity,
"I am sorry. Please forgive me. I love you. Thank you."

This energetically clears the connection between individuals or groups.
The other person may or may not accept this clearing, based on their own thinking and control, but it will always help the person saying the words in clearing and returning to a balanced state. There is also a 12 Step Ho'oponopono found online for a more complete clearing.

Undoing Mistakes

Another technique for atonement is from *A Course in Miracles*
(T-5.VII.6:3-11)
Third Edition published by The Foundation for Inner Peace, PO Box 598, Mill Valley, CA 94942-0598 http://acim.org/ & info@acim.org

"The first step in the undoing is to recognize that you actively decided wrongly, but can as actively decide otherwise. Be very firm with yourself in this, and keep yourself fully aware that the undoing process, which does not come from you, is nevertheless within you because God placed it there. Your part is merely to return your thinking to the point at which the error was made,

and give it over to the Atonement in peace. Say this to yourself as sincerely as you can, remembering that the Holy Spirit will respond fully to your slightest invitation:
I must have decided wrongly, because I am not at peace.
I made the decision myself, but I can also decide otherwise.
I want to decide otherwise, because I want to be at peace.
I do not feel guilty, because the Holy Spirit will undo all the consequences of my wrong decision if I will let Him.
I choose to let Him, by allowing Him to decide for God for me."

Fear

Fear has many purposes. It can help save someone if they find themselves in a dangerous situation.
But in this modern day story, I am clearing it.
Therefore, if I feel fear or paranoid in any situation, I'll first blow out white light (love) in all directions to transmute or chase away any dark energy that may be in the vicinity. If the fear remains, I then accept this feeling to be a reflection of something within me, otherwise why would I be experiencing it?
So, I enter into ceremony with herb, a crystal, a stone being, etc …, and/or go to the mirror to find the source of darkness within me and clear it so I may return to peace.

The ONE Major Cause of Relationship Problems!

By Dr. Margaret Paul
June 28, 2010

What if you could discover the ONE major cause of your relationship problems and it was something that you could do something about? Would you do it?

What if there really is ONE major cause of relationship problems, one issue that if you address, would change everything? The good news and the bad news is - there is!

The good news is that it makes it easier to understand why you might be having problems in your relationship.

The bad news is that to resolve the issue takes a deep personal commitment to heal.

The one cause is - *self-abandonment*.

Let's take a look at what self-abandonment is and why it causes almost all the problems in relationships.

There are many areas in which we can abandon ourselves: emotional, physical, spiritual, financial, relational, and organizational. One or more of these areas may be affecting your relationship.

Emotional Self-Abandonment

We abandon ourselves emotionally in four major ways:

1. We judge ourselves rather than accept ourselves.

2. We ignore our feelings by staying up in our head rather than being present in our body, especially our painful feelings of loneliness, heartache, heartbreak, and grief.

3. We turn to various addictions to numb the anxiety, depression, guilt, shame and anger that we cause when we judge ourselves and ignore our feelings.

4. We make others responsible for our feelings.

Once we emotionally abandon ourselves and make others responsible for our feelings, then we need to try to control them to get them to love us and make us feel worthy. Trying to control another with anger, blame, criticism, compliance, or withdrawal creates many problems in relationships.

Financial Self-Abandonment

When we refuse to take care of ourselves financially, instead expecting our partner to take financial responsibility for us, this can create problems. This is not a problem if your partner agrees to take financial responsibility for you and you fully accept how he or she takes this responsibility, but if you choose to be financially irresponsible, much conflict can occur over your self-abandonment.

Organizational Self-Abandonment

If you refuse to take responsibility for your own time and space, instead being consistently late or being a clutterer, and your partner is an on-time and/or neat person, this can create huge power struggles.

Physical Self-Abandonment

257

If you refuse to take care of yourself physically, instead eating badly and not exercising and possibly causing yourself health problems, your partner may feel resentful at having to take care of you. Your physical self-abandonment not only has negative consequences for you regarding your health and well being, but it also has unwanted consequences for your partner, which can lead to much conflict and power struggles.

Relational Self-Abandonment

If you refuse to speak up for yourself in your relationship, instead either giving yourself up or resisting, you are eroding the love in the relationship. When you abandon yourself to another through compliance or resistance, you create a lack of trust that leads to conflict and resentment.

Spiritual Self-Abandonment

When you make your partner your dependable source of love rather than learning to turn to a spiritual source for your dependable source of love, you place a very unfair burden on your partner. When your intent in the relationship is to *get love* rather than to *share love*, then you will pull on your partner for attention, approval, time, or sex. When you do not take responsibility for learning how to connect with a spiritual source of sustenance, your neediness can create much conflict in the relationship.

Learning to Love Yourself Rather than Abandon Yourself

When you decide to learn to love yourself rather than continue to abandon yourself, you will discover how to create a loving relationship with your partner. Practicing Inner Bonding® is a very powerful way of learning to love yourself!

http://www.innerbonding.com/show-article/2581/the-one-major-cause-of-relationship-problems.html

http://margaretpaul.com/

Reprinted with permission.

Motorcycles, Madness & Miracles
A Badass Journey to Empowerment
rudall30/Shutterstock.com

Empowerment

Joy
Purity
Freedom
Divine Trust
Happiness
Optimism
Hopefulness
Contentment
Boredom
Frustration / Impatience
Overwhelmed
Doubt / Worry
Blame / Anger / Hate
Jealousy / Revenge
Victim / Fear / Guilt / Unworthiness

My Walk with Fear
A True Story by Rowan Glaser

On a sunny summer day some friends, their two children, and I went on a nature hike in a local city park. The children bounded into the lead, and after a mile or so on the main trail, they came upon a less beaten path that they wanted to follow. After a short discussion about how their innocence makes them more in touch with their intuition, we all agreed to see what sort of adventure waited along this new route.

Glowing with pride, the children led the way, making sure to never get too far ahead. For the most part, the trail was easy to follow, and it was refreshing to see new landscape. Climbing over fallen trees, discovering a previously unknown pond, and using our imaginations about what might be living in a hole that disappeared deep into the earth – we were enjoying our nature experience.

After walking for a good while, I stated perhaps we should turn back and return to the park's main area. One of the children replied, "If you think we should go back, then that means something wonderful is just ahead!"

Surprised, but willing to see if this was true, I said sure! We picked up the pace with an increase in excitement. Lo and behold, we came upon a small river, about 18 feet across. The water was moving along gently and there was a tree that had snapped but not totally disconnected. It fell at the perfect location so that it crossed the stream and lodged between two trees on the opposite side. A natural bridge! The bark was gone and it was approximately 2 feet wide - ideal for us to cross and explore the inviting scenery on the other side. Without hesitation, the two kids hopped up on the log and walked over. Then, the dad went across, offering his hand to help his wife. Then, my friend offered to let me go next. I declined and said I would follow. Once she was safely on the far shore, I hopped up on the log and started to take a step, but was suddenly gripped by fear. Now, this confused me, because I don't have a fear of heights and the bridge was certainly wide enough. I also consider myself to be both courageous and well-balanced, so I was puzzled at my body's reaction. Yet, every time I tried to take a step, my legs started shaking uncontrollably. This irrational fear was so intense that the shaking of my legs was going to be the cause of my falling! Backing up to where I could place a hand on a nearby tree, I steadied myself and began an internal dialogue, trying to understand where this fear was coming from. I had no clues, so offering silent reassurances, I commanded myself to buck up and cross that bridge! But, the moment I took my hand off the supporting tree, the legs shaking resumed in earnest, my stomach clenched, and try as I might, I could not get myself to take a single step. I was forced to give up. My friends were sympathetic and offered to assist me, but shame at my shortcoming made me lie and I told them I wanted to explore something that was on the side I was currently on, and that they should go ahead without me. Well, the three adults walked around a little on the far bank as if exploring their immediate surroundings without going too far, and I acted like I was doing the same on my side. The two children hopped back onto the bridge and returned with confusion on their faces about why I wasn't joining them. To this, I mumbled something meaningless. When the younger of the two boys stood in the spot where I had experienced my intense fear, he picked up on the energy and started to become afraid. I noticed and went over to him, explaining that he had no reason to fear because he had already accomplished the crossing; it was just that his sensitivity was enough to pick up on my residual energy. The father also witnessed his son's reaction. Not wanting him to despair, he met him on the bridge and taking his hand, lead him away. Meanwhile, I waved my hands in the general area of the left-over anxiety in order to dissipate it. The father continued to encourage his son to play on the log until the boy's confidence returned to full strength. Then, everyone came back to the side I was waiting on, and we all walked back to the park, and eventually to our cars. They were gracious in not pressing my cowardice.

Returning home, I realized my error in not accepting help

from friends in the moment. Next time, I will lay pride by the side. By not taking their hand, I also blocked their gift of being able to help someone else in a time of struggle. Sigh. I sat with shame, which weakens the 3rd chakra[327] which is our place of will power. I resolved that in order to heal this newly created hole, I *must* return and cross that bridge over and back, thereby thoroughly erasing any fears that are within me. If I allowed one fear to take root, then others could follow, and that was *not* the way I intended to live.

With mind made up, I considered what I had on hand that would make my crossing easier. I decided to bring along a few bottles of essential oils designed to calm, give courage, and connect with the Earth. Then, I laced up my waterproof hiking boots and returned to the scene of my previous shortcoming.

The sun was about an hour from setting, so the shadows were long, but I had plenty of time to accomplish what I came to do. I sat on the ground and breathed in the essential oils until I felt fully confident and grounded. Then, I hopped up on the tree and gave a few jumps just to make sure it was still sturdy. Almost immediately, I could feel my legs grow nervous, so I shifted my weight from the back leg to the front, trying to determine just what was making them shake. It didn't seem to make any difference and I remained dumbfounded. Next, I tried to locate the origin of the fear. I diligently searched my memory for any time that I might have been in a similar situation. Nothing presented itself. In fact, I recalled stories from my mom about how I would walk along the top railing of a picket fence as a little girl, much to her dismay.

Returning to present time, I watched two squirrels chase each other around some trees. I smelled the clean scent of the woods. I listened to the sound of the laughing water, and then decided it was time to get a move on. I took my hand off the supporting tree and my heart began to pound wildly. I could literally, audibly hear it outside my chest. I focused on my breath and began to take slow, full inhalations and exhalations until I felt calmer - not completely calm, but enough to where I felt like I was a little more in control. Then, I started off. One small sliding step, feeling the placement of my foot on the log, making sure it was secure, shifting my weight forward, dragging my rear foot to meet the lead. My legs were shaking, but scooting forward, a little at a time, I began to make progress. Up a little incline, over a knot in the tree that was a touch difficult to navigate, now past the knot, recognizing that the supporting tree was far beyond reach, moving further, heading out over the open water, establishing a rhythm of movement, not comfortable, but not doing too badly, slow and steady…. My focus was so intent on the log beneath my feet that I wasn't sure how much further I had left to go. I stopped and looked up to gauge the distance to

→ ● ←

the other bank, but now that I halted, my legs started to tremble, and I realized I was in the very middle of the makeshift bridge over open water! Because of the trembling of my legs, the log started to bounce up and down, which caused more fear, more shaking, and an increase in the bouncing! I tried to take a step forward but my leg was frozen and unwilling to respond. I could feel fear coming at me from all directions, so with faith I yelled out, "Universe, help! God, help me please!!" Instantly, calm descended upon me and I took that opportunity to begin my slow shuffle again. Right foot forward, quick test of secure footing, rear foot to follow, repeat. I started making progress once again, step, shuffle, step, shuffle. I started feeling good as the far shore inched closer and closer. Then, when I was about 2 feet from the bank and thinking I could leap onto the shore, I saw both my boots slip off the log at the same time and SPLASH! I landed in the water on my feet, upright. Ha! I couldn't believe it! I had actually fallen in! The water only came up to my knees, so it wasn't anything major. And, I didn't hurt myself in the fall, so I just gave a little laugh and walked up the bank, shaking my head. I recognized my mistake in losing focus, but I also observed the miracle of calmness that had enveloped me when I had called out to the Universe for help. I was amazed and grateful. It worked! There *is* a Great Mystery to hear my call!

But I still had to get back to the other side....

→ ● ←

Sitting on the bank for a little while, listening to the birds chirp until my heart slowed its pace, I heard a little voice in my head suggest that since I was already wet, I might as well walk through the water and get on home. That voice was not my friend. Impeccability of word matters, and it's a foundation I refuse to let crumble. So, I placed my feet on the log to begin the return journey. Immediately, my legs started shaking. Seriously?! I've done this; I knew the procedure. What the hell was wrong with my legs?! Plus, now that my boots were soaking, I could feel them slipping on the log and I knew I didn't want to fall in a second time because then I'd see myself as a loser and no – not going there. I stepped off and considered possible solutions … then, it came to me, take off the boots. But - what if I slipped and landed on a rock? It would hurt something awful. Yet, the protection that the boots offered was getting in the way of feeling in control of my steps. Protection … or self-control … I decided to take off the boots and put my faith in myself and the Universe. With a boot in each hand for balance, I sent up a prayer to the Great Mystery for assistance and stepped forward.

With feet free of their false protection, I was able to grip the log much better than I had ever done with the hiking boots. Having a grip, I felt much more in control, and between my faith in the Universe watching out for me and my ability to feel what I was doing, I crossed back to the other side in minimal time. It was surprisingly easy without false protection! As I leapt onto the bank, I let out a whoop of joy! I had done it!! I overcame that which had made me less than I wanted to be - woohoo!!

Bach Flower Questionnaire
Read more at
www.BachFlower.com

This questionnaire can help you learn the different type of emotional imbalance that each Dr. Bach Flower Remedy addresses. You may want to read more about each of the Remedies in order to select the correct combination.

Agrimony
__I hide my feelings behind a façade of cheerfulness
__I dislike arguments and often give in to avoid conflict
__I turn to food, work, alcohol, drugs, etc. when down

Aspen
__I feel anxious without knowing why
__I have a secret fear that something bad will happen
__I wake up feeling anxious

Beech
__I get annoyed by the habits of others
__I focus on others' mistakes
__I am critical and intolerant

Centaury
__I often neglect my own needs to please
__I find it difficult to say "no"
__I tend to be easily influenced

Cerato
__I constantly second-guess myself
__I seek advice, mistrusting my own intuition
__I often change my mind out of confusion

Cherry Plum
__I'm afraid I might lose control of myself
__I have sudden fits of rage
__I feel like I'm going crazy

Chestnut Bud
__I make the same mistakes over and over
__I don't learn from my experience
__I keep repeating the same patterns

Chicory
__I need to be needed and want my loved ones close
__I feel unloved and unappreciated by my family
__I easily feel slighted and hurt

Clematis
__I often feel spacey and absent minded
__I find myself unable to concentrate for long
__I get drowsy and sleep more than necessary

Crab Apple
__I am overly concerned with cleanliness
__I feel unclean or physically unattractive
__I tend to obsess over little things

Elm
__I feel overwhelmed by my responsibilities
__I don't cope well under pressure
__I have temporarily lost my self-confidence

Gentian
__I become discouraged with small setbacks
__I am easily disheartened when faced with difficulties
__I am often skeptical and pessimistic

Gorse
__I feel hopeless, and can't see a way out
__I lack faith that things could get better in my life
__I feel sullen and depressed

Heather
__I am obsessed with my own troubles
__I dislike being alone and I like to talk
__I usually bring conversations back to myself

Holly
__I am suspicious of others
__I feel discontented and unhappy
__I am full of jealousy, mistrust, or hate

Honeysuckle
__I'm often homesick for the "way it was"
__I think more about the past than the present
__I often think about what might have been

Hornbeam
__I often feel too tired to face the day ahead
__I feel mentally exhausted
__I tend to put things off

Impatiens
__I find it hard to wait for things
__I am impatient and irritable
__I prefer to work alone

Larch
__I lack self-confidence
__I feel inferior and often become discouraged
__I never expect anything but failure

Mimulus
__I am afraid of things such as spiders, illness, etc.
__I am shy, overly sensitive, and modest
__I get nervous and embarrassed

Mustard
__I get depressed without any reason
__I feel my moods swinging back and forth
__I get gloomy feelings that come and go

Oak
__I tend to overwork and keep on in spite of exhaustion
__I have a strong sense of duty and never give up
__I neglect my own needs in order to complete a task

Olive
__I feel completely exhausted, physically and/ or mentally
__I am totally drained of all energy with no reserves left
__I have just been through a long period of illness or stress

Pine
__I feel unworthy and inferior
__I often feel guilty
__I blame myself for everything that goes wrong

Red Chestnut
__I am overly concerned and worried about my loved ones
__I am distressed and disturbed by other people's problems
__I worry that harm may come to those I love

Rock Rose
__I sometimes feel terror and panic
__I become helpless and frozen when afraid
__I suffer from nightmares

Rock Water
__I set high standards for myself
__I am strict with my health, work &/or spiritual discipline
__I am very self-disciplined, always striving for perfection

Scleranthus
__I find it difficult to make decisions
__I often change my opinions
__I have intense mood swings

Star of Bethlehem
__I feel devastated due to a recent shock
__I am withdrawn due to traumatic events in my life
__I have never recovered from loss or fright

Sweet Chestnut
__I feel extreme mental or emotional heartache
__I have reached the limits of my endurance
__I am in complete despair, all hope gone

Vervain
__I get high-strung and very intense
__I try to convince others of my way of thinking
__I am sensitive to injustice, almost fanatical

Vine
__I tend to take charge of projects, situations, etc.
__I consider myself a natural leader
__I am strong-willed, ambitious and often bossy

Walnut
__I am experiencing change in my life--a move, new job, etc.
__I get drained by people or situations
__I want to be free to follow my own ambitions

Water Violet
__I give the impression that I'm aloof
__I prefer to be alone when overwhelmed
__I often don't connect with people

White Chestnut
__I am constantly thinking unwanted thoughts
__I relive unhappy events or arguments over and over again
__I am unable to sleep at times because I can't stop thinking

Wild Oat
__I can't find my path in life
__I am drifting in life and lack direction
__I am ambitious but don't know what to do

Wild Rose
__I am apathetic and resigned to whatever happens
__I have the attitude, "It doesn't matter anyhow"
__I feel no joy in life

Willow
__I feel resentful and bitter
__I have difficulty forgiving and forgetting
__I think life is unfair and have a "Poor me attitude"

You can purchase the Dr. Bach Flower Remedies at your local Health Food Store or online at **www.DirectlyFromNature.com**
Interested in learning more? You can purchase books at **www.BachFlowerBooks.com**

800-214-2850 - info@BachFlower.com

www.BachFlower.com

Directly *from* Nature

Bach Flower Indication Chart

INDICATION	BACH REMEDY	OUTCOME
Hide Problems behind a cheerful face	Agrimony	Cheerfulness stems from a real sense of self acceptance and inner joy.
Fears and worries of unknown origin, night terrors	Aspen	A state of inner peave, security and fearlessness.
Intolerant of others, critical, They are always in the right	Beech	Tolerance and a sense of compassion for and unity of others.
Weak-Willed and easily led, You find it hard to say no	Centaury	Become in touch with what you want and follow your own path.
Seek advice and confirmation from others	Cerato	Trust your own inner wisdom and follow it. Self Assured and decisive.
Fear of losing control of your own behaviour	Cherry Plum	A calm mind and are able to think and act rationally.
Failure to learn from past mistakes and experiences	Chestnut Bud	Observe your own mistakes with objectivity, and learn from it.
Overly possessive and over protective of others	Chicory	Able to care for others unselfishly, offering genuine maternal love.
Dreaminess, lack of interest in the present. Daydreamer	Clematis	Interest in the world around, and enjoyment of life.
Poor self image, sense of uncleanliness	Crab Apple	Acceptance of oneself and one's imperfections.
Overwhelmed by responsibility	Elm	Restoration of one's normal capable personality and self assurance.
Discouragement and dispondency	Gentian	Realization that there is no such thing as failure when doing your best.
Hopelessness and despair, for people who have given up	Gorse	Sense of faith and hope, despite current physical or mental problems.
Self preoccupied, self concern or talkative	Heather	Good listener who is generous in helping others. Selfless.
Envious, jealous, feelings of hatred	Holly	Generous-hearted person able to give without making demands.
Dwells on the past, over-attachment to the past	Honeysuckle	Ability to live in the present, able to move forward in life without regret
"Monday Morning Feeling", mental weariness	Hornbeam	Certainty of one's strength and ability to face the day's work.
Impatience, people who are easily irritated	Impatiens	Someone who is decisive and spontaneous, less hasty in action.
Lack of self confidence, people who don't try	Larch	Determined, capable, with a realistic sense of self-esteem.
Fear of known things such as illness, death, accidents...etc	Mimulus	Quiet courage to face trials and difficulties with humor & confidence.
Deep gloom with no origin, unable to shake off at will	Mustard	Return of joy, supported by an inner stability and peace.

More on backside...

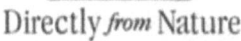

Directly *from* Nature

Bach Flower Indication Chart

INDICATION	BACH REMEDY	OUTCOME
Exhausted but struggles on, Keep going ignoring tiredness	Oak	Restores their energy and helps them recognize the need to take time off.
Lack of energy, exhaustion to point of tears, tires easily	Olive	Restoration of strength, vitality and interest in life. Peace of mind.
Self-Reproach and guilt, blame themselves	Pine	Accept responsanility realistically and have sound judgement.
Fear of over concern for others and welfare of others	Red Chestnut	Ability to care for others with compassion but without anxiety.
Terror such as after being in an accident, or nightmares	Rock Rose	Courage and presence of mind. The person is calm and self-forgetful.
Inflexible, self denial and set themselves high standards	Rock Water	Ability to hold high ideals with flexible mind. Willing to change minds.
Uncertainty and indecision, faced with two possibilities	Scleranthus	Certainty and decisiveness with poise and balance in all circumstances.
After effects of shock, mental or physical	Star of Bethlehem	Neutralize the effects of the trauma, whether immediate or delayed.
Extreme mental anguish, at point of breakdown	Sweet Chestnut	Liberation from despair and despondency. Peace of mind.
Over enthusiasm. Those with fixed principles and ideas	Vervain	Calm, wise and tolerant. Able to relax and take broad view of life and events.
Assertive and inflexible, often very capable and ambitious	Vine	Determination without domination. See the good in others/encourage.
Protection from change and outside influences	Walnut	Ability to move forward and remain steadfast to one's path in life.
Proud and aloof, calm, capable and knowledgeable	Water Violet	Warmer relationships with others, while maintaining one's wisdom.
Unwanted thoughts, mental anguish, Repetitive thoughts	White Chestnut	Peace of mind, the head is clear and thinking is under control.
Uncertainty as to correct path in life.	Wild Oat	Clear picture of what to do in life with positive ideas and ambitions.
Resignation and apathy, for those who are resigned	Wild Rose	Lively interest in life, work and the world in general.
Self pity and resentment, feel more or less put-upon	Willow	Allows people to forgive and forget past injustices and enjoy life.

Order online at www.DirectlyfromNature.com
www.BachFlower.com
www.BachFlower4Kids.com
Questions? Call us at 1-800-214-2850

7 Chakra System

7th - Crown - Violet - Pineal - Thought - I Know - Fasting. Lets in universal and divine knowledge, wisdom, guidance, understanding, higher purpose & reason, meditative self, purity, bliss. Blocked by earthly attachment.

6th - Third Eye - Indigo - Pituitary - Light - I See - Marijuana & Psychedelics (sometimes beneficial, sometimes not). Spiritual sight, clairvoyance, intuition, non-linear perception, trust, imagination, dreaming. Blocked by illusion.

5th - Throat - Blue - Thyroid - Sound - I Speak - Fruits. Vibration, communication, connection, telepathy, creativity, peace & calm. Blocked by lies.

4th - Heart - Green - Air - I Love - Vegetables. Compassion, love, balance, sharing, devotion, renewal, generosity, selfless service. Blocked by grief.

3rd - Solar Plexus - Yellow - Fire - I Can - Starches. Personal will, name, fame, acquisition of wealth, power, control, analyze, metabolic energy, clarity, focus, self esteem, joy. Blocked by shame.

2nd - Sacral - Orange - Water - I Feel - Liquids. Physical desires, pleasure, procreation & family, sexuality, fantasies, patience, clairsentience, tears, emotions. Blocked by guilt.

1st - Root - Red - Earth - I Have - Proteins & Meats. Survival, grounding, fulfillment of our physical needs & comforts, ambition, stillness, stability. Blocked by fear.

From the book: Motorcycles, Madness & Miracles

→ ● ←

CHARKA QUESTIONS[328]

From the book Wheels of Life: A User's Guide to the Chakra
System by Anodea Judith
http://sacredcenters.com/   Reprinted with permission.

Directions: Answer each question honestly

Mark N for Never, S for Seldom, O for Often, and A for
Always.

Mark P for Poor, F for Fair, G for Good, and E for
Excellent.

Score 1 point for answers in column one, 2 points for two, 3
for three, 4 for four. Add.

CHAKRA ONE: EARTH, SURVIVAL, GROUNDING

How often do you go for a walk in the woods, park, etc.?
N S O A

How often do you exercise?   N S O A

How is your health?   P F G E

How is your financial situation?   P F G E

How would you rate your diet?   P F G E

Do you consider yourself well grounded?   N S O A

→ ● ←

CHAKRA TWO: EMOTIONS, SEXUALITY

How would you rate your ability to express your emotions?
P F G E

How would you rate your sex life?   P F G E

How often do you show nurturing for others?   N S O A

Do you allow yourself to relax and seek pleasure in the form of movies, hot tubs, sensual pleasures or food in a non addictive
way?   N S O A

How would you rate your physical flexibility?   P F G E

How would you rate your emotional flexibility?   P F G E

CHAKRA THREE: FIRE, POWER

How would you rate your sense of personal power?
P F G E

How would you rate the effectiveness of your will?
P F G E

How would you rate your daily energy levels?   P F G E

How would you rate your metabolism?   P F G E

Do you accomplish what you set out to do?   N S O A

Do you feel confident?   N S O A

→ • ←

CHAKRA FOUR: AIR, LOVE

How often do you feel happy?   N S O A

How would you rate your ability to make friends?
P F G E

Do you love yourself?   N S O A

Do you feel connected with the world around you?
N S O A

Do you have successful long-term relationships?
N S O A

Do you feel in harmony with your present situation?
N S O A

CHAKRA FIVE: SOUND, COMMUNICATION

How would you rate your ability to communicate
your ideas?   P F G E

Do you listen well to others' ideas?   N S O A

Are you creative?   N S O A

How would you rate the resonance of your voice?
P F G E

Do you harmonize well with others?   N S O A

Do you engage in an art form (painting, music, dance,
writing, etc.)?   N S O A

→ • ←

CHAKRA SIX: LIGHT, CLAIRVOYANCE

Do you notice visual details in your surroundings?
N S O A

Do you have vivid dreams?   N S O A

Do you have psychic experiences, i.e., precognition,
clairvoyance, uncanny coincidence?   N S O A

How would you rate your ability to visualize?   P F G E

Do you make use of your imagination?   N S O A

Do you like bright colors?   N S O A

CHAKRA SEVEN: THOUGHT, UNDERSTANDING

Do you meditate?   N S O A

Do you have strong spiritual experiences?   N S O A

Do you spend a lot of time intellectualizing?   N S O A

Do you spend time gathering information, research,
study, etc.?   N S O A

Are you consciously aware of your thoughts, actions,
motives, etc.?   N S O A

Do you like taking tests like these?   N S O A

Using logic, compare each chakra's score to notice what is strong and what needs improvement.

For a more detailed reading of results, please purchase Anodea Judith's book at:
https://jr117.infusionsoft.com/app/storeFront/showProductD etail?productId=573

→ • ←

* Protection *

I call upon the Family of Light,
To be surrounded in an
impenetrable blanket of
pure white light.
As a sovereign being,
I intend that this brilliance hold
as a barrier against any energies
that are not of the Highest order,
and I invoke you,
Angel Warriors of Light,
to guide that process.
Let all other vibrations return
to their point of emergence,
carrying back to their source
the heightened energies
of Universal Love.

*Note – You don't need protection, unless you think you do. No one can harm you, unless your thinking allows it or unless you have opened yourself to this action by your own actions ie harmed another, used witchcraft, karma. Wisdom leads to atonement, which will release karma through Grace. Archangel Michael may be called in for protection at anytime, as well. Ultimately, non-duality existed before duality; therefore non-duality is supreme, thereby releasing all conflict.

→ • ←

The Motorcycle Journey

1. In Time - Robbie Robb
2. Not So Far Away - Glen Burtnick
3. If Everyone Cared - Nickleback
4. Hold On - Triumph
5. Solsbury Hill - Peter Gabriel
6. Fruitful Days - Big Mountain
7. Watershed - Indigo Girls
8. That's The Way - Led Zeppelin
9. The Wall - Kansas
10. Even In The Quietest Moments - Supertramp
11. In Your Eyes - Peter Gabriel
12. Return To Innocence - Enigma
13. What If I Stumble? - DC Talk
14. Amazing - One Eskimo
15. Imagine - John Lennon
16. Heaven's Plea - Michelle Kaye

The One Booth that is Always Missing on Career Day
By Robert Rabbin

I recently read an article describing how, down in Texas (a rogue fourth world country), the people in charge of public education wanted eighth graders to select their career paths.

Yes, this is true.

As I thought about what I might want to say in response to this insanity, outlining my view of education, I remembered the very first article I had ever published, back in 1991. I found it hiding in my hard drive. I read it. I didn't change a word.

Here it is. I will write another article outlining my view of education, but for now I'll let this article stand on its own.

Career Day for Mystics

I don't remember seeing an information table for aspiring mystics during Career Day in high school. I suspect that never in the history of high school career days has there ever been such a table.

What's the deal? How can kids with a sliver of awareness pointing towards reality find suitable colleges and careers?

Why wasn't someone like Meister Eckhart seated behind a table in the converted gymnasium, beckoning us as we strolled wide-eyed and impressionable down the shopping lanes of career offerings?
I don't remember anyone exhorting us, as Meister Eckhart would have:

"One should not give up, neglect or forget for a moment one's inner life, but one must learn to work in it, with it, and out of it, so that the unity of one's soul may break out into one's activities."

281

My career day was in 1968, at Magnolia High School in Anaheim, California. That sliver of light within me that wanted validation and encouragement was disappointed.

What would have happened to the legendary dancer Nijinsky had he not found a dancer's stage, or Ray Charles had he not found his way to a piano? What happens to the young mystics' inchoate yearnings, ripe for opportunity and guidance and mentoring?

Somewhere within me was the sentiment expressed by Tom Robbins:

"Deep down, all of us are probably aware that some kind of mystical evolution is our true task. Our purpose is to consciously, deliberately evolve toward a wiser, more liberated and luminous state of being."

But Tom wasn't there, and the only enticements for a compelling future were offered by the big corporations and the service academies—nobody was there to speak to me about a path towards soulful eruption. That would come years later. On that day in 1968, I did not see a sign "Career Opportunity for Mystics" up on the wall. Upon graduation from high school, I orbited restlessly for five years around and through a number of colleges, countries and continents.

Then, in India, a mystic mentor entered my life and pointed to a path that had not been evident on career day.

I have come to think that being a mystic isn't exactly a career, but a prerequisite for any career. In terms of a college curriculum, it might be called "Reality 101" and would certainly not be an elective. Everyone would have to take this course before any other courses and before one selected a career path.

We would have to learn what Chief Seattle taught back in 1852,

"This we know: the Earth does not belong to man, man belongs to the Earth. All things are connected like the blood that unites us all. Man did not weave the

282

→ ● ←

web of life, he is merely a strand in it. Whatever he does to the web, he does to himself."
This would properly prepare us for our career choices and responsibilities. In fact, we shouldn't graduate from nursery school before we are reminded about mysticism. Come to think of it, the kids in nursery school probably do know about it, but by the time most of us graduate from high school, overwhelmed with education, we've forgotten what nursery school kids know about mysticism.

Webster's dictionary defines mysticism as "the experience of direct communion with ultimate reality" and "the possibility of direct and intuitive acquisition of ineffable knowledge and power."

Alan Watts, quite the mystic himself, slyly presses a single finger to his lips when asked about mysticism. He doesn't mean that it shouldn't be talked about, but that it must be known in silence. But the twinkle in his eye is very alluring, and had Mr. Watts been seated at a booth during my career day, perhaps I and others would have signed up with him.
What did you know in nursery school that you forgot by the time high school career day came around? I think that nursery school kids play with God. As kids, our memories often stretch back to the time before we were born and retain images of the universe as it is: the big picture.

I think we know intuitively the sorcerers' secret, like don Juan, who said,

"We are luminous beings. We are an awareness. We are not objects. We have no solidity. We are boundless. The world of object and solidity is a way of making our passage on Earth convenient. It is only a description that was created to help us. We, or rather, our reason, forgot that the description is only a description and thus we entrap the totality of ourselves in a vicious circle from which we rarely emerge in our lifetime."
That's what we all tend to forget as we ingest millions of bytes of information.

Communing with ultimate reality is not as big a deal as you might think. It's as simple as remembering that we are luminous beings whose strands of luminosity are woven together with everything else.

Career people have obscured the simplicity and naturalness of mysticism.

Career people who have gone on to become presidents and CEOs of multinational corporations, business ones and religious ones alike, want to sell us things, most of which we don't really need to live happily in the cosmic tapestry, have obscured this with their attention to lesser things.

Conventional career days are so successful because high school kids have forgotten who they are. And there is so much opportunity for people who have forgotten who they are. Nonetheless, something in all of us stirs when we hear Ray Charles sing. There is a moment when our inherent rapturous selves pour out under the enticement of Mr. Charles' soulful voice. There is an instant of remembrance.

But then we forget again under the relentless pressure to go to work or shop for things we don't need.

Mystics are not special human beings; each human being is a special kind of mystic. It is very important to know this, especially in these modern times when careerists are screwing things up for all the living things on the planet. All the living things on the planet includes everything, not just humans—even the beautiful, fearless, and utterly stupid blue-footed boobies of the Galapagos Islands mentioned by Kurt Vonnegut.

Mystics know that all things are alive with the same essence. The careerists think that only their careers are alive and that everything else, including humans, is just career food. This kind of thinking is very fashionable and leads to a lot of silly ideas, which lead to more silly ideas, usually at the expense of living things. One day we may even read about over-anxious business people planning to build a papier-mâché tunnel through the Milky Way as a way of profiting from toll booth fees.

When ideas are hatched out of forgetfulness of who we are, the unmistakable stink of rotten eggs hangs in the air.

Albert Einstein said this about mysticism:

"The most beautiful and profound emotion we can experience is the sensation of the mystical. Those to whom this emotion is a stranger, who can no longer wonder and stand rapt in awe, are as good as dead."

Did you ever hear this kind of talk on career day? Neither did I. That's why I said mysticism is a prerequisite for all careers, because if we don't remember who we are, we're as good as dead.

If Mr. Einstein is correct, then we should ask ourselves why we so easily go along with the ideas of people who have not graduated from "Reality 101." Why do we sheepishly go along with plans to build parking lots and malls over the rainforests? Why do we eagerly march off to wars that are the ideas of people looking to advance their careers?

Because we all forgot how to play together in the luminosity of our true beingness. We got anxious for a career. We were encouraged to watch television and go shopping.

Ramana Maharshi was a great Indian mystic. In America, he would have had some trouble getting by because he didn't evidence much ambition. He never owned very much and, by career standards, didn't amount to much. But he knew who he was because he had let go of silly ideas about who he was and what he should do.

The magic about Ramana was that in his presence, people remembered who they were. Perhaps their inner Ray Charles started singing. Their souls awoke, their luminosity ignited, and they reconsidered what they were up to. They may have even wanted to stop steam-rolling steamy asphalt over lush forests, because they could suddenly hear the terrified screams of the Earth as the hot gooey tar was being applied like deadly mascara to her face.

Ramana Maharshi said,

"The ultimate truth is so simple. It is nothing more than being in the pristine state. This is all that need be said. All we need to do to realize the pristine state is to give up our habit of regarding as real that which is unreal. Reality is simply the loss of the ego."

The ego is nothing more than all the bad ideas about who we are that we ate as we were growing up; it's just a bad idea that keeps playing in our collective mind like a broken record. It's an eccentric quirk of awareness that corrupts the inherent wonder of our transcendent nature into the bad idea that we are separate and different from the light that streams through the cellular corridors of living things everywhere.

This feeling of being separate from the web of life gives us a terminal case of fear, anxiety, and tension, which makes us think up bad ideas.

Ramana is saying that if we remember what we knew in nursery school and forget what we learned in high school, we'd all be a lot better off.

We ought to stop remembering that we're not who we really are. The light of who we really are instantly shines out between the cracks of our forgetting to remember who we're not. The big rush of self-forgetfulness we experience when we're in love is who we are asserting itself. Not a single day passes that we don't stare silently off into the imaginary distance and try to remember who we are. We do it instinctively.

When it came time for me to choose a career, I decided to speak with other career people about mysticism. When I first started, I was as nervous as a heretic during the Inquisition. The Inquisition is when the career people of a certain religious order tried extremely hard to increase their membership by encouraging dissidents to join them or else. This went on for about 300 years, during which time at least three million humans were paved over with the asphalt of a very bad idea.

I took courage in remembering that we had all gone to nursery school, that we were all there together, learning to walk and talk and swing on swings. I remembered that we all used to play in the sandbox of luminosity and it was no big deal.

One day, I decided that if I could remember, then others could, too. Could and would, though it was a bit risky in career terms.

I started walking right up to people in big offices and conference rooms, asking, "Would you tell me about your mystical experiences?"

Guess what? They did.

They remembered their nursery rhymes, though they were a bit rusty and skipped a few words here and there.

Even presidents of big companies. Even lawyers.

Here's what they remembered about reality, which is where we ought to live, all things considered: *we are bigger than our bodies and smarter than our brains.* We know things no one has ever told us, and we can fix our bodies with the right attitude. We feel connected to other people; in fact, we feel connected to all of life, including clouds and spider webs and the Crab Nebula.
The happenings in life go on well enough without our manipulation, as when delicate flowers appear out of nowhere at the gong of spring. When people experienced who they really are, torrents of love would make their eyes sparkle like dew. They wanted to help others. They became causelessly happy.

No people have yet told me that when they were dancing like Nijinsky or singing like Ray Charles in the luminosity of their original happy hearts they got the idea to torture their friends with cattle-prods or drop mustard gas bombs on little children giggling with the secret that is still so obvious to them.

287

No one said that they wanted to pave the Earth with asphalt or crush the tender skulls of baby seals for sport or profit. Everyone said that it was good to be kind and helpful. They said there was a definite purpose, or plan, for all living things and for the whole universe.

Meher Baba expressed this essential purpose quite profoundly,

"To penetrate into the essence of all being and significance and to release the fragrance of that inner attainment for the guidance and benefit of others is the sole game which has any intrinsic and absolute worth. All other happenings, incidents, and attainments can, in themselves, have no lasting importance." This means that we should not pave the planet with asphalt. We should not kill everything that gets in our way.

We should learn to live with everything. Everyone should eat. Don't be greedy. Learn to be wise and loving.

That's what people told me they remembered about who they really are. It seems to me that we all ought to sit down right now and try hard to remember this. I know we can. And when we do, we'll also know how to fix the mess we've made. That knowledge is part of the plan of reality. We just got carried away with careers and shopping.

I know that many people are secretly sad because they rushed right up to the tables of career day and signed on.

People want to know reality. When we make the unreal real, we reap a massive harvest of sadness.

And that's what we do when we forget that we are all mystics. We sow and reap the misery of great destruction because in our forgetfulness of who we are, we become fearful and greedy and we end up wanting to hurt and enslave others, and we try to take away their freedom and pass laws against dancing with the universe like Zorba did on the beaches of Greece, thinking that if we

288

outlaw the dance of luminosity we can protect our interest in the harvest of silly ideas.

This is a very bad idea. I hope we will all remember who we are, and I hope we will remember this very soon, and I hope we will begin to act accordingly.

www.robertrabbin.com & www.speakingtruthfully.com

Used with permission.

Jesus Meditating limited edition prints available at
http://harmanvisions.com/visions_frontpg/jesus.html
Artwork used with permission of Visionary Artist
Bruce Harman -   www.HarmanVisions.com

290

→ ● ←

ENDNOTES

If you own a print version of this book and would like a pdf version sent to you for easier usage of links, simply snap a photo of the book you bought along with receipt, and email both to info@McMMbook.com and provide an email address the pdf version should be sent.

These links to websites and organizations tell a deeper story and are provided for convenience. We are not endorsing any of these groups or sites (nor do they endorse us). We are simply offering them to you for further research. If any of the links or endnotes are found to no longer work, have been altered from their original content, or are now incorrect – please feel free to email your findings to the email address provided at the end.

---

[1] http://rashani.com/arts/poems/poems-by-rashani/the-unbrokayen/
Rashani Réa wrote this poem in 1991 after experiencing 5 deaths in her family.

[2] http://www.bosshoss.com/

[3] I have noticed that those with a cloudy or dull left eye, seem to have closed off to their receptive, or feminine side.

[4] http://en.wikipedia.org/wiki/Chock_(wheel)

[5] http://www.reeseprod.com/content/products.aspx?lvl=2&parentid=9200&catID=9380&part=0

[6] https://www.youtube.com/watch?v=1kE4xnA-eEY

[7] http://www.motorcycle-superstore.com/34477/i/steadymate-soft-loops

[8] http://en.wikipedia.org/wiki/Motorcycle_fork

→ ● ←

→ ● ←

---

[9]http://www.ppg.com/coatings/refinish/en/products/vibrance/Pages/default.aspx

[10] http://www.houseofkolor.com/products/specialty.jsp

[11] http://msdssearchengine.com/local_msds.php?id=122596

[12] http://lynnandrews.com/lynns-books/ - Medicine Woman book series

[13] http://www.starchildglobal.com/channels-and-articles/the-dance-of-the-dragonfly-perspectives-from-new-shamanism/

[14] White sage, not the herb sage.
http://www.wikihow.com/Smudge-a-House &
http://thespiritscience.net/2015/11/26/study-shows-how-smudging-does-a-lot-more-than-just-clear-evil-spirits/

[15] http://sageandsmudge.com/index.htm#.Ubj05OeyCSo

[16] http://www.greenmedinfo.com/blog/killer-germs-obliterated-medicinal-smoke-smudging-study-reveals

[17] http://www.imdb.com/name/nm0000375/ - Robert Downey Jr.

[18] http://www.imdb.com/title/tt0371746/

[19] http://www.imdb.com/title/tt0988045/

[20] http://www.imdb.com/title/tt0081505/ - The Shining

[21] Typically a juvenile hall but in this case a residential program for up to 85 adolescent boys who have been adjudicated delinquent by the *Juvenile Court*

→ ● ←

[22] http://dictionary.reference.com/browse/rap+sheet

[23]

http://www.ksacc.ca/docs/sibling_sexual_abuse.pdf?LanguageID=EN-US

[24] The Glencoe parade is an annual event during Sturgis bike week. (an inside joke)

[25] https://wmeac.org/fracking1/frackingimpacts/air/fract-42/

[26] http://www.panna.org/issues/publication/pesticides-and-honey-bees-state-science

[27] http://www.ratshole.com/main.asp

[28] Currently a soccer field. http://www.sturgis-sd.gov/index.aspx?NID=154

[29] https://www.youtube.com/watch?v=AegLdB7UI4U & http://www.youtube.com/watch?v=ivk4DT4L2qc

[30] http://www.paughco.com/

[31] A billet is simply a solid piece of material that is shaped into its finished form by machining. Most finished products are either cast or molded into shape. A billet is a raw block of material.

[32] https://en.wikipedia.org/wiki/Harley-Davidson

[33] http://fluoridealert.org/content/bottled-water/

[34] http://www.wikihow.com/Get-Reflexology-Charts & http://www.reflexology-usa.org/articles/index.html

[35] http://www.urbandictionary.com/define.php?term=gixxer

---

[36] http://thespiritscience.net/tags/sacred-geometry-3/ & http://www.ancient-wisdom.co.uk/sacredgeometry.htm

[37] http://www.goodreads.com/book/show/6388946-end-the-fed

[38] http://en.wikipedia.org/wiki/Flight_dispatcher

[39] http://en.wikipedia.org/wiki/Farm-to-table

[40] Many homes in Spain have what are termed "Gypsy" Bars on the windows. These are permanent bars to keep the "Gypsy's" from gaining access to rob the home.

[41] The Life and Teachings of the Masters of the Far East by Baird T. Spalding

[42] http://www.youtube.com/watch?v=Uk7biSOzr1k

[43]
http://www.cosmicquotes.com/quotes/authors/a/albert_einstein/energy-cannot-be-created-or-destroyed-it-can-only-be-changed.html

[44] http://www.charliechaplin.com/en/synopsis/articles/29-The-Great-Dictator-s-Speech

[45] http://www.wellbeingalignment.com/violet-flame-meditation.html or the book "Radical Forgiveness" by Colin Tipping

[46] http://www.usatoday.com/story/nation/2014/04/25/suicide-rates-army-military-pentagon/8060059/

[47] https://vocesdetierra.wordpress.com/2014/08/12/depression-is-not-a-disease-but-an-indication-that-human-consciousness-needs-to-change/

→ ● ←

---

[48] http://caretakersofmotherearth.com/

[49] http://www.med-health.net/Pineal-Gland-Calcification.html

[50] http://ascensionlifestyle.org/the-pineal-gland-calcification-why-you-should-care/

[51] https://en.wikipedia.org/wiki/Medieval_Inquisition

[52] http://soundofheart.org/galacticfreepress/content/22-signs-you-are-embodying-your-higher-self

[53] http://www.sanders.senate.gov/newsroom/news/?id=c883abcf-5903-4c37-bccb-9fef9e9fb362

[54] http://www.collective-evolution.com/2015/08/13/cbs-news-investigative-journalist-explains-how-mainstream-media-brainwashes-the-masses/

[55] Apathy - lack of interest, enthusiasm, or concern

[56] http://en.wikipedia.org/wiki/Cognitive_dissonance

[57] http://en.wikipedia.org/wiki/Posttraumatic_stress_disorder

[58]
http://articles.mercola.com/sites/articles/archive/2014/03/01/body-electricity-grounding.aspx

[59] Post Traumatic Stress Disorder
https://en.wikipedia.org/wiki/Posttraumatic_stress_disorder

[60] http://www.investopedia.com/terms/f/fracking.asp

[61]
http://www.sourcewatch.org/index.php/Fracking_and_water_con

→ ● ←

sumption

[62] Cree Prophecy: 'When all the trees have been cut down, when all the animals have been hunted, when all the waters are polluted, when all the air is unsafe to breathe, only then will you discover you cannot eat money.'

[63]

https://secure3.convio.net/fww/site/Advocacy?cmd=display&page=UserAction&id=233

[64] https://en.wikipedia.org/wiki/Oil_sands

[65] http://www.npr.org/blogs/krulwich/2013/01/16/169511949/a-mysterious-patch-of-light-shows-up-in-the-north-dakota-dark

[66]http://www.reuters.com/article/2012/04/18/us-usa-fracking-emissions-idUSBRE83H0UH20120418
http://www.pnas.org/content/110/44/17768.full.pdf+html

[67]

http://serc.carleton.edu/NAGTWorkshops/health/case_studies/hydrofracking_w.html

[68] http://money.cnn.com/2013/09/17/news/global-fracking-ihs/

[69] http://fracfocus.org/chemical-use/what-chemicals-are-used

[70] Formic Acid, Acetaldehyde, Zirconium, Petroleum distillates (naphtha), Ethylene glycol, Acetic acid, Acrylamide, Phosphoric Acid Salt, Naphthalene, Isopropyl Alcohol, 2-Butoxyethanol
https://fracfocus.org/chemical-use/what-chemicals-are-used

[71] http://www.cdc.gov/niosh/idlh/intridl4.html

[72] http://www.dangersoffracking.com/ &
http://www.popularmechanics.com/science/energy/coal-oil-

gas/top-10-myths-about-natural-gas-drilling-6386593#slide-10

73

http://answers.yahoo.com/question/index?qid=20091208122134 AAP1Xut

[74] http://america.aljazeera.com/articles/2014/1/5/some-states-confirmwaterpollutionfromdrilling.html

[75] http://water.epa.gov/lawsregs/rulesregs/sdwa/index.cfm http://www.epa.gov/air/caa/

[76]http://energy.wilkes.edu/PDFFiles/Laws%20and%20Regulations/Halliburton%20Loophole%20Essay%20Final.pdf

[77] http://en.wikipedia.org/wiki/Dick_Cheney

[78] https://en.wikipedia.org/wiki/Macrocosm_and_microcosm

[79] http://www.foodandwaterwatch.org/ & http://www.nrdc.org/ & http://sumofus.org/ & http://www.350.org & http://www.organicconsumers.org/

[80] http://www.nytimes.com/2014/07/01/nyregion/towns-may-ban-fracking-new-york-state-high-court-rules.html?_r=0

[81] http://www.senrg.org/blued-trees/

[82] http://www.organicpools.co.uk/

[83] http://www.treehugger.com/gadgets/njord-portable-water-creator-condenses-drinking-water-air-reymin-de-leon.html & http://www.roots-up.org/#!Design-of-a-Dew-collector-Greenhouse/c1j2v/55082c6a0cf2031a76490f16

[84] http://www.ncsl.org/research/agriculture-and-rural-development/state-industrial-hemp-statutes.aspx

[85] http://nutiva.com/articles/the-science-behind-carbon-dioxide-reduction-with-hemp/

[86] http://www.hemp-technologies.com/page33/page33.html

[87] http://www.kingjamesbibleonline.org/1611_Revelation-22-2/

[88] https://www.youtube.com/watch?v=s9Sdr6ZWcUU

[89] http://www.hemp-technologies.com/page33/page33.html

[90] http://www.oprah.com/food/Superfoods-List-2012-Sunchokayes-Adzuki-Beans-Chia-Seed/3

[91] Fiberboard, roofing, flooring, wallboard, caulking, cement, paint, paneling, particleboard, plaster, plywood, reinforced concrete, insulation, bricks

[92] http://www.hemp.org/news/book/export/html/202

[93]

http://www.nytimes.com/2009/11/10/science/10patch.html?_r=0
http://www.plasticpollutioncoalition.org/

[94] http://www.theoceancleanup.com/ &
https://www.googlesciencefair.com/projects/en/2014/77b0af7d78
199d72bb8b7b077459fcc0c443cabde6ec353188e8c08dd551cb83

[95] http://patft.uspto.gov/netacgi/nph-Parser?Sect1=PTO1&Sect2=HITOFF&d=PALL&p=1&u=%2Fn
etahtml%2FPTO%2Fsrchnum.htm&r=1&f=G&l=50&s1=515970
3.PN.&OS=PN/5159703&RS=PN/5159703 &
https://books.google.com/books?id=KrwdbEHBd6AC&pg=PT10
7&lpg=PT107&dq=publicity+material+Dr.+Lowery+subliminal
+sounds&source=bl&ots=Oqef9lnEaQ&sig=F_3o7vNiJtc3QkE
OQef-

Bqun04g&hl=en&sa=X&ved=0CB0Q6AEwAGoVChMI3qujya
HMyAIVxZaICh0CWATW#v=onepage&q=publicity%20materi
al%20Dr.%20Lowery%20subliminal%20sounds&f=false

[96] http://www.imdb.com/title/tt0065333/

[97] http://blog.doctoroz.com/oz-experts/herb-of-the-month-
dandelion

[98] http://www.fao.org/3/a-i4021e.pdf &
http://www.youtube.com/watch?v=VBspR2p0YYM&feature=em
-subs_digest-vrecs

[99] https://www.youtube.com/watch?v=N5Lu-7FIj_g

[100] http://www.treehugger.com/sustainable-product-
design/naturhus-wraps-a-house-in-its-own-private-
greenhouse.html

[101] http://cleantechnica.com/2014/02/02/which-solar-panels-
most-efficient/

[102] http://gizmodo.com/5901464/solar-panel+in+a+tube-
generates-power-and-hot-water-at-the-same-time

[103] http://www.builditsolar.com/Projects/SpaceHeating/GregCanC
ol/Can%20Colllector.pdf

[104] http://www.extremetech.com/extreme/188667-a-fully-
transparent-solar-cell-that-could-make-every-window-and-
screen-a-power-source

[105] http://www.solarroadways.com/intro.shtml

[106] http://www.solarenergyworld.com/2014/09/12/solar-roof-will-
shoot-death-rays-kill-little-birdies/

[107] http://www.google.com/patents/US20130162057

[108] http://news.nationalgeographic.com/news/2011/10/111031-population-7-billion-earth-world-un-seven/

[109] http://www.designbuild-network.com/news/newsshimizu-unveils-plans-for-underwater-city-dome-4453154

110

http://www.cityofdeadwood.com/index.asp?Type=B_BASIC&SEC=%7BFDD11CF4-F861-473A-BF57-29C897B35DF0%7D

[111] http://auto.howstuffworks.com/fuel-efficiency/biofuels/hemp-energy.htm

[112] http://www.3m.com/product/information/Scotch-Fine-Line-Tape.html

[113] http://www.ccohs.ca/oshanswers/chemicals/how_chem.html

114

http://www.aocs.org/Membership/FreeCover.cfm?itemnumber=1120

[115] http://patients4medicalmarijuana.wordpress.com/marijuana-info/marijuana-in-the-bible/jesus-cannabis/

Exodus 30, verses 22 – 30 Anointing Oil
22 Then the LORD said to Moses, **23** "Take the following fine spices: 500 shekels of liquid myrrh, half as much (that is, 250 shekels) of fragrant cinnamon, 250 shekels of **fragrant cane** (Kaneh-bosem, 24 500 shekels of cassia – all according to the sanctuary shekel – and a hin of olive oil. **25** Make these into a sacred anointing oil, a fragrant blend, the work of a perfumer. It will be the sacred anointing oil. . . .

Converted into today's measurements:
liquid myrrh 500 shekels 5.75 kg (12.68 lbs)
cassia 500 shekels 5.75 kg (12.68 lbs)
cinnamon leaf 250 shekels 2.875 kg (6.34 lbs)
cannabis flowers 250 shekels 2.875 kg (6.34 lbs)
olive oil 1 hin 6.5 liters (1.72 gallons)
In the traditional method, all of these ingredients would have
been mixed with water and then boiled until all the water
evaporated. The oil was then strained and ready for use.

[116] http://www.openbible.info/topics/anointing_oil

[117] In 1936, Sara Benetowa, later Known as Sula Benet, an
etymologist from the Institute of Anthropological Sciences, in
Warsaw wrote a treatise, "Tracing One Word Through Different
Languages." This was a study on the word Cannabis, based on a
study of the oldest Hebrew texts. Although the word cannabis
was thought to be of Scythian origin, Benet's research showed it
had an earlier root in the Semitic Languages such as Hebrew.
Benet demonstrated that the ancient Hebrew word for Cannabis
is Kaneh -Bosem. She also did another study called Early
Diffusion and Folk Uses of Hemp. There is a reprint of this in
Cannabis and Culture ISBN:90-279-7669-4. On page 44, she
states, "The sacred character of hemp in biblical times is evident
from Exodus 30:23, where Moses was instructed by God to
anoint the meeting tent and all of its furnishings with specially
prepared oil, containing hemp." On page 41 Sula Benet writes, :
In the course of time, the two words kaneh and bosem were fused
into one , kanabos or kannabus know to us from the Mishna.
According to the Webster's New World Hebrew Dictionary, page
607 the Hebrew for hemp is kanabos.
Sara Benetowa discovered that the Kaneh-Bosem or Cannabis is
mentioned 5 times in the Old Testament. The first occurrence
appears in the Holy Anointing Oil as Calamus, (Exodus 30:23).
Sara argued that the translation of Calamus was a mistranslation

which occurred in the oldest Bible the "Septuagint" and the mistranslation was copied in later versions.

[118] https://www.youtube.com/watch?v=1miGzTwK28U

[119] https://www.osha.gov/SLTC/isocyanates/

[120] http://www.consumerreports.org/cro/news/2015/02/pros-and-cons-of-aluminum-cars-and-trucks/index.htm

[121] http://www.atsdr.cdc.gov/toxfaqs/tf.asp?id=190&tid=34

[122] http://www.autotrainingcentre.com/blog/kestrel-eco-friendly-hemp-car-canada/

[123] http://en.wikipedia.org/wiki/Mountain_Dew

[124] http://www.wikihow.com/Avoid-High-Fructose-Corn-Syrup

[125] http://www.naturalthyroidchoices.com/MtDew.html

[126] http://www.webmd.com/food-recipes/news/20130129/brominated-vegetable-oil-qa

[127] "New Stealth Chemicals Hidden in Your Food" - http://www.manataka.org/page1476.html & Genetically Modified Food - http://www.nongmoproject.org/learn-more/ & "19 Foods That Aren't Food" - http://www.prevention.com/food/19-foods-that-arent-food

[128] http://www.goodreads.com/book/show/929418.Life_and_Teaching_Of_The_Masters_Of_The_Far_East

[129] I use Frankincense, Sandalwood, and other oils on a regular basis.

[130] Home Health's Almond Glow® Coconut Skin Lotion with peanut oil, olive oil, lanolin oil and vitamin E

[131] http://www.treehugger.com/organic-beauty/20-toxic-ingredients-avoid-when-buying-body-care-products-and-cosmetics.html & http://www.ewg.org/2015sunscreen/report/nanoparticles-in-sunscreen/

[132] https://nicholas.duke.edu/search/node/fracking

133

http://newswatch.nationalgeographic.com/2013/12/20/hormone-disrupting-chemicals-linked-to-fracking-found-in-colorado-river/

[134] http://thinkprogress.org/climate/2014/09/29/3573449/west-virginia-to-frack-ohio-river/

[135] http://act.credoaction.com/sign/enbridge_scheme

[136] http://www.duluthnewstribune.com/news/health/4091119-toxic-chemicals-drinking-water-six-million-americans & http://www.waterboards.ca.gov/press_room/press_releases/2013/pr020413.pdf & http://en.wikipedia.org/wiki/2014_Elk_River_chemical_spill & https://stateimpact.npr.org/texas/2011/11/29/burying-toxic-water-texas-community-keeps-on-plugging-to-halt-it/ & http://www.mncenter.org/issues/water/mn-agricultural-certainty-program-review.aspx http://www.jhsph.edu/news/news-releases/2015/increased-levels-of-radon-in-pennsylvania-homes-correspond-to-onset-of-fracking.html

[137] http://www.waterinfo.org/resources/water-facts

[138] http://nepis.epa.gov/Adobe/PDF/30004HGG.pdf

→ ● ←

---

[139] http://www.masaru-emoto.net/english/water-crystal.html

[140] http://www.ecosway.com/ecosway/en_US/hexagon_03.jsp

[141]
http://web.mit.edu/12.000/www/m2012/finalwebsite/problem/groundwater.shtml

[142]
http://www.westernresourceadvocates.org/frackwater/factsheetfrackingourfuture2012.pdf

[143] http://mitakuyeoyasin.net/about/

[144] http://www.cdc.gov/niosh/topics/emf/

[145] http://www.safespaceprotection.com/harmful-effects-electromagnetic-fields.aspx

[146] http://www.amazon.com/Milwaukee-6509-22-Sawzall-11-Amp-Reciprocating/dp/B0000789HE

[147] High Volume Low Pressure

[148] http://www.iwata-medea.com/

[149] http://www.thequotefactory.com/quote-by/jim-carrey/i-hope-everybody-could-get-rich/57662

[150] http://www.imdb.com/title/tt0070047/ - The Exorcist

[151] http://www.janinafisher.com/pdfs/selfharm.pdf

[152] http://www.elephantjournal.com/2012/05/if-your-relationship-is-failing-heres-why-dr-margaret-paul-2/

→ ● ←

[153] http://www.originsnsw.com/mentalhealth/id4.html

[154]

http://paranormal.about.com/od/lifeafterdeathreincarnat/a/Life-Before-Birth.htm

[155] http://www.oprah.com/relationships/Forgiving-Your-Parents_1

[156]

http://lyrics.wikia.com/wiki/Wayne_Newton:Daddy_Don't_You_Walk_So_Fast

[157] http://www.catholiccharitiesusa.org/what-we-do/programs/adoption/

[158] http://www.campaignforliberty.org/national-blog/transcript-of-farewell-address/

[159] https://en.wikipedia.org/wiki/Fritz_ter_Meer

[160] http://www.vocabulary.com/dictionary/persona

[161] http://www.theqeffect.com/shadow

[162] http://www.thefreedictionary.com/psychopath

[163] http://en.wikipedia.org/wiki/James_Franco

[164] http://www.chakra-centers-heal.com/heart_blockages.html

[165] http://www.betterworldshopper.org/app.html

[166] http://www.elephantjournal.com/2013/07/the-unsexy-truth-about-sex-addiction-kimberly-lo/

167
http://articles.mercola.com/sites/articles/archive/2011/10/28/cdc-director-arrested-for-child-molestation--bestiality.aspx

[168] http://www.cbgnetwork.org/4.html

[169] http://www.imdb.com/title/tt0058536/

170
https://en.wikipedia.org/wiki/Indian_Reservation_(The_Lament_of_the_Cherokee_Reservation_Indian)

171
http://en.wikipedia.org/wiki/Homosexual_behavior_in_animals

[172] http://en.wikipedia.org/wiki/Kinsey_scale

[173] http://indiancountrytodaymedianetwork.com/2016/01/23/two-spirits-one-heart-five-genders

[174] http://www.upworthy.com/there-are-6-scriptures-about-homosexuality-in-the-bible-heres-what-they-really-say?c=ufb4

[175] http://www.cnn.com/2015/07/20/living/pope-francis-devil/

[176] I wish to acknowledge that in tribal traditions, tobacco is a very powerful ally when used respectfully. However, when used out of balance or referred to as 'cancer sticks', this powerful ally can kill.

[177] Slang for Knucklehead. Harley-Davidson's first overhead valve Big Twin engine manufactured from 1936 – 1947. The name comes from the valve covers that look like the knuckles of a clenched fist.

[178] https://www.youtube.com/watch?v=XdLyMhNdcSc &

https://thetruthaboutcancer.com/questions-before-chemotherapy-treatment/

[179] http://phoenixtears.ca/articles/hemp-oil-the-real-medicine/ & http://www.youtube.com/watch?v=6OhUtL6T6BE & http://davidkretzmann.com/2012/07/alternative-cancer-treatments-rife-machine-explained/ & http://www.thrivemovement.com/royal-rife-s-cancer-cure-and-suppression

[180] Slang for lesbian

[181] http://www.poisonweb.com/

[182] http://en.wikipedia.org/wiki/Bell_Huey_family

[183] Chemtrails may or may not contain heavy metals such as barium and aluminum. No matter. Human beings are both human and Being. The human side may take in toxins but with a fully functioning Being side, be unaffected because *well-being* is our birthright. No one and nothing can take that away from us without our permission (thoughts otherwise). We over stand and can transmute any toxin. Look to gurus in India for proof such as this. If there is concern over the heavy metals in the brain or body, then bentonite clay will draw them out. http://sonnes.com/store/product-category/7-detoxificant-32-oz-liquid/

[184]

http://www.urbandictionary.com/define.php?term=abracadabra

[185] http://www.ehow.com/how-does_4911638_what-causes-adrenaline-rushes.html

[186] http://www.wikihow.com/Control-an-Adrenaline-Rush

---

[187] http://www.medicaldaily.com/therapeutic-science-adult-coloring-books-how-childhood-pastime-helps-adults-relieve-356280

[188] http://healthland.time.com/2011/06/16/magic-mushrooms-can-improve-psychological-health-long-term/

[189] http://www.watermakesmoney.com/en/the-film

[190] https://en.wikipedia.org/wiki/Zeitgeist_(film_series)

[191]

https://www.youtube.com/watch?feature=player_embedded&v=EuGuTsExN4Q – Ecological Overshoot

[192] http://www.becomingminimalist.com/less-consumerism/

[193] https://en.wikipedia.org/wiki/Traditional_African_medicine

[194] https://www.shamanlinks.net/shaman-info/the-spirit-world/talking-to-spirits/

[195] http://globalpublicpolicywatch.org/2014/01/14/deforestation-logging-and-mining-a-deadly-combination-for-the-amazon-rainforest/

[196] http://apecsec.org/mountaintop-removal-pros-and-cons/

[197]

http://articles.mercola.com/sites/articles/archive/2016/04/24/gmo-myth-truth.aspx

[198]

https://www.earthworksaction.org/media/detail/government_data_shows_mines_will_annually_pollute_up_to_27_billion_gallons

---

#.ViKWi9KrRki

[199] https://www.youtube.com/watch?v=ewDS5ROrLcE

[200] http://www.huppi.com/kangaroo/Einstein.htm

[201] http://www.thrivemovement.com/

[202] http://www.dailymail.co.uk/sciencetech/article-3012955/How-fires-extinguished-using-SOUND-Handheld-gadget-uses-pressure-waves-remove-oxygen-flames.html

203

http://www.ted.com/talks/paul_stamets_on_6_ways_mushrooms_can_save_the_world?language=en &
https://www.youtube.com/watch?v=za-vIdak3bI&feature=youtu.be

[204] I was taught, 'Give and you shall receive'. But that's not how it works in a garden. You might do all the soil prep by the book, plant according to the lunar calendar, water and tend to the new shoots diligently, and still the plant might not make it. Then, you notice a plant growing vibrantly where no seed was planted. Perhaps the wind blew it to its location, or a bird ate the seed and pooped it there. No matter, for this plant is giving of itself so you reap the rewards of its fruit without extending effort. Now, if you share the fruit, the plant will produce even more. Basil and kale are great examples of this. The plant can become huge if you keep picking the lower leaves. Receive and share with others, so everyone flourishes.

[205] http://www.motherjones.com/tom-philpott/2013/07/bee-colony-collapse-disorder-fungicides

→ ● ←

206
http://www.fda.gov/Food/FoodborneIllnessContaminants/Metals/ucm191007.htm

207 Dr. Rattan Lal

208 http://carbonpilgrim.wordpress.com/2014/01/01/grass-soil-hope/

209 http://gofossilfree.org/

210 http://www.rainforestfoundation.org/commonly-asked-questions-and-facts

211 https://www.flashlyrics.com/lyrics/snatam-kaur/aakhan-jor-acceptance-33

212 https://en.wikipedia.org/wiki/Project_MKUltra

213 https://www.google.com/patents/US6506148

214 http://www.janinafisher.com/pdfs/trauma.pdf

215 http://www.tir.org/

216 http://www.webmd.com/mental-health/emdr-what-is-it

217 http://www.sandraingerman.com/abstractonshamanism.html

218 http://www.scientificamerican.com/article/mental-health-may-depend-on-creatures-in-the-gut/?WT.mc_id=SA_Facebook

219 http://healing.about.com/od/ethericbody/a/human-energy-field.htm

220 http://en.wikipedia.org/wiki/The_Celestine_Prophecy

→ ● ←

[221] http://psychcentral.com/lib/the-importance-of-personal-boundaries/0001112

[222] Questionnaire from: Book on Chakras - Wheels of Life: A Users Guide to the Chakra System by Anodea Judith

[223] http://www.chopra.com/ccl/what-is-a-chakra
http://www.care2.com/greenliving/chakra-101-a-beginners-guide.html

[224] http://www.reuters.com/article/2012/10/19/us-italy-phones-idUSBRE89I0V320121019

[225] http://www.drnorthrup.com/7-habits-to-boost-your-emf-protection-from-cell-phone-radiation/

[226] https://www.google.com/patents/US6506148

SEXUAL ATTITUDES

Sexual Abuse Mind-set (Sex = Sexual Abuse)	Healthy Sexual Attitudes (Sex = Positive Sexual Energy)
Sex is uncontrollable energy.	Sex is controllable energy.
Sex is an obligation.	Sex is a choice.
Sex is addictive.	Sex is a natural drive.
Sex is hurtful.	Sex is nurturing, healing.
Sex is a condition for receiving love.	Sex is an expression of love.
Sex is "doing to" someone.	Sex is sharing with someone.
Sex is a commodity.	Sex is part of who I am.
Sex is void of communication.	Sex requires communication.
Sex is secretive.	Sex is private.
Sex is exploitive.	Sex is respectful.
Sex is deceitful.	Sex is honest.
Sex benefits one person.	Sex is mutual.
Sex is emotionally distant.	Sex is intimate.
Sex is irresponsible.	Sex is responsible.
Sex is unsafe.	Sex is safe.
Sex has no limits.	Sex has boundaries.
Sex is power over someone.	Sex is empowering.

From *The Sexual Healing Journey - A Guide for Survivors of Sexual Abuse* by Wendy Maltz, who also wrote, *The Porn Trap.*
www.healthysex.com   Used by permission.

[227]

→ ● ←

---

[228] http://www.allthingshealing.com/

[229] http://www.peacefulwarrior.com/

[230] http://www.nealedonaldwalsch.com/

[231] https://www.deepakchopra.com/book

[232] www.emofree.com The Official Source for EFT

[233] http://www.emofree.com/

[234] https://www.psychologytoday.com/blog/memory-medic/201303/why-writing-hand-could-make-you-smarter

[235] http://www.loc.gov/podcasts/musicandthebrain/

[236] http://healing.about.com/od/drums/a/drumtherapy.htm

[237] http://www.bachflower.com/cure-negative-emotions-bach-flower-remedies/

[238] http://www.realfarmacy.com/essential-oils-and-brain-injuries-heres-what-youre-not-being-told/

[239] http://www.biospiritual-energy-healing.com/vibrational-frequency.html

[240] http://www.metrolyrics.com/return-to-innocence-lyrics-enigma.html & http://www.enigmaspace.com/

[241] http://en.wikipedia.org/wiki/Peace_Pilgrim

[242] http://www.peacepilgrim.org/

[243] http://www.peacepilgrim.org/book/ppbook.pdf page 27

312

→ ● ←

→ • ←

---

[244] http://www.kingjamesbibleonline.org/1611_Matthew-7-12/

[245] http://www.metrolyrics.com/soon-love-soon-lyrics-vienna-teng.html & http://viennateng.com/

[246] http://superstringtheory.com/index.html

[247] http://en.wikipedia.org/wiki/Observer_effect_(physics)

[248] http://www.youtube.com/watch?v=jVSD66ZkF4g & http://www.mindbodygreen.com/0-12124/meditation-for-people-who-dont-meditate-a-12-step-guide.html

[249] http://people.howstuffworks.com/taoism-and-chi1.htm

[250] These nightmares happened to my teenage niece after being prescribed melatonin. http://www.doctoroz.com/article/melatonin-not-magic-bullet-sleep

[251] https://www.google.com/patents/US6630507 & http://veteransformedicalmarijuana.org/content/general-use-cannabis-ptsd-symptoms

[252] https://en.wikipedia.org/wiki/Cannabinoid_receptor & http://faculty.washington.edu/chudler/mari.html

[253] http://www.advancedholistichealth.org/history.html

[254] http://www.bachflower.com/rescue-remedy-information/

[255] http://healing.about.com/od/drums/a/drumtherapy.htm

[256] http://www.laughteryoga.org/english

→ • ←

[257] http://www.laughteryoga.org/english & http://laughteryoga.org/english/laughteryoga/details/321

[258] http://www.kingjamesbibleonline.org/Matthew-7-7/

[259] http://www.tunedbody.com/scientists-finally-show-thoughts-can-cause-specific-molecular-changes-genes/#

[260] http://www.social-consciousness.com/2012/09/awakening-the-illuminated-healing-heart-power.html

[261] http://www.theatlantic.com/health/archive/2013/10/what-we-eat-affects-everything/279922/

[262] http://www.nrdc.org/breastmilk/benefits.asp

[263] http://www.parenting.com/article/corn-syrup-in-formula http://www.naturalnews.com/033926_infant_formula_corn_syru p.html & http://www.princeton.edu/main/news/archive/S26/91/22K07/

[264] I've noticed that I can tell if people are balanced, if their eyes have equal brightness.

265

http://www.abuseandrelationships.org/Content/Survivors/trauma _bonding.html

[266] http://www.innerbonding.com/show-article/2581/the-one-major-cause-of-relationship-problems.html

[267] http://science.howstuffworks.com/life/crying3.htm

[268] http://www.chakramirrormath.com/

[269] http://theforgivenessmethod.com/learn-the-method/

---

[270] http://en.wikipedia.org/wiki/Ho%CA%BBoponopono

[271] http://acim.org/ & info@acim.org (T-5.VII.6:3-11) Material from *A Course in Miracles* is from the Third Edition published by The Foundation for Inner Peace, PO Box 598, Mill Valley, CA 94942-0598

[272] The Ringing Cedars of Russia Book 2: "In order to discern the thoughts of the Creator, one must attain a purity of thought appropriate to Him, as well as the pace of His thinking. To discern the thoughts of enlightened people, one must possess their purity of thought and the ability to think at the same rate. If a given Man has insufficient purity of thought to communicate with the dimension of the forces of light - the dimension in which radiant thoughts dwell, - then Man will draw his thoughts from their dark counterparts, and will end up suffering himself and causing others to suffer."

[273] Latin word for love

[274] For those who prefer videos - https://www.youtube.com/watch?v=xmN2RL4VJsE&list=PL2C 2FBAB7E002EE3E & http://www.nick.com/avatar-the-last-airbender/episodes/

[275] http://www.ringingcedarsofrussia.org/Main/English/index.php

[276] http://www.ringingcedars.com/tekos_school/

[277] Philosophy professor Kim Ivanovich Shilin, Doctor of Social Sciences, senior researcher at Moscow State University's Institute for Asian and African Studies as well as a Corresponding Member of the International Academy of Informatisation (MAI), has written a number of articles analyzing Anastasia's sayings. In

one of them, he wrote: Anastasia = Tara = Buddha = Maitreya. Anastasia is in the fullest sense Man in the likeness of God. (A Tara is a female Buddha, a deity capable of removing interferences and putting things in perfect order. A Maitreye - the loving one - is described as the future Buddha, associated with friendliness, success and prosperity.)

[278] http://www.ringingcedars.com/seed_planting/

[279] https://en.wikipedia.org/wiki/Library_of_Alexandria

[280] https://en.wikipedia.org/wiki/Akashic_records

[281] http://www.biomindsuperpowers.com/Pages/CIA-InitiatedRV.html

[282]http://www.goodreads.com/book/show/929418.Life_and_Teaching_Of_The_Masters_Of_The_Far_East

[283] http://www.drunvalo.net/store3.html

[284] http://en.wikipedia.org/wiki/Great_year

[285]
http://www.sanskrit.org/www/Hindu%20Primer/yugatime.html

[286] 'The Ancient Secret of the Flower of Life Volume 1 by Drunvalo Melchizedek pg 57

[287] http://www.sacred-geometry.com/ancientknowledge.html

[288] http://en.wikipedia.org/wiki/Dark_Ages_(historiography)

[289] http://en.wikipedia.org/wiki/2012_phenomenon

---

[290] http://www.kingjamesbibleonline.org/1611_Isaiah-11-6/

[291] http://www.nytimes.com/2015/01/27/science/so-happy-together.html?_r=0

[292] http://humansarefree.com/2011/02/how-to-clean-up-pineal-gland.html &
http://www.wakingtimes.com/2013/05/16/the-spiritual-eye-how-to-decalcify-awaken-your-pineal-gland/

[293] http://en.wikipedia.org/wiki/Apocalypse

[294] http://en.wikipedia.org/wiki/Serenity_Prayer

[295] For those having difficulties with negative thoughts, if you prefer Bible based teachings, then Joyce Meyer's book and CD's are helpful:
http://www.joycemeyer.org/EverydayAnswers/teachings/teachingbotm.aspx?article=battlefield
For those who don't believe in demons or hell, then Abraham Hick's talk:
https://www.youtube.com/watch?v=Zmf_FLGsYNs&list=FLHxZ7_Xgr8WLltAH1n8nNyQ&index=1

[296] http://www.kingjamesbibleonline.org/Bible-Verses-About-Lake-of-Fire/

[297] By dangerous, I refer to those individuals who are an immediate threat to society. Not the incarcerated individuals, who having no influence to pay quality lawyers, and become trapped in the 'prison for profit' scheme created by privatizing prisons.

[298] "One of the saddest lessons of history is this: If we've been bamboozled long enough, we tend to reject any evidence of the bamboozle. We're no longer interested in finding out the truth.

The bamboozled has captured us. It's simply too painful to acknowledge, even to ourselves, that we've been taken. Once you give a charlatan power over you, you almost never get it back." - Carl Sagan

[299] http://www.spiritscienceandmetaphysics.com/proof-that-the-pineal-gland-is-a-3rd-eye/

[300] http://www.mayoclinic.org/diseases-conditions/compulsive-sexual-behavior/basics/definition/con-20020126

[301] http://bismarcktribune.com/bakken/trafficking-in-north-dakota-is-on-the-rise-and-often/article_c7f42282-92b7-11e4-819f-5b05c8a62325.html

[302] http://www.nydailynews.com/news/crime/woman-sues-ex-husband-du-pont-heir-dodged-prison-raping-3-year-old-daughter-article-1.1740180

[303] https://www.youtube.com/watch?v=rrjvifKXQy4

[304]
http://www.azlyrics.com/lyrics/pinkfloyd/thehappiestdaysofourlives.html

[305] http://en.wikipedia.org/wiki/Pocketbike_racing

[306] http://bacaworld.org/

[307] http://guardiansofthechildren.com

[308] https://en.wikipedia.org/wiki/Lotus_position

[309] http://en.wikipedia.org/wiki/Yoda

[310] http://en.wikipedia.org/wiki/Yoga

---

[311] http://en.wikipedia.org/wiki/Grinch

[312] http://www.foodandwaterwatch.org/food/factoryfarms/ &
http://www.hsi.org/issues/climate_change/

[313] The reason I have a crap perspective about conventional food, is because of the way it hurts the earth through monoculture practices, and because genetically modified food – food that has been genetically altered so it can survive dousing of the herbicide Roundup Ready™ - contains a bacterium designed to make targeted insects' stomach explode. I have a good friend who eats and drinks items made with GMO's, and now, she has painful tumors on her stomach. As for me, I haven't got time for doctors and their pills. Plus, I know that preservatives, which extend shelf life, cause inflammation because I feel my clothes get tight whenever I eat that type of food. Inflammation is the body trying to rid itself of contaminants and it leads to all sorts of diseases. Plus, the only time I experience hot flashes, is after eating conventional food. With my aquaponic system that uses living fish poop as the fertilizer, I am in control of the source, and comfortable in my own skin. Where it's cold, people can build an aquaponic walipini, an Aymara Indian word for place of warm.

[314] http://www.chakras.info/hand-chakras/

315

http://www.pbs.org/warrior/content/timeline/opendoor/roleOfChief.html

[316] http://www.easyoff.us/

[317] http://goodearthnaturalfood.com/

[318] http://www.pbs.org/newshour/bb/study-finds-ptsd-lingers-body-chemistry-next-generation/#.Vec1QgEL9Gg.mailto

---

[319] This happened back in Egypt when out of balance people thought to enslave others, but then realized that owning people outright resulted in pissed off slaves. So the High Priest told everyone they were free, but if they wanted to work they could, and then took back the money he paid them for food, shelter, and services thereby making them believe they were free when they really weren't.

[320] https://solutions.thischangeseverything.org/

[321] http://www.yogajournal.com/basics/822

[322] http://www.reuters.com/article/2013/05/31/us-wheat-control-idUSBRE94U06H20130531 & http://www.doctoroz.com/episode/what-food-industry-doesnt-want-you-know & http://sustainablepulse.com/wp-content/uploads/ENSSER_Statement_no_scientific_consensus_on_GMO_safety_ENG_LV.pdf & http://www.change.org/petitions/congress-support-h-r-254-sewage-sludge-in-food-consumer-notification-act & http://www.mnn.com/food/healthy-eating/blogs/arsenic-in-chicken-feed-affects-more-than-chickens & http://www.nytimes.com/2013/10/02/business/fda-bans-three-arsenic-drugs-used-in-poultry-and-pig-feeds.html?_r=0

[323] http://www.pachamama.org/

[324] I personally know several children who can read minds and heal through touch. But they won't show these skills to people who might freak out and misuse their talents, and since they can read minds, they know who to trust.

[325] http://www.melodycrystalsuk.co.uk/

[326] www.lynnandrews.com All Rights Reserved, Used with

Permission.

[327] The Sanskrit word Chakra translates to wheel, referring to wheels of energy throughout the body. There are seven main chakras, starting from the base of the spine up to the crown of the head. To visualize a chakra in the body, imagine a swirling wheel of energy where matter and consciousness meet. This invisible energy, called Prana, is vital life force, which keeps us vibrant, healthy, and alive. These swirling wheels of energy correspond to massive nerve centers in the body. Each of the seven main chakras contains bundles of nerves and major organs as well as our psychological, emotional, and spiritual states of being. If there is a blockage, energy cannot flow and dis-ease follows. For more information: http://www.chopra.com/ccl/what-is-a-chakra#sthash.YxfB4ALC.dpuf

[328] http://www.tantrikstudies.org/blog/2016/2/5/the-real-story-on-the-chakras

info@McMMbook.com or donate@McMMbook.com